Sin, with its ensuing guilt, is the central theme of ASHFORD. The novel is about a new young schoolmaster, Timothy Jordan, who graduates from Colgate to teach at Ashford, a fictional boarding preparatory school in Southwest Massachusetts. The school is conducted by Catholic laymen.

The yarn begins when Timothy attends his mother's funeral in Pompey Hollow in upstate New York in 1963. On the return drive to school, he recalls the selected events of his childhood, highschool and college years, and the drama of his first fourteen months at Ashford, during which time he is seduced by the Headmaster's wife, falls in love with the school nurse, teaches English, and coaches football and baseball most successfully, only to have it all collapse during a polio epidemic at school in the early fall of 1954.

By his return to school at the end of the novel, he has finally seen his life all as one, his guilt nearly expiated, his dues over the nine years paid, and he is ready to move on. Along the way are observations regarding secondary education and the Church.

ASHFORD is fiction. However, the scenes of farm, school, college, and graduate school have the authority of personal experience. Of course, the theme of sin and its consequence is universal.

ASHFORD

by James R. Moore

Edited by Em Putnam

"<u>Ashford</u>" is fiction. Any resemblance of depicted events or characters to actual events or people, living or dead, is mere coincidence.

Copyright © 2000 by **James R. Moore**

ISBN: 1-58721-816-X

1stBooks – rev. 7/11/00

ASHFORD

For my wife Billie -
whose support and encouragement are
the sole reasons for this book.

CHAPTER ONE

I drove home for my mother's funeral in the rain. At last, I turned on Pompey Hollow Road for the Jordan farmhouse, set amid aging maple trees, inhabited now by my brother Samuel and family. Approaching it set memories swirling. In fact, Samuel's call that she had died initiated a catharsis which found me wrestling with recollections from childhood through to that incredible fall of 1954 at Ashford School. Here I was, nine years after that chaotic season, home to help bury my mother. As I pulled in the driveway, I felt an unspeakable sadness.

Throughout the ride I experienced a clear memory of the thirties and my parents, Thomas and Kate, and my brothers and sisters subsisting very simply on this farm. We were so poor that we were rich, so motivated to escape the poverty that none had realized the Eden we had. The children, grown now, came to understand the roots of Pompey Hollow, the strength and character engendered there, but in the midst of it we'd been innocents aground.

In a wide measure, rural central New York has no specialness, isn't "the place to visit," has no canyons or real mountains, yet for the Jordans, Pompey Hollow was a total universe, where the past lingered in the lore of a time truly "Onondaga." The valley is a vast bowl, with the country villages of Oran at the north exit, and Delphi at the southern. Connecting both, Limestone Creek was usually generous with its brown trout and provided a muskrat and mink population my father depleted for profit every winter. Thomas Jordan was also the best shot around with regard to deer, pheasant and partridge. He ran rather than walked, and everyone knew him to be the smartest, most advanced farmer, even on the side hill where he grew apples, corn and kept a few grade holsteins.

Life on the farm wasn't exactly ennobling, or extraordinary, or original. But it was enriching, as I later found: the labor and expectations had formed a confidence born from the successive failures that challenging Nature provided on a daily basis. By age fourteen I had disappointed my father many times, caused in large measure by the fact that he had asked me to do so much, more it

1

seemed than was asked of my brothers and sisters. When I managed to dump a load of second cutting hay into Limestone Creek, my father simply called from the far bank, "Go get another load." When I backed the new truck into a tree and crumpled the tailgate, he held the tailgate up and had me back into the tree again. The impact flattened it - the cracks remained, but it was usable. I learned everything was fixable and by age sixteen believed anything was possible.

My first memory was at age four, sitting on Mother's lap on the side porch, watching the barn burn, from raging flames to smoking fallen beams lying on horribly dead cows. It was May. Lightning had struck at midnight, and by dawn our family had nearly nothing but ourselves, except that, by noon, my father was talking to Uncle Red about a new barn. The next day the clean-up began. I held a string so Mother could make straight rows for the beans and carrots; it was a huge garden that year - 1933. There was no money, so growing food had to be the first plan for starting again. Through the summer the barn and the garden grew, the barn a red symbol of renewal for a family of seven living in an economic depression which actually found the farmer best off of all.

The dairy gone, my father concentrated far more on the main crop - an apple orchard on the hill side of the farm. The basement of the red barn was used for storing the apples, mainly Northern Spies and Macintosh, but with no need for the hayloft, Thomas Jordan decided it would be a basketball court. That decision truly determined my future more than others. I played basketball from age five on, and in winter shot thousands of baskets wearing mittens or gloves. In later years there would be dances and parties and roller-skating in that red barn, but basketball made the Jordan farm Pompey Hollow's focus of activity.

Across the north orchard, only five hundred yards from the house, I began the first grade in a one-room schoolhouse. Children walked, rode horseback, or were sometimes driven there. In the deep winter, a neighbor, Orie Smith, even picked up students in his sleigh. School closed each day with the sound of his horses' bells, whatever the time. Even recess time was determined by the weather - good snow and sliding meant Miss Tobin delayed the return bell.

Limestone Creek ran behind the schoolhouse in a wide curve, where in January and February it usually froze for remarkably good skating.

Years later, I often reflected on this first education, the one-room schoolhouse with eight rows of desks and the round wood-burning stove in the center. The first grade was against one wall, the eighth grade against the other, which meant in winter the fourth and fifth grades were reasonably warm on either side of the stove. The older students came early to start the fire; well done meant Miss Tobin was generous with recess time. That single room would become a model for me when the '50s found me teaching. The interplay among grades, among older and younger students, the necessity for independent work, and the genius of a master teacher in Miss Tobin, found us all reading and computing ahead of our years. Achievement in school was the step out and up. There weren't any complications. Early on I was able to read the countless books lining the parlor walls, not the great classics, but good yarns by Roberts and Wren and others. The parlor was for reading or playing bridge - the table always up, waiting for four to gather. For diversion it was books, bridge, or the Atwater Kent radio - the rest of the time was farm work and school. Very simple.

As a boy, life was a wonder of family and school. Traditionally, parents and children gathered at Christmas break for a party at the schoolhouse. Orie Smith cut out a huge cedar from the swamp west of Limestone Creek, erecting it on a Sunday afternoon, and on the last day of classes the children decorated it - school-made paper ornaments, strung popcorn, with Miss Tobin's special star on top. The rush of excitement came when, at dusk, down the crossroad came Santa Claus, in a real sleigh, drawn by a horse (which never seemed to cause questions), St. Nick at the reins. It had all seemed so real. Each child received a gift, if only an orange, and for most Christmases it was the only gift - except for the indelible gifts of awe and wonder. I heard those sleigh bells long after I left Pompey Hollow forever, saw Miss Tobin and her bright red sweater; even Orie watched.

Macawber's definition of prosperity, income exceeding expense, fitted the Jordan family, especially since we never spent

3

more than we had. There was only one real flaw in my growing up, which rested in the fact that my mother was an Irish Catholic, and my father's family, who had come down from Canada, solid, staunch people, were very Protestant. Generous, Christian, frugal and wise, they allowed no room for the Catholic persuasion. My parents loved and bred, were resourceful mates, extraordinary examples, right and wrong clearly defined - but I dreaded Sundays, at least Sunday mornings.

Somehow Kate Jordan had managed that each child be baptized in St. James Church and receive First Communion, though she couldn't manage to sneak in Confirmation - for me that would come at college. The tension Sunday mornings about going to Mass frightened all the children, and my relief was enormous when the snow made roads impassable. During high school, one son stayed home each Sunday, to help our father with the chores, a sacrifice so the others could go to Mass. When my turn came, father and son marched in silence, side be side, I fearing to speak, my father stoically grim. It was a strange communion.

Finishing the chores quickly one April morning, my father finally spoke. "They stocked the crick yesterday. Want to go fishing?"

"That would be great!"

"Go behind the barn and dig some worms - I'll get the poles."

Together we crossed the field to Limestone, the worms in a tin can.

"Stand back from the bank, Tim. They're smart, but they're hungry. They'll be small, but a dozen will make breakfast."

Thirty feet from one another, we fished in silence, the warm spring sun in our faces. The brown trout did jump to the bait until each of us had several and our fishing became desultory.

"When will your mother be home?"

It was the first reference ever made by my father to the trip to Mass, and I stumbled. "Well... I'm not certain."

"You do know the church times?"

"Well, yes...I guess around 10:30 or so. Think they went to nine o'clock."

"Today was your turn at home?"

"Yes."

"Which is better, Timothy? Doin' this or dressing up for church?" And my father turned slightly to look at me, his eyes impossible to read, except that I felt an instant ache at my father's almost unfair question and at my own desperate search for an answer.

"Dad, I like doing this, and never mind trying to help. It's just all so difficult."

Nearly a minute passed before my father said, "Yes. Yes, it is."

Then abruptly we collected our catch and headed back to the house. The car was back. Another Sunday morning had come and gone.

The difficulty never dissipated, and the fear of going to Mass in those years tore at my loyalties, despite my complete embracing of the faith, of my fulfilling love for Jesus. The difficulty, in fact, enriched and strengthened my faith, even when I increasingly knew that my father was the greatest influence I'd ever have, even after his death.

There were more Sunday mornings after that when my father would change plans, and we'd go hunting, or tend the trap line, or hike up to the Indian burying ground on the Ingersoll Farm to look for arrowheads. These excursions never occurred for my brothers, only for me.

One Sunday morning my father and I sat on a promontory of the Indian burying ground, alternately looking at three arrowheads and a piece of pottery, and then out over the valley. I always felt an excitement at this place, as though transferred back in time. The wind seemed always to blow, and the pines gave off moaning sounds that made me glance behind; only once did I ever go there alone.

"Tim, we'll put these arrowheads with the others in the safe. You should count them. I found my first over thirty years ago, when your grandfather brought me up here."

"Dad, was this place a fort?"

"Not really, but there was a wall around it. The Onondagas did that - and the site gave them visual command of the whole valley, from south to north." My father paused. Then, "You know, Tim, we have great hopes for you. You make mistakes, but usually from trying. At times your aim may be too high, but you can see things better."

"I'm not sure I understand...what it is I see."

My father turned then, startling since he wasn't a loquacious man, and spoke in an even voice. "The farm is small, Tim, not enough to support all of us. You children must break out, go to college - you more than the rest. The usual thing in Pompey Hollow is that the sons stay on the farm, and the girls marry farmers - and that's okay, I guess, or used to be, but it isn't going to work any more. The small farms here won't last as we know them, not more than twenty, maybe thirty years. Anyway, if ours did, it just isn't big enough for everyone. You have ambition, a lot of talent, potential. Honestly, it's a selfish thing, too." He grinned. "My hope is you will succeed, make some money, support your old man when the time comes."

Then he stood, the conversation ended, and we slanted down the ridge to the path back home. Later, I counted the arrowheads in my box - the day's find brought the total to seventy-three. I was twelve years old.

The next December 7th Pearl Harbor changed everyone's world. The war took our family from subsistence to real prosperity. Our crops took on a new value. Farmers could get gasoline, but other folks were rationed, and friends came trying to buy gasoline, since my father had plenty. Older sons in the valley left for war, but I, my father and my two brothers were too old or too young, which meant man-power for the farm, so we planted more fields, over two hundred acres, with sweet corn, tomatoes, potatoes, melons - and always the apples, whose price doubled in one year.

My older brother, Samuel, and I spurted in size and strength, each well co-ordinated, but I had the speed. There was always basketball, but when the first hay was in, we would hit fungoes to each other on the mowed fields until it was too dark to see for pitching or catching. We made a pitching mound in back of the house, sixty feet, six inches from plate to rubber, and we would pitch to the Babe and Gehrig and Dickey - always the Yankees. Left-handed, I was fast and wild, had a hook and a slider. Samuel always pitched over the plate. He never walked anyone. Samuel was always true, in everything.

CHAPTER TWO

My only solace was that no one knew the truth but me. Home at last from the cemetery from Mother's funeral, I sat under an apple tree in the hill orchard, able to scan north and south the five miles of Pompey Hollow, my home so long ago now, though details of that life in the '30s and '40s rushed back to combat not the sorrow of Mother's death, immense as it was, but the private Hell of my indescribable fall from grace. I had stamped it down, laid it to rest, I'd thought, stored it away in a hidden recess of the heart. But the funeral had found it.

I had never truly documented those events of 1954 at Ashford, nor outlined the preliminaries, nor seen it all in context, so terrifying was the circumstance. It seemed now, like it or not, I had no choice but to go back, perhaps to find some anchor, or event to placate, or to bandage the wound that bled continuously - such bleeding - how had I lived these nine years and not drained white, to wake up again and again, still alive, but so weary?

Coming home this time did force recollections of my mother, and of my beginnings. It was likely the place to start, for what happened had to be connected to what I was, how I became what I was, how I became so susceptible while thinking myself invincible. Obviously, the story could never be revealed, but if I told it to myself, just *for* myself, perhaps I could retreat from the edge of madness to which I so often felt drawn. I ached from the enervating battle for sanity I waged each day, and too often all night, since that plague, that terrible Autumn of 1954.

I stood and trudged slowly higher up the hill to where it leveled at the Macintosh trees, where I could see they were now old, broken, not bearing much anymore. What apples there were Samuel used to make cider, actually making more profit that way than from a bushel, and cider was just as good from small apples as large ones; a worm or two didn't harm the flavor.

My mother ... recollections swirled, an eddy of grief. Kate Ryan, all Irish. Two miles down Pompey Hollow Road was the Ryan farmstead where she'd grown up always fearful of her father's major drunks, so afraid when he rampaged Saturday nights that she'd hidden in the cornrows, often until dawn. She'd survived, grew wise and became statuesque, slender but full-bosomed. My father came calling despite her Irish Catholicism. Somehow she managed Teacher's College in Cortland, and taught school in one-room schoolhouses, at Bethel and Limestone, the latter just five hundred yards from the Jordan house. They had married at age twenty-seven.

One night she came to my bed where I lay sick and feverish. She leaned down to wipe my forehead with a cool cloth, her nightgown slack, so that I saw her full breasts.

"Mother, what are those?"

"Timothy, I am your mother. They are me." She took my hand to each for a moment, and I closed my eyes, her full warmth in my hand, and then slept.

The sudden clarity of this memory horrified me, but it was there. I had never remembered it before, not the next morning, not the rest of my life, until this moment. The incredible honesty and rightness of her move - and now the sorrow of her death ... I cried for the first time and reached for a connection.

Kate Ryan Jordan never cooked well, but the family seemed to eat well, ordinary foods from the farm, three meals a day. She still found time to drive the tractor when needed, fish Limestone Creek, talk with neighbors on the telephone. About housecleaning she would say, "Well, I'll just give the house a lick and a promise."

My father was her idol, and her five children were her prizes. The teacher in her made us study, and she always expected each child to do well, and each did. She expected us to be stalwart and firm in moral purpose and righteousness. In time, whenever I was about to leave on a date, taking the family car, she would remind me, "Remember, Timothy, your mother is a Magrill!"

I never knew exactly what that meant, nor had I ever asked for an explanation, but understood that my conduct should be beyond reproach, that somehow the family line demanded it, that a tradition was to be upheld, that one's reputation was everything and that one's name was to be honored by all. Mine still was but shouldn't have been. Sadly, I wondered what Kate Jordan now thought, and could only pray for her heavenly forgiveness.

My mother's faith had been obdurate, unstinting, rosary-bound, but necessarily pragmatic, faced with his her husband's equally rocklike blind spot. It had to be a blind spot, she had often said, for Thomas was so good, honest, fair, even noble in her eyes. He had been an incredibly Christian man, right up to seven years ago and the flip of the spraying machine on the side hill. When he hadn't returned to reload the sprayer, she had walked up through the orchard and found him, crushed. Again her faith persevered, she knowing that despite his blind spot, he was in Heaven. My brothers and sisters decided I should give the eulogy, and though the task was incredibly difficult, I actually enjoyed extemporizing for the large crowd at the funeral home.

In our formative years, my mother's manipulations to secure the faith in the children were a marvel. We didn't always make Mass in the winter, when my father's mood was especially foreboding or when, mysteriously, the Nash wouldn't start, but she always said, "God will understand," and she would lead everyone in several "Our Fathers" and "Hail Marys" - and always "Glory be to God, the Father, the Son, and the Holy Ghost." At the end, she would say, "God bless this family, and especially your father." As a result, the Masses they did get to were precious. During high school, I had even walked the five miles to Mass a few times.

I shook my head - the memories were so rambling - but now I was into it, relieved that my mood seemed lighter, more at ease, even amused.

And why on earth was I now remembering riding the bus to the Consolidated Central School when Limestone Elementary closed, and fourth grade with Miss Pratt as my teacher? Then it was only Miss Pratt in my mind - dark eyed, dark hair, handsomely formed, usually clad in a purple knit dress disturbingly defining her large breasts. I'd watched her closely and had awakened to that larger world of the womanly form. She knew I stared, and when she had stood by the desk and leaned down to ostensibly look at my work, my whole body had come alive. She gave me "A"s in everything. But then, for her I did all my work.

My walk took me to the last row of Macintosh; beyond lay the woods I had roamed fearlessly as a child. Now they seemed dark and ominous. I stood still, gazing into them, remembering the oak sapling dug up and brought to Mother when I was ten. Together we had planted it just beyond the side porch. Remarkably it had survived - we had once counted the leaves - and now it was ten inches around at the base of the trunk, and in the fall its leaves made a pile. I had brought trilliums and mayflowers for her, and together we had picked blackberries from the hundreds of wild, prickly bushes around the wood's edge. Once, Mother had set down a full pail of berries to retrieve on the way home, only to find on return a snake coiled on top.

"It's a snick," she had whispered. I was enthralled, then terrified.

"Leave it," she said. "One should never leave anything behind, or a snick will come."

I now walked along the same berry patches, but not into the woods, and returned, down through the orchard, in a sort of torpor, the tranquil recollections of Mother now agitating the crises of my life and, pointedly, the crucible fall months in 1954 at Ashford. I felt an Oedipal reflex that made her death more troubling than simply the inevitable passing of one's parent, and yet her death also printed a pale cancellation stamp on the other, enough that perhaps now some perspective could come, but not fully racked in pain or shame. Moving on seemed too arduous, but standing still could become bearable.

Samuel, still lanky and slim but nearly bald, stood by the porch and my oak tree, watching me come down the hill into the yard.

"Still know your way around? Did you go to the woods?"

"Nothing seems to change up there. Mother's berries remain. You know, the woods are still sort of scary."

"It's just the day - your mood. My plan is to keep it all the same, as much as possible. The trees are getting old, especially the Spies and those Rhode Island Greenings. The Greenings are no loss. Besides, they were never any good. Not even in cider. Anyway, our mother would like it if we kept it on. Sort of: 'the Jordans still here in the Hollow.' For Dad, you know."

I nodded. Knowing Samuel was right, and was the one to do it, who wanted it.

"Samuel, I'm for you. Do as you wish. It's your right. You are here. Just so I can visit."

"You know, Tim, it's here for you any time."

The next day I bade good-byes to brothers and sisters, and drove down Pompey Hollow Road to Route 20, through Cazenovia, and then steadily east.

I was numb with sadness. The only reason ever to return was nostalgia for my beginnings.

After Morrisville, Bouckville and Madison, Route 20 becomes four-lane, and I put the car on cruise and just steered. By the time I got to Sangerfield I was thinking of the Colgate years.

CHAPTER THREE

My path had been defined by academic excellence, studious work habits and a seeming pleasure in always doing "the right thing" - no errant ways among them. At Colgate, superior performance was expected, and more than once I chafed over the example everyone expected me to follow. Worse was the fact that my younger brother, coming behind, was a genius.

My particular flair was sociability, for both good and ill. From somewhere I'd been bestowed with an ease with others, an obvious confidence and open good nature. Simply, I was popular, admired, sought after, with the girls intently conniving for dates that the distance of the farm, as well as circumstance rarely permitted. I managed good grades, played a euphonium in the band, edited the yearbook, even played the king in <u>Androcles and The Lion</u> - all the while playing all the sports, even track and baseball in the same spring season. Once, during a home track meet and baseball game, I pole-vaulted to a first place, between innings, in my baseball uniform. Samuel had set the scene in sports - a splendid, calm, steady performer; but I achieved the larger acclaim. I was simply very fast.

All those endless games at home came to fruition - the fungoes, pitching, basketball shooting, even the padless games of tackle. At the farm Samuel and I stuck apples on three- foot sticks and threw them for distance, the elongated arm providing the long arc of a giant pitching machine. Of course, it hadn't all been easy. Once, at a football practice, after the coach had instructed the backs on a certain play, he had called to the sideline, "Jordan, do you think you can do that?" I was a tenth grader and a sub.

"I...I don't know."

Coach Rhymer lost it, tore off his whistle, threw it in the air, and bellowed even more explosively than usual, "Don't you ever say 'I don't know,' even if you don't! We have to have players who *do* know, who *want* to know, who will *kill* to play. We want Goddamn fearless players out here! Don't you - or anybody- ever say that again. You all can do it, Goddammit, or you better want to even if I have to beat the living shit out of you. Now, Jordan, get in here. You're supposed to be the hotshot around here."

I never forgot that day, or Harry Rhymer, and I ran with a fear-rush of adrenaline that made me the wingback by the end of practice.

Picking apples in the fall was a task for the whole family: father, mother, brothers and sisters. As a saving, my father never hired pickers in those years, but also because the family could pick apples faster and less bruised than anyone from the outside. The boys had contests for the amount picked in a day. Picking Spies from the ground in a good season, each was capable of one hundred bushels, and my father would pick the top ones from a ladder. Of course, none of the boys could match our father. Thomas could glean, using both hands, into his shoulder bag with a smooth, flowing motion at which I marveled. My father's speed set such a high goal.

One October Saturday morning, when I was a junior, the family was in the orchard when up from Pompey Hollow Road walked Harry Rhymer who, with a bow to my mother, approached my father.

"Morning, Thomas. I see you're all at it today."

"Hello, Harry. What brings you here on a Saturday morning? Aren't we playing Oneida this afternoon?"

"We certainly are, and I heard about your family and Timothy all working Saturdays. God, Thomas, don't you know Timothy has this game at two-thirty?"

"Oh, we sure do. But not to worry. Tim will meet his quota in time. He'll have forty bushels picked. Look - he must have twenty already."

"But that's what I mean. He's going to be tired out. This is a big game. Can't you send him down the house to take it easy?"

"Harry, he'll be fine. When he's done here, he'll just be getting up to speed. Don't worry. We'll have him there on time."

Harry Rhymer stood, shaking his head, but with resignation on his face. Turning to leave he said, "Well, at least he's not on a ladder."

16

I finished my task by noon and, indeed, made the gym locker room on time. That year I was running Harry Rhymer's single wing out of the tailback position, from which I could run and throw left-handed bullets both short and long. My speed and change of pace gave an elusiveness talked about around the league. Oneida was very good, and the first half of the game found my passes either dropped or off the mark, and one tackle flattened me with no breath left. Oneida led at the half, 14-0.

In the locker room Harry yelled, with a snide reference at the end of his diatribe to "our apple-picking quarterback." As I left the locker room, I found my father standing at the top of the stairs. This had never happened before. He touched my arm.

"Tim, you're playing with little conviction. You must believe you can beat Oneida, that you can win. Then everyone else will. You can beat this team, but you must believe it."

I remembered that amazing second half, Cazenovia receiving the kickoff, how I ran and passed with dizzying success, even intercepting the other side to return the ball for a touchdown. All on the team came alive, stymied Oneida at every turn, a reversal so dominating that victory saw the score 27-14.

My father may not have been a Catholic, but there had never been any other man like him in my life, not anyone. How I had loved him. But, sadly, I could not remember ever telling him.

I stopped for the light in Bridgewater. West Winfield and Richfield Springs lay ahead. I knew this route so well. Over the years I had been stranded in each of these towns, as I hitchhiked back and forth on Route 20, often to Skidmore, and then very often to Albany, where Marjorie had lived. We had dated steadily for two years, and then she had broken it off under pressure from her mother to stop seeing "that Catholic."

In high school Harold Webster had been my very best friend. The Websters lived on Seminary Street in Cazenovia. Harold and I often stayed overnight at each other's home. Harold's father William taught English, and it was likely it had been he who had influenced my interest in English, augmenting the extensive reading I had done growing up on the farm. In fact, the English faculty was remarkable at Cazenovia High School. One of my teachers was

17

Walter Van Tilburg Clark, who wrote <u>The Oxbow Incident</u>, and many short stories.

William Webster was a Colgate man. Harold was headed there, and, with the friendship and William's influence, my own interest grew. Colgate offered War Memorial Scholarships, the only way I could consider attending. So began the process of testing and recommendations and application. I'd continued to run off tackle with recognized success, and Syracuse University beckoned with a football scholarship. In April of my senior year, on a Saturday morning, I was in the Spy orchard, up in a tree pruning, when two men in suits picked their way up the hill, directed there by my father. They found my tree and squinted up at me, smiling. The balding older man said, "Timothy Jordan, is that you way up in that tree?"

"Yes, it is."

"My name is George Deming, Dean of Students at Colgate, and this is Arthur Chase, Assistant Dean of Admissions. We wanted to meet you and find out something about where you come from. What, exactly, are you doing up there?"

"Well, I'm pruning the tree. You see these shoots? They have to be cut out each spring. Otherwise, they use up the tree's energy and clog everything. We also cut out dead limbs. An apple tree has to be sort of open - open to the sun."

"Is there anything else you do?" asked Arthur Chase.

"Well, yes, mowing the grass and when the apples come, if there are too many, we thin them, so we have fewer but bigger apples. And there are several sprays for worms and scab and aphids. The sprayer is sort of tricky on this side hill, so my father does it."

I had climbed down, awkward in my overalls and knee-high boots, but they didn't seem to care.

"Timothy, can we walk down to your house and talk for a while?" George Deming asked.

On the way I wondered if Mother had neglected to give the house a "lick and a promise," and I agonized that I might be embarrassed.

But my mother knew what was going on, and drew them into the parlor where she had readied some of her molasses cookies and coffee. To my relief, her housedress was fresh and stainless.

"Mrs. Jordan, we didn't expect this," Arthur Chase said pointing to the cookies, "but it looks delicious. How long have you lived on your farm?'

"My goodness, a long time. It's over a hundred years old - not that we're that old!" She laughed merrily. Then she was off again with "Mr. Jordan's family..." and went into the history of the house all the way back to 1880 and right on up to a description of the fishing and the berries while I squirmed. But Deming and Chase didn't seem to mind. In fact, they gave every appearance of immense enjoyment - these high-positioned college men in their suits, smooth silk ties, and polished shoes made somewhat scruffy from tramping up the hill to find me.

George Deming asked about Kate's other children and then about her diversions, and she was off again, this time about my Holstein yearling, who, being haltered for the first time, had dragged me full speed around the ring at the State Fair.

Why on *earth* did she have to tell them that? And why on earth were the men laughing so gleefully? While they and my mother were having a wonderful time at my expense, my scholarship was being swiftly flushed down the drain.

When, half a dozen cookies and several cups of coffee later, they finally rose to leave, George Deming said, "Timothy, you live in a special place, and it has been a wonderful visit. We'll think about it, and you'll be hearing from us."

All lost, I had despaired. All lost. Without a word to my mother, I had returned to the Spy tree, realizing Colgate left nothing to chance. Well, they'd seen firsthand the hayseed I was, and they had seen the hayseed's mother. I could just hear them in the car back to Hamilton: "Well, after all, what could you expect?" I wondered if Syracuse would send anyone, and if I could somehow avoid another disaster.

Syracuse sent no one, except a coach to talk to Harry Rhymer. Two weeks later, gloriously, Syracuse notified me that I had a football scholarship of generous proportion, and, on the same day, a letter arrived from Dean Deming awarding me a War Memorial Scholarship, of much less proportion, but still a thrilling recognition. Decision time was upon me, more upon my parents, but most of all upon my father. There seemed to be no way he could afford his son at Colgate; even Syracuse would be more than a sacrifice.

"We're all proud of you, Tim," Thomas Jordan said. "Winning the scholarship says a lot about you. How do you feel about the two places?"

"Dad, that's the trouble. I never thought, really, about playing football at the Syracuse level - or if I can, or if it's the right reason for going to college. It was sure impressive that Dean Deming and Mr. Chase came to see me and Mother. But I know Colgate's a real bunch of money. Dad, I'll be fine at Syracuse."

"But deep down you want Colgate. Look, we'll figure it out somehow. You can get a job there, and weekends you can get home to help here. Maybe I'll hire you to pick by the bushel. Hopefully, if you do well, the scholarship will increase. Dean Deming hinted at that. If you want Colgate, we'll just work at a way."

Why hadn't I told my father <u>then</u> how much I loved him? All I could do was mutter things like, "Do you mean it?", "Are you sure?", "Is it really possible?"

Then my father said, "Tim, just assure me of one thing: We're not sending you to Colgate to become a teacher. Promise me that. Your sisters are into it, but that's different. There isn't any money there. After all, your mother and I will need someone to look after us down the road."

CHAPTER FOUR

My Freshman year was fabulous athletically. I ran off-tackle for forty yards to beat the Army Plebes, and, ironically, threw a three-hitter to shut out the Syracuse Frosh. Best of all, I started every Freshman game in basketball; it was a unique season, the most rewarding of all.

Basketball tryouts found at least sixty candidates, including Harold Webster. The format was simple: the coach, Rudy Wilson, lined us up and had us count off by fives, then stood on the bleacher in the gym and watched one five play half-court against another five for five minutes. The winning five stayed on the court. By sheer luck, I had lined up with the four best other players and, incredibly, we kept winning, until we nearly dropped from exhaustion, and went on to be the team starters.

Harold Webster was cut on the first round, and for four years he barely spoke to me.

That first year found my grades mediocre, with five Cs. I found myself in classes with men from the most prestigious prep schools who all seemed to know everything. Even more competitive were the G.I. Bill veterans - mature, purposeful men who intimidated professors. Freshman college courses daunted none of them after the foxholes and beaches and far-away Pacific atolls. They were nerveless and focused, celebrating being alive in nightly beer sessions.

I worked at the library nearly every night but was usually tired from the year-long practices and games. I just didn't "catch on" like the others, hadn't learned to distinguish trivia from the heart of the matter. Still, I managed to do better than those whose too frequent nights at the Inn doomed them from any return. Increasingly confident and aggressive on the court and field, I was naive, tenuous, uncertain in the classroom.

In late May Dean Deming called me to his office. The Dean was off-hand, but clear in his words: "Timothy, I can't tell you the pleasure your play has brought me - and the whole campus. Great stuff. Good show. But you are a War Memorial Scholar, and five Cs just aren't enough, even figuring the adjustment from the farm and public school. I recommend you select one season to get some balance in your life. You'll likely be better at both the books and whatever one sport you choose. Mind you, I'm not telling you, just recommending. In any event, keeping the scholarship means better grades all around. Besides, you're already waiting on table, so your time is pushed. Think it over - over the summer. Talk to your mother. She's a wise lady - a better counselor than I."

. . .

So I settled on basketball, returning in the fall committed to the library and to trying to make the Varsity. All summer I practiced a one-hand shoot in the barn, at least one hundred a day, and ran the Pompey Hollow roads in heat and rain, and often in darkness, a flashlight in hand for wandering coon and farmers' cars.

Practice and tryouts began in October. I also found my way to morning Mass that month at St. Mary's Church at the other end of town, and went on the day the coach posted the twelve selections for the traveling squad. I went to classes and then circled the gym for an hour, not daring to look at the bulletin board. When I thought people would be at lunch, I brought myself to go look. Mine was the twelfth name! I would come to realize that no success would ever rival that moment, or impact my life so fully - not graduate degrees, not promotions, love - nothing would come close.

. . .

The remaining years at college now seemed to merge, one unit of ascending experience. Academically, I grew more assured, settling on an English major. I could read quickly, usually taking the novels on the basketball trips.

Matthew Mussler was Colgate's English professor of choice; only English majors could take his special course, The World Novel. He behaved as if his students weren't real, that they were just an assembled audience, that he didn't curry their favor or applause, but just gave horribly long reading assignments and

22

required papers that if not researched thoroughly would surely fail. Nonetheless, his presentation, lectures, and insights were all electric, a level I'd never yet experienced. Mussler graded severely, and when one of my papers was returned with the hook grade, a paper on which I had truly labored, I asked for an appointment. I'd be late for practice, but so be it - there was always that expectation to hold for the Scholarship. My left-hand hook shot wouldn't keep it, not at Colgate.

Mussler was a tall, thin man, mustached, his glasses rimless and a sort of brown color, his jacket drooping from his shoulders.

"Sit down, Jordan," he said. "Why are you here?"

"Professor, I'm on scholarship, you know, a War Memorial Scholarship, and, you see, the Dean expects certain grades in order to keep it.'

"I see. Are you doing that?"

"Mostly, yes, but in this course I can't seem to measure up, at least on this last paper. I spent hours on it, and to get only a C just doesn't seem the right thing."

Mussler said nothing for a while, apparently unmiffed by the unintended insult. Then: "Jordan, do you enjoy the course?"

"Yes, I do."

"Do you find Thomas Mann and The <u>Magic Mountain</u> a significant literary experience?"

"Oh, yes. It is very challenging - some things I've never thought of before."

"Then you do think you are learning something, Jordan?"

"Absolutely."

"Then, Jordan, since you have entered this office, you certainly know your way out, especially since you are a War Memorial Scholar."

My grades improved - to Bs by the end of the course.

CHAPTER FIVE

While some fraternities rushed me as a freshman, they ignored me in the bidding. My dorm entry-mates all pledged, but I didn't feel left out, and certainly I was in no position to afford the life-style. I waited on tables and served food at the Student Union, played the sports, attended class, and went home as often as possible to help, especially with picking the apples. I made the varsity team as a sophomore, and the Dekes came calling. When the hazing started, with the sleepless nights and the bizarre, inhuman flagellation of the spirit, I found himself in a migrant workers' shack five miles out of town with other pledges, expected to return to the college by foot - and naked. Somehow I had managed to stuff away my trousers and keep them from collection, take to the fields and, alone, make my way back to Andrews Hall. I knew it was over - the craziness had affected my play and my study, but more so, rudely shaken the dignity, probably the desired effect, but hardly within my self-esteem. Back in the room at two in the morning, I wrote a brief resignation to the good brothers and fell into bed, saying a prayer of thanksgiving that I had made a decision to be myself. They did everything to persuade me to return, but I stood firm and told my roommate Archie Wilson, "I'm your man. You'll be my brother."

Archie had never been rushed, was from New Jersey, talked about his mother constantly, and sought my approval on everything. He grieved that he had no niche, no athletic skill, no apparent goal or real ambition. Short and slight, he simply wasn't visible; his alliance with me was both touching and suffocating. He saw every movie that came to Hamilton, much to my relief, for these times I could study in the room rather than the library. Archie came to all the games and was a sincere, loyal fan and analyst of the game. Archie called me "Lefty."

One movie night Archie returned late, but I had not noticed, reading "Young Goodman Brown" and "Rappacini's Daughter," making notes and drinking cider brought from home. Around midnight Archie, face aglow and smiling, floated in, walking straight rather than in his usual slouch.

"Lefty, old man, it's been some night. I'm telling you, some night."

"Good flick?"

"I don't know. I never got there. But the night began at the Inn. Stopped in for a brew or two."

"Or three of four."

"Nope. I did something crazy. Two dames came in, kinda older, ya know, and sat in the corner, one tall and dark and the other shorter with glasses. The bartender asked me to take 'em two beers - save him steps and all. So I take the beers over and they're all smiling and grateful - and Jesus, ask me to sit down! Can you imagine?"

"No, I can't."

"Well, just so's you know, I did. Turns out they teach down at the high school. We have the beer, and I buy another, and we chit-chat until they say it's time to go. So I says I'm coming back here and - can you believe it? - ol' Archie offers to walk them home! - and they'd 'be delighted.' God, Lefty, the tall one is something, and the other is okay, just she has glasses. Anyway it's Betty and Marion. They live here on College Street in an apartment. So we get there, and Betty asks me to come in - I can't believe it. So we go in and look around a bit, and Marion says she's going to bed."

Archie paused, threw his head back, raised his arms in the air and froze.

"Well?"

"Well, Lefty Jordan, big star athlete, guess who just got attacked by a Home Economics teacher. Archie Wilson, that's who!"

"I don't believe it."

"Believe it, baby. Believe it. We sit on the sofa, and, shit - she's all over me. I mean wild - and ripping and laughing until - Christ, she's naked and on top and just goin' nuts. God, I can't remember it all, but she did a job on me - and I didn't have to do anything. Lefty, do you know what I'm saying?"

"I don't believe it!"

"Believe it!"

"Okay, okay, calm down, Archie. Calm down."

26

A few nights later I was called to the phone in the entry. It was Archie, at the Inn.

"Lefty, I'm with my friends, and we all think it would be dandy if you got away from the books and came on down. Whaddya say?"

"Forget it, Archie."

"Lefty - come *on*. You need something. Besides, be my good roomie - it would make things kosher, ya know."

"Archie, you've been doing fine without me - if it's all true."

"Look, they're fans of yours - they watch you play. Besides, you know - I'd like them to know you're really my roomie."

Finally, at that last plea, I threw on a jacket and walked to the Inn. Outwardly, everything was as Archie had said. The tall woman, Betty, was indeed stunning, affable, most aware of the Red Raider team and its lefty guard Jordan. Marion was a sidekick, funny, self-deprecating, Rubensesque in a red pullover. I found it amazing, these young teachers, apparently at ease with two younger college kids.

Once we were inside the women's apartment door, the plan was obvious. Betty pulled Archie to the living room, and Marion led Timothy to the kitchen to find drinks. She turned on a small light over the sink and said, "I doubt they'll *really* want anything, do you?"

"But the drinks were Betty's idea."

"Well, Mr. Basketball, that was just conversation. She has other plans for Archie, so we should stay out here - unless you'd like the bedroom."

"No - no. It's okay here."

There was a pause, and then, still by the sink, she pulled her red sweater over her head, and with a flick undid her brassiere, turned with her amazing breasts exposed, one cupped in each hand, and flicking her nipples, walked to him, smiling and saying, "These are for you, Mr. Jordan."

Somehow I felt violated - like I had in the migrant shack, my trousers clutched behind me - and then flashes came, of my mother bending over me, of a poor girl in high school showing her breasts on the school bus on a dare, of the illustrations in the big, bound volume of the Inferno I would sneak off to look at in his Aunt

Harriet's attic, and of the invariable and continual fantasies I had of women's breasts, my ever o'er-weaning, constant indulgence in contemplating their shape and size, this beauty that I wanted, craved to touch.

I reached out, but too late to slow her determined effort at belt and trousers. I was frozen, eyes shut, for some minutes the food of her voracious appetite, until my legs quivered to the point of collapse. Afterwards, she was incredibly calm, effiently zippering and buttoning, pulling on her top, ushering me to the door - and only then kissing me on the mouth and saying, "Be gone Mr. Basketball, but come again."

Archie didn't come back that night, and I didn't see him until the next day when he came along the food line for supper. He looked under the sneeze guard and said to me, serving food behind the counter, "You okay, roomie?"

"Not really."

"What's the matter - lousy time or what?"

"No - well, yes. I forgot my mother is a Magrill."

Archie walked away, shaking his head.

I went to confession the next Saturday, and Father enjoyed my presence at daily Mass for two weeks. Eventually I convinced myself it had been fantasy. Anyway, I never returned to College Street.

CHARTER SIX

Approaching Richfield Springs, I recalled how I had once been stranded there almost all night while hitchhiking back to Colgate from visiting Marjorie in Albany, from the usual cold reception by her mother, from the intensity of our physical attraction that, at least for intervals, overcame the fact that she was a Lutheran and I a Catholic.

I met her on a party weekend; she had been the date of someone else - who had passed out at the Inn. The details of our meeting were now lost to me - I remembered dutifully walking her to where she was staying. I also recalled, after summer had passed, how, in the early fall of my junior year, I called her Syracuse sorority. She remembered me and agreed to come to Hamilton for a football game.

Marjorie was not particularly sophisticated or preppy and had no idea what impact she had on men: though not beautiful, she was simply extremely attractive: at a party all eyes found her. She had a physical symmetry that dazzled, a laugh that distinguished her presence, a warmth that made me want to hug her. I could hardly believe it when, in the note she wrote to thank me for the weekend, she said at the end: "Be on guard, Timothy Jordan, because I think I've started to fall in love with you."

She had loved coming to Colgate, "Away from the city and all the crazies" she maintained populated the Syracuse campus. A Physical Education major, she feigned interest in my English major but was enthralled with my talent on the court. She danced acrobatically, taught me tennis, and completely cowed me on the golf course. I could beat her from the foul line, but not by much. She was graceful, poised, perfect - and Lutheran. We talked about our religious differences some, but never to conflict, or to any seeming real difficulty. Such conversations usually ended with her tongue deep in my mouth or my mouth attempting to devour her whole right breast. Though we frolicked, we both seemed to agree, without actually saying so, that postponing consummation was best.

. . .

I broke into the Varsity lineup my Junior year, and Marjorie came to Boston to see me play Holy Cross in the wonderful, old, packed Garden. It was another public relations stage for our star, Ribicoff, and he made the most of it, especially in the final quarter when he scored five unanswered baskets on direct feeds from me. I got but nine points but defended and rebounded for two halves better than ever. Marjorie screamed from the fifth row as I flew through the game intercepting, assisting, and, remarkably, staying out of foul trouble. The winning margin was just three points on a final turnaround from Ribicoff on which he was fouled. Certainly it was that game that settled Ribicoff for basketball's All-American team. In the locker room he came over to me. "Tim," he said, 'you were numb out there. You made it all happen. You made the greatest night of my life."

And Marjorie couldn't contain herself, devouring me in the taxi on the way to the train station. She said "I love you" a hundred times. Boarding the train without her that night had been hard, but I decided it may have been best - she was so dear, such a terrific pal. I glowed from her idolatry but wasn't sure I loved her, and wondered what would it be like to be a Lutheran. Her Lutheran. Perhaps her mother's point of view had been right.

"Find a Lutheran, Marjorie," Marjorie had reported her saying, "or at least a Protestant. You can never go to confession with a priest in that box. Do you know what they do?"

Now, at the stop light in Sharon Springs, Route 20's infamous speed trap, I thought about how my dear Marjorie had finally conceded to her mother, her loyalty flawed just enough for some doubts about a lifetime with me - and this without my ever bringing up that possibility. Somehow God, or my own unreadiness, or fear of commitment, had held me back even though she had everything a woman could bring to a marriage - but for an upbringing that taught her Catholics were bad people. During a tempestuous night in her car, parked in a quarry pit beyond the west hill of Pompey Hollow, she wept and fought her doubts, but finally rearranged her clothes, smoothed her hair, and dropped me at the farm. I watched the red tail lights for a mile down the road. Once, they went on bright. She was stopping! She was coming back! But then they went off, and she drove out of sight. My Lutheran lover was gone.

32

CHAPTER SIX

Of course, that all had come to pass near the end of my last year at Colgate. It was a year that found me the most comfortable with my classes. I had discovered the knack of doing well, of enjoying a bemused yet detached association with Archie, of an apparently intimate connection with Marjorie. The Melville seminar was rewarding and great fun - adult, English majors only - and met all afternoon once a week up at Tom Donovan's house in a gully behind the golf course. One fellow had an old station wagon, and all ten students would load in and on it and careen up the dirt road to where Professor Donovan was ready with coffee and donuts, piercing insights into Herman's life and work, and the requirement that each student conduct on entire seminar himself on a significant Melville work. My fate had been <u>Omoo</u>, but somehow I managed it after a month's research and reading. In fact, Donovan smiled at the end, saying, "You know, Jordan, you just might make an American Lit Scholar some day."

Not if <u>Omoo</u> is the text, I thought.

But it was a pleasure to tread in the field of literary research, to write some hard prose about it, to know I might know something not even the American Scholar knew. It was okay!

Ribicoff had graduated and gone to New York and the Knicks. At Colgate few thought the basketball season would be much without him. We had little size, no depth, and a new coach, Coach Russell, who knew his football but not much basketball strategy. But the starters had such speed, defense, and tremendous desire to prove everyone wrong that we would play until we fouled out, or nearly dropped dead.

The season ground along, up and down, but the team proved valiant as we were usually the underdogs. We played with injury - my right knee taped daily - and by February the first five were drawn and fatigued to the extent that all had lost too much weight - I was down fifteen pounds - and most had colds. Our record, with a game to go against Syracuse, was 13-8 - not bad at all, rather a triumph. On the last Monday at practice Coach Russell looked us over as we came on the court, and then sent us back to shower. As we dressed Russell told the starters to report to the infirmary. We stayed there a week, ate steak, drank orange juice and walked about a mile a day. We could read or study, but lights were out by ten. Nothing like this had ever happened with any Colgate team, so we felt special, with a few faculty even stopping in to visit. We almost reveled in our boredom, broken only on Friday by an hour's shoot-around before going back to the infirmary for steak dinner, and bed.

At the Monday check-in Nurse Bromley had signed our admission cards. She was a legend at Colgate for her toughness, especially with athletes. A widow in her fifties, slatey-grey haired, she stood tall, her figure trim and full-bosomed in her whites. Gazing straight at me, she said she had seen me play.

"We weren't much last time out."

"You know, you look awful. You all look awful."

"I guess that's why we're here. Coach said you could fix us up," I lied.

"Well, I don't know about that. I just know what you're supposed to do and make sure that's all you do." Then, "You're from Cazenovia."

"Yes. Yes, I am. Well, just beyond Cazenovia, in Pompey Hollow."

"I go through there to see my sister in Seneca Falls. I always wondered who lived in that big valley. Now I know: old 'Lefty' Jordan."

"You know about 'Lefty'?"

"Yes. Archie's been in here. The flu. He talked about his 'roomie Lefty.'"

"Ole Arch."

"Well, Lefty, you have a single. Room Five at the end of the hall. There are pajamas and a robe on the bed. Get into them and get into bed. I'll be by in a bit."

She came by often. For all her toughness, she treated us all kindly, often lingering in my room. She seemed to enjoy talking to me. I told her about the farm, my parents, how I came to Colgate, about many things, including Marjorie. She listened carefully, her eyes on me always. She even smiled more as the week wore on.

Her apartment on the third floor kept her on call for all patients, for evening bed checks, and for juice. Assigned our care, she gave detailed instructions to the other nurses about meals, medicine, vitamins, and proper conduct. To me she appeared very professional, but also alive, vibrant, firm, and very female. She moved smoothly, gliding around the infirmary, her posture revealing remarkably high breasts. I remembered the farm requirement from my father: a cow's udder conformation should have a high attachment. And I brooded on why, as a young man, women kept proffering me their breasts without provocation, as if I were some sort of lost Billy Budd in need of suckling. Or was it that most women simply wanted to proffer this gift, if only there be a proper receiver. For me, it had been a pattern, one that had climaxed in shattering sadness.

But now my memory was of that Friday, the shoot-around, the steak supper, and early bed. The next night we were to play Syracuse in a last show. I felt better, at least in my mind, and soon slept. Startled, I woke, a hand on my forehead, Nurse Bromley's, her robed form in shadow.

"How do you feel, Timothy?"

"My God, you scared me!" I tried to sit, but her hand pressed my head back.

"I'm so sorry, but I wanted to check you all this last night, and I thought I heard you - maybe you were talking in your sleep. Just lie back. We all hope you do well tomorrow."

"Uhm - yes - the game. I'd almost forgotten. Yes - well - will you come?"

"No. Besides, I don't think I could bear it, after a week of you all." She moved toward the open door, turned as though to say goodnight, but then, closing the door, walked slowly back, and went to the window.

"I must tell you, Timothy Jordan, that you are so like my son."

"Oh. Is he - is he here, or around?"

"No. He was killed near Utica." I could see her outline against the dim, early-March light. "He was hitchhiking - at night - returning from a date at Skidmore, and a car veered at him, going very fast. He never had any chance, they said. The people in a car behind saw it happen, but no one was ever apprehended. He died in the ambulance."

I was awake now, but her unbending, shadowed form, this midnight communion, left me silent, groping for words. Finally, I managed to say, "I'm so sorry."

She turned from the window, and as she moved toward my bed, she untied her sash and walked out of the robe, her body majestic, like moving marble, breasts, belly, arms, and legs all conjoined so harmoniously that I never resisted when she lay atop me, moving and murmuring over and over, "My son, my son."

I never forgot the ecstasy of the next thirty minutes of her almost clinically consummate sexuality. She led me beyond any edge into a maturity of sensation that must have stemmed from her loss. She had lost her son, and lover, but in Room Five, she had exhumed the past. The violence of our connection took us off the bed, around the room on the hard, disinfected floor, muted panting heating swollen parts. I ate everything thrust at me and was consumed in return. She called me a carnivore, trailing her tongue everywhere over me, cleaning me of her own blood, till she finally straddled me on all fours, her breath beginning to slow somewhat.

When she lay spent against me, her mouth near my ear, she spoke slowly, saying that she loved me - or perhaps her son, I now thought.

"Of course, you must never speak of this." And then, "You must sleep now, dear boy. Sleep and dream of winning. Dream of me. Dream of me." Her robe back on, she leaned down to kiss my mouth, her tongue lingering, salty, wet, still suggesting.

"Remember, not a word.'

"Of course not."

At the door, she turned to look at me. I said, "Will you admit me if I come in here with a temperature?"

She smiled, whispering, "It depends on how sick you are."

When she had gone, I came to understand, before I slept, how much older I now was.

CHAPTER SEVEN

Of course, Syracuse had known the Raiders had no depth, so had run three teams at us. By the middle of the third quarter Colgate was drained. Losing the last game was a whimper; the infirmary experiment had perhaps failed, but God knows how bad it might have been otherwise. Anyway, my athletic career had ended, and I rejected the idea of playing baseball in the spring. I was ready for a spring on my own terms - a time to enjoy, to look for a job. I had two flu-like flare-ups that spring which needed infirmary confinement, resulting in two serious confessions and two or three attempts to remember distinctly the admonition: "Remember, you mother is a Magrill." It was a spring of maturing, not wisely, but I did age somewhat.

Marjorie had had a reason why she couldn't come for Spring Party weekend. Now, so many years later, I couldn't remember what it was, only that it hadn't been very convincing. The crack in the vase had begun to lengthen until the night in the quarry found it broken.

Trying to re-order events in my mind as I slowed for the speed signs in Carlisle, I noticed once again the snowplow planted in front of the firehouse - orange, with CARLISLE painted on both blades.

After three interviews for jobs - one with Scott Paper, another with Sun Oil, where training programs seemed appallingly sterile, uninspiring, and restrictive, I had despaired for the future. But one end-of-May day, a week before graduation, and still with no prospects, I had run into the Colgate Director of Admissions.

As we stood on a bridge looking at the swans, George Buntz said, "Well, Tim, what's the plan? What corporate giant will you go out to control?"

I told him the situation.

Buntz thought, and then said, "Look, I've just returned from a school trip to New England - Deerfield, Choate, Westminster, and for the first time I stopped at Ashford. I'd heard of it, and we've taken boys from there, but I'd never visited before. Tim, it's a beautiful school. What a setting! It sits on a plain in a big bend of the Housatonic River in Massachusetts. The Berkshire Mountains are to the west, and Mount Everett rises just to the right of the setting sun. I haven't been on a more impressive school campus. The school was founded and is operated by Catholic laymen. Tim, you're Catholic, do very well in English, and are a terrific athlete. Ever think about teaching?"

"Can't ever think about that! No way, Mr. Buntz." Then I told him of my promise to my father never to teach, a pledge I had to keep.

"Okay, Tim. I understand. It's just that I'm not that easily impressed, and it was the best school I saw. Certainly Henry Clare was the epitome of my idea of a school Headmaster. Anyway, good luck."

The encounter focused my thinking again. I had to work, to join one of the companies where no one would ever ask me about Hester Prynne or Mr. Starbuck.

The following day I again met Buntz, this time in the Student Union. At lunch together Buntz again mentioned Ashford, and after some questions I asked if Buntz would call Henry Clare to see if I could interview - all this while telling myself I could never go there.

The next day I found a note in my mailbox. In it George Buntz said Mr. Clare had called back to say he would like to meet this Timothy Jordan. So it was arranged - an interview the Wednesday before graduation. I had told my father I needed the car for a job interview in Massachusetts, omitting with whom. There was certainly no need to upset him for no cause. Yet, I had felt tangible guilt in taking the car.

I recalled that first drive in nearly every detail. It was June, 1953. There was no New York Thruway nor Massachusetts Turnpike then, just Route 20. My father had always said the three most beautiful towns on Route 20 were Skaneateles, Cazenovia, and Cherry Valley. I knew the road to Albany well from the Marjorie and Skidmore visits, but when I crossed the Hudson I was on new ground. Nosing my father's Ford Forty-niner southeast to the Massachusetts line, I felt both a serenity and a sense of adventure.

I went over the mountain, staying on 20 past Shaker Village into Pittsfield, where I hooked south on Route 7.

It was mid-afternoon when I came to Stockbridge and saw my first sign that I had crossed the Housatonic River. From there I crossed and recrossed the river at Great Barrington, and again south of Sheffield - before turning toward Ashley Falls at the Ashford sign.

The campus lay bounded on the north, west and south by an arc in the river. Route 7 formed the straight eastern edge. The land sloped toward the river, leveling near its edge in acres of green immaculate football, soccer, and baseball fields, bespeaking the pride and emphasis the school placed on athletics, which pleased me. I swung around the fields and headed toward the school buildings.

I parked near a man planting flowers along the edge of the drive, who rose from his knees.

"Could you tell me where the Headmaster's home is?"

"Sure. I'm Wilbur. You must be Timmie Jordan."

That a maintenance man knew my name amazed me, and I extended my hand. "Well, yes. I'm <u>Timothy</u> Jordan," I said correcting the diminutive in as polite a way as possible.

"Been expectin' ya. Mr. Clare told me to keep an eye out for a young fella - and I guess you sure are a young one. He said to send ya right over - over there at the end of West House." He pointed the direction, toward the river. To the northwest I could see a mountain, blue now in the late afternoon.

"That must be the highest spot around. Does it have a name?"

Wilbur followed his gaze and said, "Oh, yes. It's Mount Everett. Sometimes the boys go over there and climb it - on a free day - and they have lunch at the top. The Appalachian Trail runs right over the top of it."

We stood and gazed across the fields and the river at the small mountain.

"Go to the end of West House," Wilbur said. "Mr. and Mrs. Clare live in the big apartment. See the brown door? Just knock."

I was struck by the serenity of the place, the beige stuccoed buildings - relieved, I fancied, from the school-time comings and goings of its boys - properly accentuated by the stone chapel standing above the rest on the highest ground. I felt stirrings of the notion that Ashford might be the place to come and nervously rang at the brown door.

The Headmaster answered - Henry Clare. Tall and bare-headed, likely in his late forties, he resembled Gary Cooper, except when he spoke he was anything but laconic.

"You're Timmie Jordan. Good. Come out to the garden. It's a perfect afternoon to sit outside." He wore a brown jacket, tie, button-down-collar shirt, not crisp, but conveying a formality even now with school out. We sat in canvas chairs in the shade of two huge maples, and I wondered if Henry Clare's chair would hold up under his large frame.

"Timmie, I regret that as it's summer vacation, you won't see us in action, but, of course, this has all just come up. You should know we are pretty well set, but George Buntz was so in your corner, so high on you that I wanted to meet you. Why don't you tell me something of yourself. I understand you majored in English when you weren't playing ball."

So I spent the next hour talking of myself. Then Mrs. Clare appeared with iced tea.

"Timmie, this is Eunice. Mrs. Clare thinks iced tea goes with the garden - and so do I."

She had just returned from golf, her skin still warmly glowing from the sun and effort. Her face was flat-planed, eyes wide apart, nose fine and flared, mouth exquisite. Seeing her bare legs, I was startled by the way her calves dove into her ankles in a symmetry rarely seen in any woman. As she stooped before me offering tea, I gripped my glass at the sight of her perfect, tight cleavage.

"Welcome to Ashford, Timothy Jordan," she had said, looking directly at me. It was then, that first connection, her calling me by my whole name - with no diminutive - that I knew her to be both apart and compelling. She left at once, her retreating figure tall and full and lithe. And I had known that, if asked, I would come to Ashford.

"Timmie," Henry Clare had said, "I've arranged for you to stay over in East House. Clyde Carlow is Housemaster there, our Senior

Master. He's a great Latin scholar, Rhodes Scholar. He's been at Ashford years and years, and he's a sports fan. You can have a good chat about the school's history with him. Come along and I'll introduce you. He'll bring you to breakfast in the morning, and we'll talk again."

CHAPTER EIGHT

James Connaught had founded Ashford School in 1915, a school for boys to be operated and conducted by Catholic laymen. It was heresy, but it was a mission for young, thirty-four year old Connaught.

James was the only son of William and Mary Connaught, an affluent Irish couple, whose wealth derived from William's devious and successful pursuit of acquisitions of oil rights in western Pennsylvania. His cheating of ignorant landowners never surfaced in New York City, where his family lived in luxury contradictory to general economic circumstances of the city's Irish population. The Connaughts' abundance defying all experience, their life was certainly a millennium mile from the poverty and famine that had plagued their ancestors.

James grew in manners, propriety, true elegance, and in the faith at St. Thomas Church on Fifth Avenue. Despite his father's business dealings, his parents were devout Catholics, rigorously obedient to all the ritual and expectation, and he duly went off to St. Benedict's - and all-boys high school - along with many others of the New York Catholic royalty. James proved a fine scholar - he led in Latin - and a robust athlete as well. St. Benedict's began each day with Mass in the chapel. Here James learned all the Latin responses, and was appointed sacristan in his senior year, the highest honor the school gave a student.

His father's natural ambition was that James go to Yale or Harvard, but the Benedictines urged James toward Catholic colleges, broadly suggesting they could not well recommend James to "those philosophic wastelands" in New Haven and Cambridge.

James had seriously thought of becoming a priest and was imbued with the wonder and challenge of the proposition. When the Connaughts summered at their Great Barrington home in Southwestern Massachusetts, he had thought of it when hiking the high hills and canoeing down the Housatonic River. A favorite camping stop over the years had been Ashley Falls where he had set up for overnights on the riverside just north of the village. How many times he and friends had stopped there, watched the sun set behind Mount Everett! The Housatonic was not a great river, not always high enough even for a canoe, but it had been his Mississippi, his Nile, his adventure. He had fallen asleep on its bank, wondering about becoming a priest. It was a place his mind and heart often returned to in dream and reverie, when in college, while on his tour of Europe and when, eventually, he taught at Exeter.

But William Connaught overcame the Benedictines, and James went to Harvard in 1897, his father's plan being for James to assume the family oil business. So certain was his future, he hadn't the audacity to broach with his father a newly formed idea of teaching, to say nothing of his recurring thoughts of the priesthood.

Dutifully, he returned to New York and became the "and Son" in the Connaught firm. It was only then that he came to see the method and foundation of his family's good fortune. Though loyal to his tasks, James bridled at the tactics and policies so contrary to the ethics espoused in his faith, in the family adherence to the mechanics of worship at St. Thomas. The business made a mockery of it all - and he found himself increasingly distressed to the point of obsession even during the summers in Great Barrington, and the river trips to Ashley Falls when he lay at his campsites, staring at the sky. He had to make a break, he decided one night in his thirty-third year when God intervened and took his father in an untimely death, felled by massive heart failure.

Free at last, his mother as comfortable as possible in her grief and her wealth, and wealthy himself, he sold the family business. In the summer of 1914 he retreated to Great Barrington to decide his future. He began to understand that while the priesthood would not be his vocation, he felt a strong adherence to his Catholic faith. He examined what role might be for him, as a layman, in serving Christ in a significant way.

It was in that summer of 1914 that Clyde Carlow had met James Connaught, quite by accident, hiking on the Appalachian Trail north of Sheffield. Carlow was twenty-two, just out of Princeton, with no special future plans. He had come home to Pittsfield to search out what possible future might come to an ordinary liberal arts major, who concentrated in history simply because he enjoyed it. This meeting resulted in other hikes and an invitation to canoe down the Housatonic. Like Connaught, Carlow was Catholic. Unlike Connaught, his father had been a grocer, and he had waited on tables through college, serving the wealthy, and playing football as a hundred-and-sixty-eight-pound guard.

Connaught purchased a hundred and fifty acres of land from the farmer whose property occupied the arc formed by the Housatonic north of Ashley Falls, his purpose to found and build a school, a Catholic college preparatory school for boys and run by Catholic laymen. He asked Carlow to join him as the first faculty member, to teach and coach, in an endeavor not before attempted or thought acceptable. Connaught had already visited the Bishop of Springfield and, remarkably, secured his patronage, which meant that if the school were successful, the Bishop would provide a chaplain, "to insure the propriety of and rightness of the Catholic philosophy."

The name of the school must not be after a saint, but rather have a secular ring, one from the English heritage that lingered in New England. The memory of a village in England James had visited and delighted in persisted: Ashford.

That summer of 1914 Connaught and Carlow lived in the farmhouse, daily walking the property, planning a campus, first selecting the site for the future chapel, then for the first building, one with space for resident students, a dining room, and four classrooms. By fall construction was underway. Boldly, Connaught advertised the new school, locally and in New York, and he toured surrounding farms and towns attempting to recruit boys. His plan was to take only ninth graders - to be called Third Formers in the British tradition - so that he could build carefully and slowly academically, in reputation, and in practical recognition of the costs of the project. In fact, the first recruits paid little, but then the faculty received little. Persistence and commitment completed the building; remarkably twenty-four boys, whose parents had bet their sons' future on but a dream, began at Ashford School in the fall of 1915.

• • •

Clyde Carlow stood, indicating his recounting of Ashford's history had come to an end. "Mr. Jordan," he said, "you must be tired. Should you come to Ashford, there will be time for more, but I think it's good to know the concept. There's a room for you on the third floor. Come with me."

The next morning I ate breakfast in the school dining room with Carlow and other faculty still on campus for posting grades and final meetings. Near the end Henry Clare walked through, motioning me to come with him. We stood on the lawn outside.

"Timmie, we like what you might bring here, would like to make a place to teach one or two classes to start, help all around with sports, the dorms - and other things that always have to be covered. Mind you, we're set with teachers, but you could get your feet wet. Mrs. Clare thinks it's a good idea."

Fleetingly, I had wondered why she thought so, from so brief a meeting. "Mr. Clare, it all feels right, but you know - well - it's only that there have been offers from businesses, and I have to decide which direction to go. If I could have an idea of a salary."

"Timmie, I believe we could manage fifteen hundred. Of course, you'd have your room and board." Clare smiled as he added, "You would always be warm and well-fed."

"Is that fifteen hundred per month?"

"No, no, no, Timmie! It's fifteen hundred a year!"

I simply stood, amazed, and had difficulty in keeping a straight face. Seconds ticked by.

"Go back and think about it," Clare said. "I'd like to know by Wednesday. Just call, one way or the other. Drive carefully and remember - stay in and pitch."

All the way back to the farm to return my father's car, I had laughed at the absurdity of it, and felt relieved that at least one channel of my future lay shut, not to be traveled. My father was right, of course. Never be a teacher.

On Wednesday morning I rose, breakfasted, walked to the Colgate Inn, and wired Henry Clare at Ashford School accepting the position. Recollecting my action so many times over the years, I had never come to understand why I did it. But each time I thought of it, and the course of the interview, the one moment that lept to mind was Eunice Clare serving me tea.

CHAPTER NINE

It had been a summer of intense labor on the farm. I had felt I owed it to my father, whose disappointment in me informed each day, especially when he learned that Ashford was a Catholic school. As the time of my departure approached, my mother began to pack a medium-sized wooden trunk, a family heirloom, and on the appointed day, took me to Syracuse to catch the train. Between us we carried the trunk to the platform.

"Timothy," she said, "your father will survive. He has survived me, and secretly I think he's proud of you. I am - I am so very proud. Whatever you do, just remember your mother is a Magrill."

I had to change trains in Pittsfield and rode south on the New Haven Railroad for the brief trip to Sheffield. At the station Wilbur, who'd been planting flowers when I had visited Ashford for my interview, stood waiting beside his pick-up truck.

"I knew you'd come, Mr. Jordan, and when Mr. Clare told me to meet you this morning, I got the junk out of my truck - even hosed it down."

Wilbur delivered me to East House, Clyde Carlow's dormitory, and helped me with the trunk to the same third floor room I had stayed in the first time. It had a narrow bed, a desk and chair, a closet, and a tiny bathroom where the roof sloped, so that using the toilet meant always sitting down. But it was mine, all mine. It opened onto a corridor of ten rooms housing twenty fourth formers. As it was three days before school opened, after settling my things I roamed each room on my floor and the second floor. The first floor was one large room, with French doors leading onto a long, south-facing porch. It was in this room I would find that Henry Clare held his nightly all-school meetings, the boys sitting knees up on the floor. Along a small hallway was Clyde Carlow's apartment where he lived with his wife Millicent, whom some faculty referred to as "Silly Milly." She was indeed silly, but a good soul, and the one softening touch to an otherwise masculine, post-puberty clan.

All-day faculty meetings began the next day. I was the only rookie. Right away I liked Bill Warren, a Ashford alumnus and

Harvard graduate, who was beginning his second year as English teacher and Housemaster in West House with the Third Formers. Bill was so enthusiastic in his nearly total disorganization that he was refreshingly engaging. After the first meeting he took me to his quarters, lay on the bed, and grilled me on how and why I had come to Ashford.

"Well, Tim," he said, "you're going to work for a good man. Henry has been here three years - tough act to follow old Connaught and deal with the crusty old guard. In fact, I think he's too patient. Carlow is the only one to really back him, but then Carlow is a class guy. Clare's starting to bring in some fresh blood - like me, like you - and he has only one absolute rule for us: Whatever you do, never miss breakfast."

"Are you serious?"

"Absolutely. He doesn't mind us getting out for a few beers, or what time we come in, so long as the dorm is covered. But you're not long for this scene if you're not at breakfast. And don't get Carlow on your ass!"

"Does Mr. Carlow pretty much run the school?"

"Well, yes and no. He's on top of all the day-to-day stuff, especially where it concerns faculty performance. I suppose that's good. Of course, the kids are afraid as hell of him, but he's the first one to defend a boy in trouble. They're a team, Henry and Carlow, but everyone knows who's in charge. Carlow defers, even if he thinks Henry is off-track, but he's done a lot to steer Henry the right way. Any way you shake it, this is a helluva school - better than when I was a student here. Then it was a bastion of machismo. I think Eunice Clare has really helped. She's something."

"What do you mean, 'She's something'?"

"She's aloof, kind of mysterious. She's probably ten years younger than Henry. Thirty-eight, maybe. I think there's a lot of bed talk about school. She's an influence here, which isn't all bad. She's also devout - rarely misses daily Mass. She doesn't have much to do with me, probably because she caught me staring at her legs. You'll see. Her calves and ankles are devastating." I remembered. "Anyway, she and Delaney, the Chaplain, talk a lot."

"I assume they've been married quite a while. Any children?"

"Nope. Something wrong, maybe, with one of them. Maybe they don't want any, which doesn't square with church rules. Anyway, Tim, it's wise to be on her good side - her's and Carlow's."

Obviously, the faculty had been informed of my hiring, and Warren had been tagged to fill me in on my English classes and study halls.

"And you and I will do the J.V. football this fall," he concluded.

CHAPTER TEN

The following day I met Father Delaney, a youngish priest who had his own apartment in the Main building, away from the students. He taught all the Theology classes, said Mass, and heard confessions. He often visited the Clares in the evening, and I would come to wonder what they talked about. He was warm toward me, and before school started, I served Mass for Father. Eunice Clare was there; Warren arrived in time for communion, but curiously no other of the twenty-four faculty could make it.

The Chapel made a spectacular center of the school, philosophically more than geographically, rising from the high ground so that from its front steps one could survey the campus as it sloped away to the river, the sports fields in the distance. Built of Indiana stone, its symmetry broken only by the organ tower, it could seat the entire student body of two hundred, and the faculty. The organ was precious, its quality of tone not often found even in the most affluent of parishes, its acoustics near perfect. No amplification had ever been required. Father Delaney knew he was in a special place, a unique assignment, one he had courted for years.

When Father distributed the host to the one communicant that morning, Eunice Clare, her head draped with black lace that hung to her shoulders, I thought I saw the structure, the rather aquiline portrayal I had often observed in paintings of Christ.

In the sacristy after Mass, Father thanked me for helping.

"Who serves Mass when school starts, Father?"

"The boys. There's always one Sacristan here each morning. Four Sacristans who are Sixth Formers. To be a Sacristan is the highest honor in the school. We have that instead of class officers, and it's right for what we are. They take care of me very well, train the others to be altar boys, serve Sundays and Holy Days, and help with benediction every Sunday night. Of course, we have chapel every evening before dinner. That's when we sing, and usually I have something to say, or Mr. Clare does."

"It sounds like you're pretty busy."

"Oh, I manage to stay out of trouble, with my classes, and then there's a good deal of counseling, one-on-one."

"What, generally, do the boys come to you for?"

Father didn't answer the question right away, pulling his vestment off over his head and hanging it next to the others.

"Could be anything. Usually about sin, or what is a sin. Or about their parents. Or maybe a girl - or a boy."

Before I could ask about it, Father went on to mention homesickness or problems with a faculty member, rushing, it seemed, to bury his last comment. Then he suggested we hurry so as not to miss breakfast.

It was the first of many conversations I had with Father; often I sought counsel, or felt need of someone other than a fellow faculty member. Usually it was after lights out; Father always had coffee and cookies, and sometimes it seemed the talk was for himself, especially when he called and invited me over to his apartment. Most of the dormitory personnel found Father's apartment a gracious relief from the burdens of control and discipline. Father's role in the school was to serve everyone, including the Headmaster and his wife.

In time I grew to know all the faculty, some as friends, some as colleagues, some as peers, a few as not really wanting to be at Ashford. I couldn't understand why the Headmaster kept Joe Ryan, a holdover from the earlier days, who had been at Ashford thirty-five years. He didn't teach; rather, he supervised study halls, his ponderous, beefy presence controlling the scene. Otherwise, he sat in the faculty room and smoked, told tired stories of the old days, criticized nearly everyone and everything - but still apparently was an asset to the Headmaster. Henry Clare referred to him as his "number three man." Clearly, Clyde Carlow was number one. No one seemed to know who was number two, but Ryan enjoyed a tenure secured by his years of service, if not by the Headmaster's sympathy and patience. Joe thought himself an expert, though not necessarily in academia - he did know that limitation - but certainly in sports and the expectations for new, young masters who needed their edges pared by his blunt directives. In that first fall season in football, at least in the beginning, Joe Ryan thought to change the approach Masters Bill Warren and Timothy Jordan planned for their Junior Varsity team.

It was Warren's idea that as Head Coach he would concentrate on defense while I would determine the offense. The very first practice, in shorts and helmets, found us with thirty-two lads who knew little of football and who were woefully lacking in athleticism but for one: Pat Donnelli, a smallish, wiry Italian boy from Syracuse, whose speed and agility stood out. In a passing drill Donnelli threw the ball with nary a waver. We had a quarterback, and that night in Warren's room we were elated.

"Tim, I played here, single-wing, and the varsity runs it, so anything else we do just might not fly."

"With whom - not fly? What does that mean?"

"Well, Smitty looks to the J.V.s to train kids for his varsity, to use the same formations, you know, so when he gets them he doesn't have to teach 'em. And there's the old guys who don't want ever to change anything. What's good enough before is good enough now. Carlow's the Athletic Director. When he coached, he even line-blocked the kids. Joe Ryan will blow it around if he sees us using the kids as "guinea pigs," as he would say. I can hear him now: What's good enough for Princeton is good enough for us. Just be ready for some major flak, and if we get hammered, it'll be some real shit."

"Then why don't we be a little cozy, just some practice, keep it simple. The worst thing is when coaches make everything complicated. I think that kid Donnelli can learn to fake and then throw a delayed pass. The blocking is simple and straight ahead. We'll catch 'em off guard."

Grinning, we agreed, and for the next week, at the end of each day's practice, we put in two plays, running them over and over - twelve plays in all, six from each formation, with Donnelli improving rapidly, faking, putting the ball on his hip, throwing darts accurately, though half were dropped. The boys became enthused, invigorated. Warren held our practices at the far reaches of a field near the river, well away from other squads. His own enthusiasm and great booming voice soon developed pride among his defense, well ahead of my experiment.

On the fifth day of practice I glanced at a figure under an elm at the far south corner of our field. It was Joe Ryan, watching. At recess the next day, Ryan accosted me.

"I watched your practice yesterday, Jordan."

"I know. I saw you."

"Look, Jordan. You're new around here and don't understand the way things are done. We've run the single-wing for years and will now. This 'T' formation crap isn't for us - too complicated - won't train 'em for Coach Smith. You probably didn't check with him. He's the head honcho. It's his program. Just get rid of your tricky stuff and teach these kids some football. Word to the wise, eh, pal?"

"Smitty hasn't said anything'"

"He's busy with his own squad. We've had others who tried to jazz around - until we straightened things out."

"You mean until *you* straightened it out."

I had been stunned by my own brazenness. Ryan glowered, his face bloated and blood red, his trembling hands, fumbling for a cigarette.

"Look, kiddo, be smart. Someone said you are. I'm not giving you advice. I'm telling you the score, even if I don't have to. Wise up. What's good enough for Princeton is good enough for us."

"Someone said you'd say that."

"Warren? Well, he's a wise ass, too. He's supposed to be in charge, but then he's a Harvard man - they're all wise asses. And now it looks like we got another one. Just listen good - no need to go to the Headmaster. I'm doing my job - to let you know how it is."

With that he shuffled back to the schoolhouse in the short steps that his obesity required. I converted my next class to a study period, while I tried to calm down, doodling plays on a sheet of paper. I looked at Donnelli in the third row, dutifully reading a book, and concluded I couldn't waste this young athlete. He deserved this chance; he wasn't from New York, or the Catholic social register. He was from Syracuse, likely a lad whose parents sacrificed mightily to send him to Ashford. I had to talk to Donnelli - beyond grammar or football. I'd visit his room that night.

Warren said, "I told you so," when I told him of the exchange with Ryan. Nevertheless, with some trepidation but great excitement, we decided to change nothing. After practice that afternoon, Coach Smith cornered Warren and me. He was a middle-aged, slight man, quiet, certain; the boys responded to him. He was Chairman of the History Department and in most ways represented the qualities sought in an all-around school man. Studious, understanding, patient, he never lost control on the practice field or in the height of a game.

"How're you guys doing? I'm sorry I haven't checked in, or been more help. We've got a game with Gunnery coming up, and they're always after the Catholics."

Warren told him about the boys' condition, the helplessness of most, the enthusiasm of most, and that we were putting in a few, simple plays - but said nothing about the "T" or Donnelli or Ryan.

"Look, we need to see some other faces," Smitty said. "Bring your guys over tomorrow. I think everyone is in good enough shape. We'll run some controlled stuff from the thirty - fifteen or twenty plays, both ways. What do you say?"

"Sure," Warren said. "Give us a yell when you want us. Just make sure we don't get killed. Blow the whistle fast."

"Don't worry, Bill. I only want to see where we are."

That night Warren and I planned. We would ask to play defense first, so the boys could shake the nerves. Our squad wouldn't know until the call came. I planned ten plays, in the order I wanted them used. Tactics planned, Warren said, "Christ, Tim. You'd think this was the Rose Bowl!"

CHAPTER ELEVEN

Word got around the next day about the scrimmage. Apparently, the game against the Junior Varsity was an annual event where all of Ashford came to see what was in store for the fall. During calisthenics, I noticed Joe Ryan trudging across the field, and Henry Clare and Eunice were there along with other faculty when Smitty gave the call. Eunice wore a light brown tweed suit, a dark brown scarf looped around her shoulders; she seemed younger than before. By the time both teams had gathered on the game field, soccer practices had broken off, and the players stood along one sideline. My agitated adrenaline shook me until Warren said, "Calm down and don't worry, Tim. My defense will eat 'em alive."

Indeed, his defense was remarkable. They played with a ferocity, even when giving ground. Warren had showed his linemen how to turn sideways in their defensive stance, upsetting blocking assignments. He rushed linebackers all at once, hitting their ends on the line of scrimmage.

Smitty was shaking his head when he told Warren it was their turn at the thirty. "See what you can do," he said.

My first play was from the old single wing, except that at tailback I had Donnelli two yards deeper than usual and my wing back three yards behind his right end. The center managed to reach Donnelli with the ball; the right side of the line let the defense rush, drifting to their right while Donnelli flipped the ball to his wingback, now behind a wall of blockers. The varsity caught the wingback twenty-five yards down the field. In a rare show of emotion, Smitty called his defense into a huddle while the sidelines erupted.

Our second play was from the 'T', a straight 'T', my linemen no longer toe-to-toe but spaced by nearly a yard. The varsity defense never changed, and Donnelli took the ball from center, faked a direct dive to his right halfback - which the entire defense went for - and raced off tackle to the end zone. No one could catch him.

With the sidelines gleefully jumping and screaming, our offense scored twice more, the Varsity and Smitty helpless to stop us.

Finally Smitty called it a day. Ryan walked away by himself. After Warren and I had clapped each other's backs, roaring with laughter and stomping about, Warren went with our team to the showers. Eunice Clare came up to me. "That was marvelous," she said. "Your team is truly good."

"Thank you, Mrs. Clare. I'm amazed myself. Never thought it would be like this."

"Henry was very impressed with your new plays. He said, 'That Jordan boy has really done something.' Aren't you proud?"

"Of course, of course, and Bill's boys were terrific. The job they did - it fired us up. But we know it won't last. Smitty will get us next time. He's probably already figured it out."

She put her hand on my arm. "But by that time you will have something new. Timothy - I'm so happy you're here. We all need you."

She was looking directly into my eyes, holding me in her gaze, her hand lingering just a moment. She turned away to Henry, who was striding their way, and put her arm though his. Over his shoulder Henry Clare said, "Great job out there, Timmie. Great job. Think Smitty will want to talk to you."

Why did he insist on calling me Timmie?

· · ·

That scrimmage day was our undoing. We lost Donnelli to the Varsity. I dutifully drew up plays for Smitty. The Varsity beat Gunnery handily, and everyone else. Our team won half of our games, but without the boy from Syracuse it wasn't the same. Warren was furious, and Joe Ryan avoided me as best he could. Despite everything, it seemed that, early on, "Timmie" had become a fixture.

During the faculty meetings and the opening of school, I met Mrs. Malley, the school nurse, motherly, Irish, just the right sort for the boys. She was a godsend, the only relief for the students who were confronted daily by a male faculty whose sympathy could never reach the maternal. In fact, she was too lenient - saw no wrong anywhere, kept boys too long in the infirmary, mothering and doting.

In addition to being in charge of the dining room, the waiters, and the onerous, weekly task of changing the table seating - over which there was always a master or two who complained of having kids to mind for a week - I had been asked to act as a sort of liaison with the infirmary. This rather pleasant assignment found me stopping in to visit Mrs. Malley almost daily, usually at recess, or visiting confined students, especially any with injuries. She wasn't like the sexual - and tragic - nurse I had known at Colgate, her demeanor and attitude suggesting that probably sexuality was long forgotten.

She was always happy to see me, looking forward to my visits, fussing if I didn't show up. Her central problem was that it was she alone who handled the physical, and often emotional, problems of a student body of two hundred. Though she rarely complained, she one day related to me a comment from the school doctor.

"Dr. Haley says we need another nurse, that all this is too much. He keeps bringing it up and asks why I don't see Mr. Clare about it."

"He's right, Mrs. Malley. You're great, but it is too much, especially the way you take care of everyone. You should discuss it with the Headmaster. There are two empty rooms upstairs. There should be someone to help you."

"I know. I know, but the dear man has so much on his mind and likely not enough money to pay."

"Henry Clare is very resourceful, Mrs. Malley, maybe the wheel should squeak a little. Another person would mean you could get your rest and be better than you already are."

The conversation was repeated between us until one day Clare asked me how things were going in the infirmary. With this, I lauded Mrs. Malley and Dr. Haley but made a case for another nurse.

"Timmie, I know you're right. We've needed help for a long time - had even interviewed a couple of possibilities - but then I found you. So you see, it's all your fault..."

He was enjoying his humorous twist, but the economic aspect was real. There was no endowment; the school depended entirely on its enrollment and only now was climbing out of the austerity from the War.

After the Thanksgiving faculty meeting when Henry Clare had announced that two more students were coming for second semester, he held me back.

"Timmie, maybe we can find that nurse now. Two prospects are coming Wednesday for interviews. Why don't you join in? It's your cause and, anyway, I'd like your input."

The first interviewee though experienced, but not in schools, was too stern. They agreed Mrs. Malley would never do with her.

The second, Rachel Mackintire, captured us both, even though she was twenty-two and just out of nursing school. She wasn't actually beautiful. She was supple and lean, but not all muscle and sinew. My eyes had dropped surreptitiously to her rounded breasts. She had a delightful smile, auburn hair haloed her face, and freckles decorated her nose and cheeks.

"Well, nursing is nursing, wherever one is," she responded to Henry Clare's query as to her handling of the job's scope. "I really have no concerns - only that Mrs. Malley would want me, and like me. I know there is much to learn, but I can do that. Caring for people - it's my profession, and if anything, I'm a professional."

Eyebrows arched, Clare indicated me. "Mr. Jordan here sort of looks after things - you know - sees what Mrs. Malley's needs are. Timmie, do you have a question for Miss Mackintire?"

I tried desperately to think of one while staring at her large, crinkled-corners eyes that seemed to say, 'Here I am.'

"Well," I finally managed, "I have no problem at <u>all</u>."

Rachel looked radiant.

Shaking his head ever so slightly, Henry reached for his phone.

Mrs. Malley took Rachel Mackintire in tow, whisking her away to the infirmary, the two of them as disparate in appearance, I thought, as Mutt and Jeff.

Clearly Henry Clare had made up his mind, perhaps partially because he was taken with the girl, and perhaps because he felt he could afford to pay a novice.

So it was done, and it turned out the Headmaster's decision that day would impact my life forever.

CHAPTER TWELVE

Parents' Weekend always came in October - at the height of the fall foliage display - planned so parents would have a good reason for a trip to the country, a motivation greater, I felt, than coming to see their sons - at least for some. It was a time Henry Clare wanted to go well, the best advertisement for Ashford being parental word-of-mouth, so a major faculty meeting always convened on the previous Thursday for the Headmaster to review and emphasize the agenda.

Events always commenced at chapel at 10:00 a.m. on Saturday, with Father celebrating Mass. The boys had rehearsed the hymns, and Father had honed a seven-minute homily on the virtue of courage. The Third Form was excused to free space for parents and to make a last minute scavenge of the campus for litter, down to the tiniest gum wrapper. Varsity Football and Soccer played at two, followed by a massive tea for parents and guests in the dining room.

The Headmaster stood at the head of the table ticking off each activity. "We've planned a fine buffet luncheon. Chicken a la king, which you all know the chef makes so well. You should mix around, talk to as many parents as possible, and remember: Try to find something good to say about each boy, even if you have to lie a little, even" - he coughed a little - "if he's a total dunderhead. After all," he hurried on, "we're really just underway. Talk about the boy's potential for growth, that you expect a good response to counseling, maybe that he's just beginning to find himself. Whatever we do, we want parents leaving here feeling good about their day, about Ashford. If that means omitting one or two comments, at least now, in October, so be it."

As the senior faculty murmured and nodded in understanding, he went on. "At school meeting tomorrow night I'll go over all this with the boys. Meanwhile, become totally familiar with your students' grades. Dorm people, know how your minions are doing on corridor and for God's sake make sure their rooms look the best ever. No slacking here. We want parents to see what we're about, and you know how mothers can be."

. . .

Saturday had dawned cloudy, but still a crisp fall day, with the leaves aglow against the gray sky.

By nine o'clock Lincolns, Cadillacs, and various limousines were parking on the slope that slanted down toward the main campus. Clearly these weren't the Catholics of my acquaintance. I recalled not seeing even one ordinary car. These vehicles bespoke Ashford's clientele, for the most part truly affluent Irish from Boston and New York and a cosmopolis or two in between. I did spot Donnelli's parents and three sisters parking by the gym in their Dodge sedan. I would make certain to tell them their son was a special boy, the finest, I honestly thought, of the lot.

Mass had gone well. It was amazing how the boys could rise to an occasion. They sang with gusto not usual at evening chapel, and Father spoke persuasively, having picked up on the Headmaster's wish that they leave that day feeling good, assured that their sons were truly young men of God.

I worried, needlessly, about the luncheon, but the chicken a la king was a hit. It was unfortunate, I later learned, that so many ate so heartily.

Near the end of lunch, when most had trailed off to the football game, it began to drizzle. By half-time, it was pouring, the football field a quagmire, with twenty-two muddy bodies sliding into each other. From there the day fell disastrously apart, and most left without feeling good about anything.

The first attempts to depart by the Lincolns, Cadillacs, and limousines found wheels churning on the sodden turf, mired up to their hubcaps as they threw mud and grass at any unfortunate who stood behind. People pushed, even some socialite mothers. Then some cars lurched forward, down the slope, leaving rutted, slushy trails like plowed furrows in a field. Tow trucks came, but in the end, the green sward from the chapel to the dining room became an oozing, gouged battlefield of furious, shouting people. Henry Clare stood bareheaded in the midst of it all, splattered and drenched, his hopes for the day quite smashed.

66

With the last car towed, the Headmaster, Carlow, Ryan, Warren, and I stood in the rain, sadly surveying the carnage that was once their graceful campus.

"Did we win the game?" Clare asked.

"No, lost by a fumble in the end zone - a safety," Ryan answered.

"God should have known we didn't need this." Henry Clare said it, the closest he ever came to questioning any divine action. Then together we headed for the hot coffee in the dining room where Mrs. Clare met them, her umbrella diverting a shower from her shoulders.

"Henry, Tom McGrath is on the phone. It hardly sounded like him. He's ill, very ill - and wants you now. Please hurry."

McGrath, one of the wealthier parents, who Henry Clare had been hoping would donate to Ashford, was calling from the emergency room of a hospital in nearby New Milford, and was certainly ill, as was his wife. His call would be the first: most of the Ashford parents who had eaten the chicken a la king were ill, some desperately, and all were angry, hysterically implying Ashford had poisoned them all.

Then many students became sick, and Dr. Haley had come. Mrs. Malley's infirmary was full, and the dormitories were wretched substitutes, foul smelling and unhappy. The football team had escaped - having eaten a training meal of hamburger and toast - and fortunately, few faculty members had eaten lunch, busy, as they were, with parents. Oddly, those who had were not ill, accustomed, perhaps, to school fare. The only time I ever witnessed Henry Clare lose his temperate nature was that day.

"Jesus Christ, Jordan, aren't you in charge of the dining room?! What the hell happened?! Do you realize we have an enraged body of parents, some so sick they could die?! The McGraths, both of them, are in the hospital! Your damned dining room has screwed up, really screwed up. We may never recover from this. It has to be that chicken a la king. Everyone was perfectly Goddamn healthy until they ate your Goddamn lunch. Do you know what you have done?"

"But do we really know it was the lunch?"

"What else is there? Anyway, they all think it was. You better damn well find out what went wrong - not that it'll do any good now. God, I can't leave anything to anybody. Jesus, help me. Why did I ever take you on?! Jesus!"

And he stalked away, leaving me feeling destroyed, stunned by the immeasurable anger, thoroughly discouraged about my future. Sullenly, I went to the kitchen and told the chef what had happened. The chef argued about the meal preparations, pointing out that they had cooked and diced the chicken on Friday, mixing it with the sauce, and stored it in large metal bowls, only... he hadn't refrigerated it! I made sure the leftovers were dumped.

Somehow, the day wound down, I finally alone in my room and slumped in the chair. Never had I been so distressed. All the headiness of recent weeks had been obliterated. I knew my days at Ashford were near an end.

At eleven my phone rang. Who would want me now?

"Timothy, did I wake you?" It was Eunice Clare.

"Hardly. I'm afraid bed is the furthest thing from my mind right now."

"Then if you're up, we want you to come over. Henry wants you to come, and so do I."

"Mrs. Clare, it's quite late - and I don't think the Headmaster wants me around right now."

"No, no, no. That's not it. We want you to come. It's important. It has been such a day. Please come."

Her tone, as always, overcame my reluctance, my fear, really.

"All right. I'll come by."

I dressed, refitting my tie, putting on my only jacket. I combed my hair, thinking it was going to be an assessment, with Ryan and Carlow likely there. Almost sure it could well be my last visit, I walked forlornly to the Clares'. The rain had stopped.

Eunice Clare opened the door. She was in a robe, holding a drink. Her hand on my arm, she walked me to the Headmaster's study where Clare sat slouched in his armchair, also in robe and pajamas, a drink on the side table. He motioned me to sit.

"Timmie, thanks for coming this late, but it's been an extraordinary day."

"Yes, sir, an extraordinary day - a terrible day!"

"Well, perhaps. It will be one we'll all remember, for me because you didn't really deserve my outburst. Mrs. Clare knows it can happen, but not often, and she's right: You didn't deserve it. Hope you can put it aside."

"Yes, sir. Of course. I'm all right - and so sorry."

My relief was so immense I even accepted a drink when Mrs. Clare offered, which I'd never done before. It burned at first, and then I relaxed.

"Did you see the chef?"

"Yes, sir. It was the chicken. Also saw Dr. Haley, and he's sure it's food poisoning, but won't be certain until it's tested. He took some with him."

"God, Timmie, what a thing to happen. So many are so sick - boys, parents..."

"Henry, I'm sure it won't be the disaster you think," Eunice said. "When people feel better, they'll understand. It wasn't on purpose. It was a mistake. Let's wait for the doctor's report before judging the chef."

During this my eyes were fixed on Eunice Clare's feet. She had removed her slippers, crossed her legs, and was wriggling her toes, accentuating the perfection of her ankle and the full, firm calf that met it in exquisite conjunction.

"What do you think, Timmie?" I heard Henry ask.

I started. "Excuse me, sir. About what?"

"About that plowed field we have by the chapel."

So much less disastrous than the a la king, we discussed what to do with the ruined lawn with some humor, until clearly it was time for me to leave. Eunice escorted me from the study to the front door. As I opened it, she reached her hand to my face and kissed my cheek.

"Timothy, don't worry. You're here to stay. Sleep well."

Left standing in the dark, I felt my cheek, trembling from the touch of her lips.

CHAPTER THIRTEEN

My corridor consisted of twenty Fourth Formers. In a public school they would be sophomores or, for Cicero, "wise fools." They had prevailed through the Third Form and were now in their postpubic manliness. They well knew their way around the block, understanding all the gambits for survival, even if most felt little motivation toward excellence, their prospects for college so far from their tomorrows. Often gangly and awkward, growing out of their jackets and trousers in only days it seemed, they were the most unmolded lot in the school, and therefore the most unpredictable.

It was with these boys I learned control, that boys would measure up if they could trust their Master to be fair. They would accept any stern measure so long as they could trust my being just in all matters. I made sure not to favor anyone, even though Donnelli was on the corridor. Most of all I tried never to be grim, meting out discipline evenhandedly, surely, without condemnation. They all felt recovery possible, even if bad, so generally they tried to cooperate with the rules.

Perhaps the major test came just at the end of football season, when on impulse I decided to walk the corridor around eleven o'clock on a Tuesday evening and check in a few rooms. I found all twenty boys missing.

Back in my room, I couldn't imagine how they had escaped without my hearing. I remembered then that they had gone to bed so dutifully that night - not a laggard among them, lights out promptly - that I had been smugly pleased with the fine corridor I managed. I realized I had to talk to Carlow.

"I'm astounded," I exclaimed. "Can't believe they got out without a sound."

"Oh, they have resources you never imagined, but now we have to find them. I'm sure they're all okay, but their safety is foremost."

Carlow didn't seem overly concerned and showed none of the frenzy I felt.

"They're probably at Murray's Diner, over on Route 7 just before you get into Canaan. Take my car and check it out. If they're there, let them finish, and you can deal with it when they get back."

I stopped the car in the parking lot. They were all there, including Donnelli, filling the available booths, laughing and furtively downing burgers and shakes. As Carlow counseled, I returned without going in, relieved I had found them, angry at their disobedience, yet humored by their clever escape.

"It's your call," Carlow said, "but check with me, and you should see the Headmaster about it."

It was past midnight when they sneaked back, each to find a note on his bed, "Welcome back - see you all at Mass. Mr. Jordan."

I alerted Father before Mass about my charges, asking him to announce at dismissal that Mr. Jordan's corridor should stay behind. They all came, sitting together halfway down the aisle. All took communion and all sat, heads bowed, when Father made his announcement. When the others had left, I walked to just in front of their pews, took out a paper, and read: "I hope you've come seeking forgiveness. In disobedience you have sinned against your Master. Whoever says that he belongs to the Lord must turn away from wrongdoing, the Bible says. Be sure the Lord knows who are His. Be sure I know who are mine. Another sin, singly or by all, will incur the Lord's wrath, and mine will mean each or all of you will be unable to walk because of broken kneecaps. Last, I shall not find one stray leaf on this campus come Saturday morning, else you all will join me on campus for Thanksgiving weekend."

There were a few leaves blown in from the north, but they were alive. Henry Clare had paled at the thought of twenty for turkey and even was found raking with the boys on Friday afternoon.

Later, Eunice Clare noted, "Father said you quoted the Bible, Timothy II. Do you know who Timothy's mother was?" I didn't, but checked it out later - and rather wished I hadn't...

· · ·

Wiggins and Conroy had the last room down the hall and seemed aesthetes, whitish of face, both lanky, both dutiful, neither

72

athletic. Wiggins had his violin which he played at free times and very well. Conroy did pencil drawings, caricatures of anyone, but also some effective campus scenes, one of the chapel. Although Third Form roommates were separated the second year, for some reason Carlow had allowed these two to room together again, likely because of parental pressure. The Wigginses and Conroys appeared at school nearly every weekend, with food and constant concerns about their sons' room, their grades, their acceptance by the other boys. In the beginning I hadn't really noticed their constant companionship to the exclusion of others, and the others' willingness to leave it just that way.

One night Donnelli was in my room talking about the game ahead against Westminster and about noun clauses and gerunds. He just shook his head. "Grammar is harder than the whole play book. Football is easy, makes sense. But you've helped me - now if I can just remember it for a test."

He seemed reluctant to leave, a silence coming between us, until he said, "Sir, you ever scared - nervous before a game? You played in a lot of 'em."

"Every time. Butterflies, churning stomach. I don't think any athlete ever goes into a game without some nervousness, and probably isn't much of one if he isn't nervous. Are you upset about Saturday?"

"Guess I am. They're awful good and practice hasn't been so great all week."

"Poor practice, good game. It's that way lots of times, Donnelli. Don't worry. You'll pass Westminster dizzy."

At the door Donnelli hesitated again. "Sir, once in a while you go around at night, checking on rooms - you know - to see if we're in bed?"

"Yes, when I get a feeling it might be a good idea. Why?"

"Well, some time, if you do, don't forget the end of the hall."

"Donnelli, is there something you want to tell me?"

"No. Just check all the rooms when you do it again."

And he was gone, to leave me wondering if this last wasn't the real reason for Donnelli's visit. He hadn't sought help before and had never before seemed worried prior to a game.

The next night I did do a check, not all the rooms, but I included that of Wiggins and Conroy. I tapped first, as usual. The room was dark, but in silouette in front of the window the two stood facing each other, naked, their hands reaching to each other's groin. They'd never heard my knock and never ceased their work, so concentrated were they on finishing. I reached for the light switch, but before I could turn it, they simultaneously groaned. For the moment I paused, reluctant to illuminate their mutual agonized pleasure and because, I later realized, perhaps not wanting to see what I knew I witnessed. Instead, I stepped back, closing the door carefully. I had stepped into their privacy, my heart saddened that I found them. To what had Donnelli sent me? It was a connection, an activity, about which I had never thought nor had I desired. I didn't know what to do, if anything.

Finally I decided to see Clyde Carlow.

"Sir, do you ever make a room change with the boys?"

"Yes. Sometimes two lads just can't get along. They fight and argue. It's an unhappy thing all around. If it won't work, we try a change, but that isn't easy when most of the others are just fine. Anyone you have with problems?"

"Not ... problems, exactly. Let's say there's a room where the relationship may be too close - not healthy."

"Are you sure of this, Tim? Why do you suspect them?"

"I walked in on them while checking the corridor."

"I see. Well, of course you won't say anything of this to anyone else - you understand that. In things like this you should go see Father. See what he says - maybe he knows the right thing. It's better I don't know - it's a terrible thing to have in the house. I'm sorry, but it makes me angry. I couldn't be fair with the two of them. I don't want to know."

Suspecting Carlow's position, I hadn't planned to identify anyone. I had reasoned that the House Head had to know, and perhaps knew from previous experience, what to do. But Carlow had clearly never dealt with a homosexual situation, either never admitted there were any, or had ignored them if there were. I felt a like repugnance due to lack of understanding and from ignorance, especially since I plainly felt it a sin and therefore to be avoided, even if someone was tempted. The possibility of such a scene at Ashford had never entered my mind, so naive was I, or perhaps so set on converging with the opposite sex, I couldn't imagine any other choice.

My talk with Father was sobering.

"Father, I should likely not tell you who they are."

"Don't worry, Tim. It's just as likely I already know."

"Well, Father, then - well, I guess I don't know where to go from here. If you've known ... I mean, why wasn't I told - and what the hell do I do? Do I just ignore it and the fact another student knows and alerted me?"

I kneaded my forehead with his fingers and sat heavily into Father's couch. Father said nothing for some moments. Then, having served coffee and settling himself in his armchair, he said, "First of all, Tim, you must surely understand that your boys are at a very vulnerable age. There is experimentation, exploration, a coming to grips with this incredible new experience. God made sexuality very exciting. Masturbation can lead to mutual experimentation."

"But isn't that perversion? An abominable thing?"

"Not always. We have to be careful not to confuse the gropings and 'trying out' of growing up with a settled sexual preference, as something of a permanent way of life. It well could be the boys you saw are just fooling around, not all that uncommon."

"But these guys lived together last year, too." Then I realized I had identified them.

"I know."

"Well, then, isn't it possible this is a long-time affair? Why did Mr. Carlow not separate them? Isn't all this a reason for changing roommates? What is it, Father? Does the school just turn its back on it all? Hell, in the Old Testament they are killed. In 'Timothy' the law is for sexual perverts - along with the murderers, rapists - all in one pot."

"I know. I know, but I don't think Jesus may have been as quick to condemn, even though Paul is very clear about it. After all, God created adolescent boys, and all the problems they face in their teens. I understand your shock, your natural aversion. Just don't be too hard. Did they know you were there?"

"I don't think so - at least, they didn't stop, or even notice - and I just closed the door."

"You did the right thing, Tim. Let me dwell on things. We'll talk again in a week."

"Father, do boys confess this ...?"

"Sometimes - in the beginning - and then they either stop or just don't confront the sin any more. My sense here is that we're not into homosexuality, but if you have further cause for concern, well, we'll deal with it then."

"Then I should do nothing."

"For now," Father said. "You know, Tim, I think you have good judgment, even though you've just begun. So do Henry and Eunice Clare. Don't rush into it."

While my talk with Father didn't bring satisfaction or resolution, I did come to see Father's role at Ashford with new appreciation. My respect for the man had its first grounding with this incident, and was to escalate in the months to come when my own problems made this one seem minuscule.

CHAPTER FOURTEEN

Robert Kinney was Head of the English Department, was thirty-five, and lived off-campus in Canaan with his wife Imogene and three young children. He helped with a dormitory, covered meals, and coached whenever needed. A fine scholar and athlete, he was over six feet four - the Headmaster liked to hire tall men, imagining they exercised more control - a very large man with thinning hair and dark-rimmed glasses which often slid down his nose when he read.

Imogene was dynamic, also tall but stringy, whose tennis prowess meant most of the men avoided playing against her but were delighted to have her as a partner in mixed doubles, or even against two men.

The Kinneys enjoyed taking care of the men, especially the young ones in Robert's department, and paid special attention to Warren and me. Between the Kinneys and Father that first year, I found attention and support without which I might well have been kept from the second. There were suppers with the family, often wild, with the children all at the table. Imogene had a startling calmness in the face of flying potatoes or meatloaf, retrieving food and dishes while she remained well engaged in adult conversation. These meals distracted me from school concerns, keeping me in touch with family reality.

. . .

One night at the end of October near eleven o'clock - I had finished correcting a grammar quiz, the corridor silent, all asleep - the phone rang. It was Bob Kinney.

"Imogene's gone off, I'm ready for apple pie a la mode, my friend, and there's enough for two. Whaddya say?"

"You're on!"

"I'll pick you up. Be out front in six minutes and thirty seconds."

I was always stimulated by Kinney's enthusiasm for literature, his philosophy of selection, his feel for the needs of the students, his clever insight into how best to persuade the boys to achieve - and the conversation that night did not disappoint. Of course, Kinney's command of the reading and entire process naturally raised feelings of my own inadequacy, of how much I had to master.

After about an hour of discourse, Kinney said, "Tim, my spies tell me you're doing great - all around. Are they right?"

"I hope so, but there are times... All of it, together, is overwhelming. I'm getting the knack of the grammar, finally. It's fun really. I do most of it on the board - lots of arrows and stuff."

"That's okay - that's good, Tim. One lad told me you're a wild man with the chalk. Anything else - anything a problem?"

"Only Joe Ryan," I lied - my confusion based on the discovery of Wiggins and Conroy, the subsequent conversation with Father, and my attraction to Eunice Clare. These I would keep to myself. "He's been a pain in the ass. I just don't get why he's around here. Warren feels the same way. He was always snooping around the football, and seems to watch me all the time, trying to catch me up."

"Good old Joe. Don't let him get under your skin, and if you have to, hard as it is, be deferential. He's been here forever. He used to be good, they say, but now he's clearly gone to seed, and he's Henry's hardship case. Only Clyde Carlow has bridged the gap, but then he's in another league as far as schoolmen are concerned."

We had demolished the pie, and it was past midnight when Kinney delivered me to the dorm, saying before driving away, "Tim, we're doing Moby Dick after Christmas. How about taking a class - anything you want on Melville. You're probably more up on him than I. Think about it. See you at Mass. All Souls' Day tomorrow."

I watched his taillights disappear beyond the chapel, and then stood for some moments, looking across the way at the yellow light from the Clares' bedroom. I turned abruptly, shivering at the autumn night's damp chill, aghast at my emotions, wondering if Eunice Clare would be at Mass.

As I lay on my back in the darkness of my room, staring, unseeing, I pondered my own temptations until an uneasy sleep finally descended.

. . .

The next morning I was out on the corridor hustling the boys along, telling them I wanted no one late for Mass. All Souls' Day, a holy day of obligation for all Catholics, found the whole school trekking to Chapel. It was an obligation Henry Clare had regularly rewarded with a sumptuous breakfast afterward, a Sunday-brunch-like meal that made rising early most worthwhile.

Ahead of me I saw Eunice Clare walking slowly, without her husband. Despite my better judgment, I fell into step with her, and she smiled at me so engagingly I felt a tingling down my arms and an undeniable elation.

"Good morning, Mrs. Clare. Is the Headmaster checking the boys inside?"

"Henry's in New York. There's a Trustees meeting today, and he caught the afternoon train yesterday. He likes to be there ahead. It gives him time to collect himself, not to be nervous."

"I never thought Mr. Clare was ever nervous. He's so in command all the time."

"Timothy, Mr. Clare is also a fine actor." She grinned at me as if implying she was sharing a little secret. Then she said, "Sit with me, Timothy, up front in our pew."

"Really, I rather shouldn't. It's for you and the Headmaster."

"Nonsense. It's for us and anyone else. Besides, I don't want to be by myself. Bring two or three of your boys if you like."

I couldn't argue, properly couldn't decline, so nabbed Donnelli, Wiggins and Conroy, ushering them ahead of me. I positioned the three between Mrs. Clare and me, prompting her questioning glance at me. I was more comfortable, feeling less vulnerable. I concentrated on Father, on the Mass, on praying for Henry Clare's success in New York, my parents and myself. From the corner of my eye, I watched Mrs. Clare kneel at the rail for communion and noticed again how her calves slimmed to meet her perfect ankles.

At breakfast my table fell to their feast with an unholy gusto. The whole dining room was at decibel level quite beyond the usual breakfast cacaphony. The waiters even seemed cheerful, bringing platters of waffles and bacon that disappeared in an instant.

While I was attempting to control the noise, a folded note was handed to me. It read: "Timothy, please come to the house after lunch. There's a special task with which the Headmaster wants you to help. Eunice Clare." I read it, read it again, finally sticking it in my shirt pocket. At once I felt foreboding, and excitement, and I knew I certainly could not refuse. Had Henry Clare left this instruction? There would be no boys to hide behind as he had in church.

I was distracted in class, my concentration hampered further by the way the morning rushed by. It seemed I was already at lunch while still full from waffles, and then the meeting was upon me without any time to find a way out. She had apparently known I had no classes after lunch, a disquieting fact that said she knew my comings and goings. I was unnerved by that, but headed for her place in a businesslike manner, determined to dispose hastily of whatever task needed to be done.

I wasn't ready. She stood in the hallway, dressed in a flowing maroon slack suit that clung to her body, with nothing about her throat to interrupt the downward line to the tops of her breasts. I took in all this in a glance, terrified that she knew I quivered. She walked behind me to the study, the perfect smell of her an aura that surrounded me.

"Did you say your prayers this morning" she asked, "away at the other end of the pew?"

I was quite unprepared for this question. I stood near one end of the sofa, and she sat at the other, legs crossed, one foot moving in a small circle.

"Yes. I said some prayers - for all of us," I added.

"I had hoped we'd sit next to each other, Timothy."

"I never thought sitting together mattered at Mass. I mean, you know, the Mass is the thing."

"Of course. You're right. It isn't important. I guess it's what Henry likes about you. You have a good sense about things, he says. Is that right, Timothy? Do you have a good sense for things?"

"I just go through each day as best I can. If I do...have a good sense - and I certainly don't know that - it's just instinct - and a lot of times that isn't too good. My father didn't think it was very good at times - my judgment, you know."

"Tell me a time it wasn't very good."

"Mrs. Clare, there are some things I really must get back to. What is it the Headmaster wants?"

"Oh, so rushed, are you - with no classes left today. If you won't tell me about yourself, I'll just have to guess. But I've read your resume, you see, so there is much I do know. Of course, I read all the resumes. Henry insists on it. He thinks I can see things he can't. He didn't see in yours what I did - at least in the beginning - but he is wise. He makes good judgments. It's why he's a Headmaster."

"I am glad he decided to offer me this job. Despite everything, Ashford is a fine place."

"Despite everything? What does that mean?"

"Oh, I don't know. It just has to do with things at home, with not doing what my father wanted, with just wondering, I guess, if I can afford to do this."

"Timothy, would you like to talk about your father?"

"No."

"Is there anything you want to discuss with me?"

"No - just whatever it is you meant in the note. What task is it?"

She shrugged, stood, went behind the desk, eyed me for a moment, a new mein about her as she clasped her hands. She said, "Henry has you as the Master in Charge of the Dining Room. After Christmas we begin our weekly Sunday night suppers here, at the house, until we've had all the boys. It's a way for us to come to know them, and hopefully it's a warm break, especially from the baloney sandwich suppers in the dining room." She smiled at me as if for corroberation, and I grinned back. "The Headmaster feels you can be of great help by arranging things - which boys, when, which faculty member each week - generally assisting with details, menus and the like. You, yourself, should plan to attend all the suppers, or as many as you can."

She smiled encouragingly at me, though she didn't have to: I knew her arrangement could not be denied, that the Headmaster's request for my help could not be questioned - even if the idea had

81

been hers. Clearly I had no choice. I felt uneasy, sure that I was being maneuvered into some involvement that had nothing to do with the suppers. When I said nothing, she said, very softly, entreatingly, "You will step in with this, won't you?"

"If you think - if the Headmaster thinks I could be of help, of course - but things like menus... I have no idea!"

She laughed, a wonderful laugh that all but dissipated my anxiety. "You'll learn. We will have some sessions with Chef. He is very good with Lobster Newburg. Do you like Lobster Newburg, Timothy?"

"I've never had it."

By now I was feeling quite composed, my earlier feelings of trepidation dispatched, and I sat on the end of the sofa.   But she said, "Come with me. You must see all the rooms since you should know the lay out."

She led me to the kitchen, then through the dining room, back through the long spacious living room, to an enclosed porch, all the way pointing out paintings, photographs, a grandfather clock, never ceasing her descriptions and observations until I nearly forgot my discomfiture, the uneasy feeling that I wasn't supposed to be there. It was all so gracious, so comfortable, so beyond the rusticity of the farm, that I felt as if I were in a New England palace, each room high-ceilinged, painted in just the right tones of pastels.

But when she headed for the stairs, I stopped.

"Oh, do come with me," she entreated, "You must see my two Norman Rockwells and catch the marvelous view of the campus and the river."

With that she took my arm, and we went up the stairs to see the two guestrooms, and then into the master bedroom. I noticed the two twin beds as she led me through French doors onto a generous outdoor balcony that faced west toward the fields, with the campus to the left. It was indeed a splendid scene. I could hear the bell - classes were getting out for the day - and shouts from pent-up boys released from captivity.

"This is my favorite place" - she breathed deeply - "even in winter. All year you can see everything grow and change." She gestured, almost incidentally. "The fire escape goes down to the

garden. It's handy when I don't want to traipse through the house."
Then she said, almost in a whisper, "It's also an entry."

She turned to face me, taking my hands in hers; her breath quickened, and she smiled at me. "Timothy, we will have some wonderful times this winter - with the boys on Sunday nights. It's always good to have them here. Most of the time it's so... quiet, empty. And now, you will help make it truly special. I hope you don't mind."

"No, no. It will be good. Thank you for asking me - and thanks for the tour."

Finally she had seen me out. I remembered then feeling entrapped, that no matter how I might dodge, there would be no escape - and I remembered wondering if I could ever find the will to try.

. . .

It was dusk when I reached Esperance and stopped at the cheese store to collect myself and determined not to dwell on Eunice Clare, to concentrate on the road and the darkening night. I bought a wedge of sharp cheddar, a box of saltines, a styrofoam cup of coffee. Fortified with food and nostalgia, I headed on east across the bridge that spanned the Schoharie River. Each time I drove on that bridge I would remember the January night, so cold and snowy, when, driving Father's car, I had spun on the frozen surface - a full 360 degrees - coming out of the spin still headed west for my grandmother's funeral. I had hit no abutment and continued at the same speed - too fast, of course - the cause of the near accident in the first place.

CHAPTER FIFTEEN

That first year Rachael Mackintire had been my counterbalance, though I'd never perceived it then. My increasingly troubled feelings about Eunice Clare - a perilous situation, I sensed in my heart, in which I saw myself a passive recipient of an attention I couldn't fathom, coupled with a secret excitement I regarded as immoral - propelled me to overtly seek Rachel, first as a friend, but perhaps as a romantic dalliance, even as my lover. But Rachel Mackintire wasn't about to be my toy, though she enjoyed - at a distance she repeatedly defined - what I found to be an infuriating flirtation.

I was expected to check in on things daily at the infirmary, a task I rather enjoyed with Mrs. Malley, and one I relished once Rachel came aboard. One Wednesday in mid-October I found both of them in the dispensary, chatting over coffee.

"Why, if it isn't Timothy Jordan, the coaching wizard of the year," Mrs. Malley said.

"Mrs. Malley, you really kissed the blarney stone, and it appears you don't have a problem in the world."

"Not now, my dear boy, not with Rachel here. You know she's up-to-date about things, and she's such a darlin'."

"Tim's right about that blarney stone," Rachel said. "You're the one who really knows everything."

"Well, I do know about sick boys. Now then, I must go and see to a project in my apartment. Why don't you two just sit here and chat. Rachel will fill you in on our boys, Tim. We have two in. Bye-bye."

We both grinned at her retreating figure.

"You know," Rachel said, "she's a conniver, an old matchmaker. Can't understand why we aren't out on the town."

"So what's wrong with that? You keep saying you can't leave her alone, and she wants you to go."

"Boarding school's no place for it. You know very well about rumors at a place like this. Besides, you've never asked me out - like... to dinner, for example."

"God, Rachel, I can hardly afford a haircut. Do you have any idea what I make? It comes out to seventeen cents an hour."

"Maybe you're overpaid! Oh, I know. I shouldn't have embarrassed you. Okay. Let's forget it for now. It probably isn't a good idea, anyway. It's what I said before: people talking, even if it would only be a way to get off campus."

"But it wouldn't have to be only that! Look, Rachel, I'm with Mrs. Malley. I think about you all the time, and I want to get to know you better - outside this infirmary, away from the pills. Ever since that first day in the Headmaster's office I've wanted that."

She laughed. "Oh, <u>that</u> day. I was a little forward, and you both were so nice. I must admit meeting you then put a good slant on the job. I was thrilled when Mr. Clare asked me to come - and...I did think about you, Timothy Jordan."

Encouraged, I pressed her to see me, but she demurred, claiming demands of the job. Then, when I was out the door and on the sidewalk, she called to me. "How about Sunday afternoon? We could walk down by the river. I could bring something to eat."

I looked at her framed in the doorway, her white uniform unable to conceal her lovely figure, her auburn hair peeking from under her cap, her oval face alive - and I gave a thumbs-up.

• • •

That afternoon my football team played South Kent, but now, without Donnelli, we scored once and lost by two touchdowns. My lads did their best and fell short, but unlike after other losses, I felt resigned, indeed almost fine, with the Sunday river walk on my mind. I wondered what would happen with this remarkable young woman. The fact that it had been her suggestion made the date intriguing.

On Saturday, a perfect fall afternoon, I rode the bus with the Varsity to see Donnelli destroy Westminster on their turf. The boy's faking paved the way for unerring passes caught most of the time, and I knew I watched a young athlete of promise, one far beyond my own skill when I'd played for Cazenovia.

On the ride home, Smitty said to me, "Thank God we stole your quarterback and your system. Next year everyone will use the "T" formation, but for now we're king, thanks to you. I knew you were upset about Donnelli, but he deserved the shot. He's the key. He makes it work. Everyone plays up to him. What a boy!"

The good weather held on Sunday. I could see Rachel and Mrs. Malley together, well ahead of me on the walk to Mass, their whites standing out against the stream of blue blazered students headed for the chapel. Henry and Eunice Clare stood at the door as the boys and faculty trooped to their places. It was the twenty-eighth Sunday in Ordinary Time. Luke's gospel spoke of the ten lepers Jesus cured, all but one, a Samaritan, returning to praise God. Father's homily neatly tied the theme with the season of harvest and thanksgiving. Though not profound, he did capture the attention of the students, and I again understood how Father met the needs of the boys. Only a few of the faculty could speak to the boys with significance about anything beyond their discipline. This shortcoming kept most from becoming full schoolmen, I had concluded, not then, but soon enough to modify my own performance. Clyde Carlow had often said that if one out of six new masters became a good school man, a Headmaster were lucky.

After breakfast I corrected compositions all morning. I was trying to have my students become aware of the importance of verbs, to avoid the passive voice whenever possible. The students' progress was painfully slow, but they wrote regularly, and I was happy that at least they were coming to understand about paragraphing!

After each paper I found himself thinking about the afternoon, and Rachel. I felt warmed by the prospect of such a perfect fall afternoon with a woman, a lovely creature of bewitching prospect, and my peer.

She was ready at the door. It was the first time I had seen her not in whites. She wore brown-plaid slacks and a red turtleneck sweater. A jacket was over one arm and a tote bag with what appeared to be sandwiches and a thermos over her other shoulder. On her head was a rakish red tam. She looked a bonnie lass.

"Rachel, you're spectacular! You'll blend right in with the leaves. Think we should bring a blanket - you know, to sit on?"

"It's bad enough that people will see us walking across campus, but with a blanket? I think not. All we'd need is for gossip to fly."

"Never thought of that," I said, disappointed. "The fishbowl we live in. I should have gone down ahead and stashed one under a log."

Laughing, she replied firmly, "We won't need one."

Together we traced our way across the playing fields, the sun in our faces. At first we walked in silence, relishing what was likely to be one of the last best days of October, the turning leaves at their fullest brilliance, a time when New England is the only place to be. We could trace the flow of the Housatonic by the leaves floating and dancing on the surface, swept swiftly here, locked in swirling eddies there, finding the river's pulsing course. Little wonder we did not speak, so full were we with the season's last explosion, like the final rockets at a display of fireworks. Halfway around a curve a fallen tree lay half in, half out of the river.

"Look, Tim," she said, "a natural picnic table."

Astride the log we faced each other, the bag of sandwiches between us. Her cheeks were flushed, enhancing her few freckles, a perfect embellishment to her glowing face.

"Hungry, Tim?" she asked.

"Always hungry...for you!"

"Tim, please, that's not why we're out here. Promise me no more of that. Please don't spoil things."

"I don't want to spoil anything. It's just that when you asked me - well, I thought maybe... Oh, I don't know. Forgive me for that. It's just that you have become...on my mind, even though we've never been on a date. Well, I'll try, but won't promise." I was grinning.

In silence we chewed on the by now slightly soggy sandwiches and drank the now tepid hot chocolate from paper cups. After a minute, I said, "Rachel, did you have any other job offers, other than Ashford?"

"One at the hospital in Holyoke, and one in a doctor's office. Neither felt right, especially the doctor's place. I didn't like the interview, the way he looked at me."

"How did he look at you?"

"Well, let's just say I felt he was after more than a nurse."

"I understand how he felt."

"Now, Tim! Anyway, when Mr. Clare called, I wanted to look, mainly because Ashford is a Catholic School. This environment is very important to me - the Catholic part, I mean. I was sold at the interview."

"You mean I sold you with my charm!" I exclaimed, hopefully.

"No, Tim. By the Headmaster and then Mrs. Malley."

"And then," she went on, my mother was so happy about my possibly coming here, because it was Catholic. That's so important for my parents, not so much for my brothers and sisters, but it is to me. You see, there has to be more to education than itself, as with nursing. Here, at least, there is a philosophy about how to do things, even if it's just having crucifixes in each infirmary room. I like being in a place with a chapel, daily Mass, prayers in the schoolhouse, people blessing themselves. It's comfortable."

"Safe and protected?"

"Is that wrong?"

"No. No, it's not wrong. I guess I hadn't thought of it that way so much - the Catholic part. I grew up where it wasn't so close around me. It couldn't be. But that's another story. Sounds to me you might have become a nun, with your feelings the way they are."

"I thought about it, Tim, but it wouldn't work for me. I couldn't. Despite my faith, I have strong emotions. I like them, too, though I'm embarrassed saying that."

"Don't be. For me, it's a good sign. I'm so glad you're not a nun. Can I have hopes, about us, I mean?"

"There's always hope, Tim."

Then I told her of my life, from farm to Ashford. At dusk we stood, gathered the picnic things into her bag, and standing close, looked out over the river.

"Have you read Pastoral by Nevil Shute?" I asked.

"No, I haven't."

"In it there comes a point where the hero asks the heroine - Gervase is her name - when it would be he could make a rude suggestion."

89

I paused, then said, "Do you think there will ever be a time when I can make a 'rude' suggestion?"

"It will depend on the time - and how...'rude' the suggestion."

"I have one now, just a slightly rude one, given the circumstance."

She looked at me for a long moment. "All right. If it's only slightly rude, I'll hear it."

"Well, since it's almost dark, and there's little chance anyone could see us, I thought I'd like to kiss you - here by the river."

She set down her bag and turned to me, putting her arms around my neck. "Tim, you are very dear. That's not rude."

In the lowering twilight shadows of an October afternoon, Rachel and I kissed, long and passionately, our mouths and tongues hungry, lusting, her right leg hooked around mine to draw me closer. Finally parted and headed back hand in hand, we both knew it was a beginning neither could likely end. When I left her at the infirmary door, her face bespoke a frightened wonder that somehow she had unleashed a force she could not control even though she had to try. As for me, I couldn't imagine where this one small victory would lead, but I knew I must pursue the path, for on the riverbank I had felt the first tremors of falling in love. How little I knew then about the torturous turns that path would find.

CHAPTER SIXTEEN

The afternoon at the river had started it, and thereafter we continually sought ways to see each other without causing a campus to-do. It wasn't easy. While I thought her much too sensitive, I respected her judgment, her personal wishes in the matter, even though I didn't like skulking around. The reward each time was one, very thorough, kiss. She extricated herself each time with a practiced routine, developed, I supposed, long before we had met, and, in a sense, that made me proud of her, even in my frustration. All the while, I was totally charmed by her wit, zest for life, and amazing depths of knowledge in my own academic discipline. Any works offered at Ashford that she hadn't read, she read, including Shakespeare. One day I found her in the library checking out Wordsworth and Coleridge; her plan was to "do' the Romantic poets.

After two more excursions to the river, we decided that sojourn might be becoming too obvious, and for me, too full of talk for any more than that one long kiss.

One night I daringly called the infirmary after ten, told her I had Father's car, and asked her to dash out when I pulled up, to go to the Canaan diner.

"Oh, Tim, should we? I mean, is there anyone about?"

"Not now, and the night watchman doesn't hit your place until eleven. We could come back after his rounds at eleven or twelve."

"It's so daring. I don't know. I'd have to tell Mrs. Malley."

"I thought she's all for us."

"Yes. Well, all right. I'll be watching. Don't blow the horn or anything. Gosh, I'm excited. Can you imagine?"

She made it to the car, out of breath from the prospect. She scrunched down as we pulled out of the campus.

"Sit up, Rachel. You don't have to hide. After all, we are adults. This is getting rather stupid."

"I know, but I'm quivering all over. When did you think of this, and what did Father say?"

"He said, "It's about time you took Rachel somewhere'."

"You told him!"

"He knows. There's not much he doesn't know. Besides, it's safe with him. He's not about to tell the world. In addition, I think he thinks it's healthy."

"Oh,you!"

She surveyed the diner to see if there were anyone they knew. Then, satisfied there wasn't, she took a booth with me in a far corner. We ordered cheeseburgers and coffee, and felt like high schoolers on a date.

"This is marvelous," she sighed, "and I was starved. Only thing is, it does worry me some. The hour, being off campus, Father's car - but then, of course, with Father's car nothing bad could happen."

"You mean you're worried about the real 'rude suggestion'."

"Sort of, and maybe not so much about you as about me. The last several days have been glorious. I'm so happy but so scared. It's like I have a ball in my stomach all the time, bouncing around. I find myself looking out the window every morning at 7:45 when you walk to the schoolhouse, and I'm upset if some patient keeps me away. Am I absolutely crazy?"

"You're absolutely devastating. Why do you think I check the Infirmary twice a day?"

"I've noticed that. You too, Tim? You too?"

"Oh, yes."

We ate then, not as hungry as we'd thought, dawdling over half-finished food, carefully sipping coffee.

"Well," I began, "I did have in mind another route home."

"I knew it. Am I supposed to ask where that would be?" She was trying to be coy.

"There's a dirt road across the river no one ever uses."

"And you've scouted it and found a place to park."

"As a matter of fact, I have."

She searched my face, serious now, her eyes a little misty.

"If we leave now, we'll have only thirty minutes. Then I'm to be back. Agreed?"

"Yes, ma'am."

In the time allotted, I found her breasts, ecstatic that she had worn no brassiere. But they were all I found. She had designed the

92

course, I realized, but even so, I reveled in this monumental victory, and she gave them to me so wantonly, so completely that I kept saying, "I love you" over and over while she answered, "I know, I know," sobbing in her passion, her shoulders shuddering.

But she also murmured, as if in a different sphere, "God help me. Jesus help me. Mary pray for me." Then with her top back on, she took my hands in hers, asking me to pray with her. Together we said the "Our Father," and with some inward objection on my part, the "Act of Contrition." I drove her back between night watchman rounds, her body up against my side, her mouth at my cheek. She bolted from the car, her dark figure gone in the night before I could touch her again.

Father's light was still on, so I stopped with the car keys.

"You're back early. Did you eat?"

"Cheeseburgers. Rachel and I thank you very much."

"She's a splendid girl and a fine nurse. You're lucky she's here."

"Yes, very lucky. I must get to bed. Thanks again."

"Any time, Tim."

It was a breakthrough of a kind, for after that night Rachel was much more at ease with being seen, even though to a few she insisted we were not an 'item.'

· · ·

Father was generous with the car, so when Rachel asked if it were possible for me to drive her to visit her parents, I - as the football season was over - borrowed it with the promise to Father to check the oil and fill it with gas.

I was filled with the prospects for the day - not so much with meeting her parents, but with the drive back to school, the length of which would be of no consequence to anyone but the two of us.

Once in the car, however, Rachel appeared subdued. Conversation was desultory, often with long silences, and her gaze was directed out her window at the now fast fading fall. No quip or attempt to be light-hearted cheered her, and after some miles, I suspected my earlier hopes for the end of the day could well founder. Her mood puzzled me, and I felt ill-equipped to deal with it, to say nothing of guessing the cause. I was truly at sea when she asked him to pull over to a roadside phone in Westfield.

"Rachel, what's the matter?"

"Nothing, really. It's just that I should call my mother. I wasn't absolutely certain we could get the car, so I said I'd call - and didn't."

She went to the booth, and it seemed to him she talked too long to simply announce that they were on the way. Returning, she sat in the car, not looking at me.

"Let's find a place to eat, to talk," she said.

"Okay. What's going on?"

"Please, just let's find a place, and we'll talk over lunch. I've told Mother we won't be coming."

Thoroughly confused, I located a diner I could afford, and we found an empty booth. The waiter was on us at once, and out of habit, I ordered cheeseburgers.

"I'm sorry to be out of sorts, Tim. I just didn't want to go home, with you along, feeling the way I do, especially when I don't know what's wrong."

"You're not sick?"

"No, no, not that. I'm just down, and I'm not used to it."

"Is it about us, about me? I have been trotting out...the 'suggestion' a lot lately." She smiled slightly, for the first time that day.

"No, I'm used to that. In fact, I love it now when you do. I guess, though, that's part of it, or I think it is, or ...Oh, I don't know. It's just that something happened Wednesday that's thrown me out of whack, kept me awake, and it's just awful."

"God, Rachel, what on earth is it? I can't stand it if you're not happy - you of all people."

"Do you remember last Wednesday when you were in the infirmary, and we were doing rounds?"

"Gosh, I'm in every day, though not to see the boys! Let's see...What happened Wednesday?"

"Well, while we were making the rounds, Mrs. Clare came in. Remember that?"

94

I did, of course, and as I did I felt a foreboding, even without cause, for there was outwardly nothing to that. Still, I hesitated, on guard.

"Yes, I do remember. She met us in the hallway."

"And she said, 'Miss Mackintire, you have a boy up front. You should go check on him.' Do you remember that?"

"No, not really. I remember you left, and she and I went on visiting - two more rooms, I think. Why?"

"There was no boy up front, Tim."

"So? Maybe he'd left."

"I don't think so. I don't think there ever was a boy."

"What are you saying?"

"I'm saying that she didn't want me there, wanted me to leave, wanted you to herself!"

We sat staring at each other, her lips pressed together as though to keep them from quivering, a moistness in her eyes that unbalanced me, my mouth half open at what she had said. I erred in bowing my head, if only slightly, for that indicated she might have a point. As evenly as I could, I said, "Rachel, that's just not possible. Look. She was just visiting the infirmary. I mean, there's no reason she would want...what you say."

"That's what I keep telling myself, but it won't go away. But after you left, she stayed and talked to me, actually sort of lectured me about how important you were to the school - that you needed to concentrate on your job."

"Oh, that. Well, I guess she does think I've done well at times, but really, that's not all bad."

"Of course it isn't, given who she is and who she sleeps with, but that isn't all. She said she's seen me sneaking out at night - to Father's car, of all things - even though she knew it wasn't Father. Tim, she's been watching us! Why in God's name is she doing that? And then she says, 'Miss Mackintire, Timothy is like a son to us, and we don't want anything to hurt his chances at Ashford.' Tim, oh Tim. I'm so unhappy, so unhappy, so worried."

"Dear love, please don't worry. Please."

"But why do I feel something is wrong. Why do I feel she's jealous?"

95

"Rachel, <u>stop</u> it. Stop it right now. She's completely out of line, and I'll take care of it. God, Rachel, she could be my mother!"

I was arguing forcefully to overcome my lack of conviction, to overwhelm Rachel's unnerving sense of the truth.

"Oh, I know. I know. But she is so beautiful and clever - so powerful. And you are so beautiful, so wonderful - and I'm so afraid."

Now she was crying, quietly and steadily, her shoulders hunched in agony. I rose and slid into her side of the booth, my arm over her shoulders. We sat that way until she at last calmed enough for me to pay the check and for us to leave.

The ride back was grim, for I was of little use to her, almost afraid to say anything, for at the moment there was little that I could say to assuage the nightmare she felt. Before leaving the car, she did turn to me. "Tim, forgive me, please, for ruining the day, for us, my parents - for everything. You see, you have become so much a part of my life, I can't bear what happened. I can't bear the consequence of my crazy thoughts. I have this unreasonable feeling I can't understand. Be patient with me. I know you are so good, really, deep down."

With that she threw her arms around me, kissed my neck and face, then jumped from the car and ran to the door without turning back. I knew I loved her, so much, and yet I wasn't happy now, and even less so when reviewing our conversation over and over most of the night. The next morning I was at the chapel door, checking the boys into Mass. As she entered, her flicker of recognition was indeed just that, the slightest nod, the faintest smile. I prayed for assistance, hoping God could help my dilemma, knowing He had far greater vision than I.

CHAPTER SEVENTEEN

There was a scurry as school pressed toward Christmas break. Final exams loomed; it was between sports seasons, and the boys were frenetic with unspent energy and anticipation of vacation. I dreaded the Sunday suppers which would commence after the holiday, what with the recent complication of Rachel's worry and the contact I couldn't avoid with Eunice Clare. The situation gnawed at me, especially since it appeared Rachel's fervor and joy in our burgeoning feelings now seemed more calculated, less spontaneous - each meeting carefully controlled, with an unspoken reserve that I found disappointing, worrisome, increasingly irritating. We didn't address the issue she had raised, and I avoided any reference to Eunice, at the same time attempting as best I could to be both playful and loving. For her part she was available, conversant, though often dismissive of my desire for physical contact, and more than once "on duty" when I knew she really could have been free. And too, there was the constant pressure of my doing my part to hold firm a school ready to explode into the holiday. There were late nights of patrolling, of always being on tap, and of tutoring boys whose lack of daily preparation left them panicked about exams.

School would be breaking on a Saturday morning after breakfast, following a Friday night play - "Stalag 17 - directed by Bob Kinney. A play before break was an Ashford tradition, and Kinney had fumed about it for days, trying to put on a production at the end of exam week. Learning lines just didn't fit preparing for exams, but Henry Clare insisted, saying that the arts were important for the boys, that the parents expected it.

Two days before the performance, Henry Clare called me to his office. He was leaning back in his chair, hands behind his head, looking expansive.

"Timmie, how goes the battle?"

"Fine, sir, fine. The boys are pretty jumpy - ready to go. Some have been packed for days."

"I know. It's always a tense time for everyone, but we've had a good run overall - if you forget Parents' Weekend! Guess that's the way with pain - you forget it, or don't remember it, thank God. Anyway, you've done well, Timmie. You can make decisions, and a lot can't. The thing is, it doesn't usually matter that much whether a decision is right or wrong. What matters is just making it."

"You're right, sir. I never really thought about it that way."

"Do you have plans for Christmas?"

"No timetable. I want to prepare some lesson plans for January and then go see my parents at the farm. Christmas is a big time in my family. Everyone will be there."

"Good, good. You should get away; the faculty needs the time as well as the boys. Now, Timmie, you know that a large group takes the train to New York, and needs supervision. It's not the greatest duty, but I'd like you to do it. Think you could do that for me?"

"Well, I guess so, sir, if you think I could. I've not done it, but if you think I can."

"Of course you can. You're the right person."

"Have there ever been problems?"

"Not really. We just don't want them to be rowdy. If anyone tries to smoke, just confiscate the cigarettes and let Clyde know when you get back. Eunice and I talked last night about who should go, and we both agreed that Timmie Jordan was the man. And that's another thing. Eunice wants to go to New York city to do some Christmas shopping. She'll take the train with you and the boys. She's even suggested that it would be an extra pair of eyes. What I'd appreciate you do is to stay on in the city and help Eunice with her things onto the train back here, probably in the late afternoon or evening. It would make me feel better knowing you were there to help. Why not make it a day in New York? Hope you don't mind. My own mind will be at ease."

Probably Mr. Clare hadn't thought me very enthusiastic, and he would have been correct. The proposal of chaperoning the the boys had seemed a challenge, and been a compliment. Escorting Eunice changed everything. I remembered starting to tremble, sweat came, and my stomach felt that heaviness one usually connects with fear.

Trying to cover my disquiet, I mumbled my way from the office and distractedly wandered until I reached the river, where, quaking and disconsolate, I sat on the log where Rachel and I had picnicked. Even in this generous outpouring of nature, I felt compressed, shrunken in a narrowing, uncomfortable cell. I had to get out of this train ride, but how? The Headmaster, my boss, my idol - and Mrs. Clare. Rachel was right! Everything had seemed so right, and everything was so wrong. I felt as if in a vortex from which climbing up and out was impossible.

Had Eunice Clare engineered my Ashford success? I never perceived the reality of my situation, lacking Rachel's intuition, and likely refusing to see, my ego so inflated that perspective was lost. I knew I must go to the Headmaster to withdraw from the assigned duty. Sadly, I didn't.

· · ·

Friday evening the school attended Kinney's play, ingeniously proffered in the round at the center of the gym floor. The cast was superb and took everyone's minds from thoughts of holiday, finished exams, and for almost two hours created the reality of prison camp with its humor and heroics. Kinney had pulled it off, and at the end he stood at the door, relieved and pleased, accepting faculty congratulations.

"Next year, my friend," he hooted, "you are the man!"

"But I know nothing about directing a play."

"Don't worry, Tim, you just have to be a glutton and a little nuts - and you qualify," Kinney said.

The Clares stopped to shake Kinney's hand. They were effusive with praise, Eunice glowing, acknowledging the group in a sweep of her gaze that drew all eyes to her, except for Rachel's. She looked at her feet; she appeared frail.

Then Eunice turned to me and put her hand on mine. "Timothy, I suppose you'll walk to the station Saturday morning with the boys. I'll drive and park the car, so we can ride back together, since it might be late. I'll see you on the train."

I looked past her to see Rachel turn abruptly and walk away, her coat hunched over her shoulders, her rapid stride determined to escape before I could move.

The evening's elation withered on the spot.

"Yes, yes. That's the plan. On Saturday."

As soon as I could, I trudged wearily to my corridor, an ache in my body that I knew meant no rest that night. With the boys finally in bed, I sat on the edge of my bed, head in hands. I sank into a kind of despair I'd never before felt. I must talk to Rachel, try to explain, tell her I'd had no polite way to turn down Henry Clare, but that I loved her. I dialed her number.

"Can I come over? It's important we talk."

"It's late. You have a big day tomorrow - and I must pack."

"It won't take long. I can't leave without seeing you, and there's the whole break to plan for - you know - a time away from campus with no eyes on us. We have to talk about that."

"Tim, it's busy at home at Christmas. Besides, you have no car, so maybe we should just take the holiday - like the boys."

She sounded so sad, so far away. I didn't know how to proceed. Desperately, I said, "I'm coming over!"

"No!"

"I'm coming over - now!"

I hung up, threw on my coat, ran the full way. She was sitting behind the dispensary desk. Clearly she'd been crying. Her hands were clasped on the desktop, and when she didn't rise, didn't smile, offered no greeting, the moated castle wall seemed impregnable.

"Rachel, this trip to New York was not my idea. The Headmaster asked me to take it. I didn't know she was coming, until he...sprang in on me. Believe me, I didn't know! There's nothing I can do."

"I know that."

"Then why are you in such a mood? You look terrible, and - and I love you so. I'm upset - crazy, frustrated, angry -everything."

Looking at her hands, she whispered, her voice breaking, "Tim, I don't know what's the matter with me. Ideas just - just keep swirling around - about her - you - terrible things. That she doesn't just want you for a substitute son. That she - she just...wants you.

Don't you see, she's after you! My God. I can't believe I said that - but over and over I have this awful feeling - Eunice Clare wants Timothy Jordan for her lover!"

"Oh, God help us, Rachel. You are mad. God, don't you know? Even if that crazy idea were true - My God - it's all so <u>stupid</u>. You're my love! Don't you believe that?"

"Yes. I believe you, Tim, but you may not be able to help it. She's so - so overpowering, so dominating. You said yourself she influenced the Headmaster to hire you. Now she's manipulated him - and you - into a day in New York. I can't believe it! Can't you see it?" Now she looked directly into my eyes. "Can't you see what's going on, Tim?"

"No. No. The Clares are happily married - older - adults. She adores him and he, her. God, Rachel, things have run away with you."

"Perhaps. Perhaps I'm dead wrong. Perhaps I'm so in love with you that the slightest attention - or look - or innocent arrangement I'll find disturbing. Perhaps you <u>are</u> right. But - just perhaps <u>I</u> am. Even the 'perhaps' is enough to set me off."

I sat looking at her. I wanted to hold her. I wanted to assuage her fears, even knowing they had some merit. Eunice Clare held strong strings to my future, my job, but Rachel had become my life. We sat quietly looking at our hands, aching, dying, unable to push away this barrier - one without life, yet so real.

"Is Mrs. Malley asleep?"

"Probably. I guess so. Her light is out. Why?"

"Any boys in?"

"No. Everyone feels fine before holidays. Why?"

I stood then and faced her. "Why don't we go down the hall, find a room. No one's around."

"Tim, you <u>know</u> that won't do. I couldn't, and I don't really think you could. You shouldn't be here at all."

"Right now, Rachel, I'm capable of anything - of everything. To hell with what people think. To hell with Eunice Clare, the Headmaster, the rules, rumors, night watchman. Oh, Rachel, the hell with everything."

I sat heavily on the chair before her desk, rubbing my face. She came 'round then, put her hands on my bowed head, knelt by the chair and took my hands down into hers.

"I've distressed you too much. Believe me, I want you to be mine, can't bear any other thought. And I'm terrified by my feelings. I do trust you, but I don't trust her. I'm praying about it. I need help. I need Jesus for us, for me. I'm so weak, so lost - all because I love you, and because I'm not as strong. But I shall get better. Go on your trip. You'll be fine, and true, and I'll say many prayers - for all of us. I can't...go to bed with you, as much as I want to - because - because when we do that, everything should be clear. It's such a sacred thing, and there can't be any...any...shadows."

I felt like crying. She pulled me to my feet, kissed my right cheek, and led me to the door, both hands pulling my right arm.

"Remember, Tim, what you mother always told you."

"What was that? Remind me."

"That she was a Magrill."

"Oh, yes. I told you that? Amazing. All right, I'll remember."

And I walked away from her, nothing resolved, no plan laid, nowhere to turn, but toward a truly uncertain future. The night watchman saw me, but I didn't care.

CHAPTER EIGHTEEN

We sat at the rear of the car. The boys actually forgot our presence but were remarkably well-behaved, I only once feeling compelled to walk the aisle. At Grand Central they shot out of the train and away, with Eunice and me left standing at the information booth. We agreed on the four o'clock return train and to meet at the same spot at three thirty. I watched her ascend the ramp to Forty-second Street, then stood there among the hurrying throng, recalling the only other time I'd been in New York, when the Colgate team had come to play New York University at the Garden. It hardly seemed possible that it had been only a year ago. Looking about me, I felt years older. I headed for the street with no real plan in mind except to visit St. Patrick's Cathedral.

I got there in time for a noon Mass, marveling at the crowd for a Saturday, at the miles of pews filling rapidly. Some had holiday shopping in tow; for most it appeared part of a regular routine.

I debated going to communion, then did receive, concluding my times with Rachel weren't 'fornication.' We'd been loving, and she'd kept me from sin, I reasoned. If there were any transgressions, it had been in my thoughts about Eunice Clare, but I'd never fully accepted the teaching that thoughts were equal to, if not worse than, actions. Besides, my intentions were to escape any future encounter with Eunice and to give everything I had to his relationship with Rachel. I prayed that the train ride home would be uneventful.

I sat in the cathedral after the dismissal - a good time and place to think about all these things and events that had happened - to me, it seemed, rather than because of me. I realized how very tired I was, then how detached in a place far from Ashford. I could barely stay awake, the fatigue of mind and body overwhelming, until, indeed, I nodded, slept. Jarred upright by the sounds of a new crowd for the next Mass, I left, walked down to Macy's, eyed many items I would have liked to give Rachel, but for so little money. I settled on a Christmas-stocking cap, red and white, with a ball of red yarn at the end. Not much, but I could see it on her as she walked across the campus in the winter months ahead - a sign to me of our connection.

I was at Grand Central in ample time, and shortly after three-thirty, Eunice appeared at the top of the ramp, a shopping bag in each hand. She carefully began descending, eyes down, and halfway stopped to look around. Seeing me, she smiled - devastating even at a distance.

"Oh, Timothy," she caroled when she got to him, "what a marvelous day! New York is so wonderful this time of year! And believe it or not, I'm almost done. Are you all right?"

"I'm fine, just fine."

"Watch my bags, will you? I want to run and call Henry - let him know we've made this train. I think they come through with sandwiches on the train. It will have to do."

Shortly, she returned, bubbling. "All's well at school. It's snowing there, and some parents' cars skidded around, but everyone's gone. Henry says hello."

On the journey she was humorous, delightful, happy; she talked even while relishing her sandwich, and I ate mine ravenously. Neither of us had had lunch.

Finally, well along in the trip she said, "Enough of my day. What did you do, Timothy? Did you get around?"

I told her I'd gone to Mass at St. Patrick's.

"Goodness, Timothy. It isn't many a young man who would go to Mass with a few hours in New York City. What a wonderful thing. Did you enjoy going there?"

"Yes, I did. It was a great experience. And all those people - so many at Mass."

"Yes, it's amazing, isn't it? I hope you said your prayers."

"Of course. I have much to be grateful for."

"Tell me."

I felt tongue-tied, not expecting the personal question on recalling what, if any, prayer I had said. I looked out the window - snow was now swirling in the passing lights, the ground white - and hesitated.

"I'm sorry," she said. "That wasn't an appropriate question. Forgive me."

"That's okay." And, self-consciously, I rattled off all the benefits of being at Ashford, not the least, the people I'd met there.

"I think you have learned much already," she said, "and so does Henry. The other night Father suggested to Henry he appoint you to the Discipline Committee, the group that recommends to Henry on the serious cases - and Henry thought it a good idea. People see good things in you. There are a few who've been at school for years and haven't yet grown as you have."

After a pause, she said, "Now I am sleepy. It you don't mind, I'm pushing back my seat to rest a bit."

I watched her from the corner of my eye, and soon I, too, felt tired - in the way I'd felt at the Cathedral. For many miles we both slept.

Awakening first, I thought I needn't have worried. The whole event had gone without any complication. Perhaps my nerves and Rachel's were based on sheer fantasy. Perhaps, in Eunice Clare there was a genuinely caring and warm person who had come to admire me as a new young master who brought a dynamic dimension to her husband's school.

Her head lolled toward his seat, a faint smile on her lips, her eyes closed, half-inch lashes definitely her own. Even asleep, her regal beauty was startling, discomfiting, and I turned away to the window. The snow fell steadily on the Connecticut countryside, perhaps a coverlet until spring. Wondering if Rachel had left for Holyoke, I hoped she'd stayed at Ashford for the night, that she wanted to see me. That last time with her had been fragmented.

Eunice awoke, startled. "Oh! Where are we?"

"Getting there. Just north of New Milford."

"Look at the snow. I hadn't counted on there being so much."

At Ashley Falls I carried her shopping bags as she reached in her purse for the keys. As we approached it, we saw the station wagon she'd left in the parking lot was covered with snow. She slipped in and started the engine and unlocked the passenger door. After handing in the packages, I swept the snow away from the windshield with long swishes of my arms.

The snow was falling very hard; it was cold, and the wind swirled around the station house, its lights dimmed by the snow.

By the time I slid himself into the passenger seat, she'd adjusted the heat. "We'll sit for a while until it warms up," she said.

"It isn't far."

"I hate cold steering wheels, and the defroster will work better with it warm."

She revved the motor a few times and finally drove slowly to the road where she turned in the opposite direction from school.

"Mrs. Clare, school is the other way."

"I know where the school is. I'm taking another way."

"Should you, in this weather? This is a good car, but these roads can still be tricky. Why don't we find a place to turn around?"

She looked at me then, and I saw a different face, a determined set to her mouth, a wideness in her eyes. At first I was perplexed, then distraught, sensing this was contrivance, a plan, a frightening prospect - alone together in a car, no one around, in a storm.

"Mrs. Clare! Look, this doesn't make sense. We can get stuck! Mr. Clare will be worried."

"Henry thinks we're on the six o'clock train! I told him we were on the six o'clock."

"You did _what_?"

"And now we have at least two whole hours all to ourselves."

"You mean you set this up. Lied to your husband! For God's sake, Mrs. Clare, where are we going?"

I suddenly realized she'd orchestrated everything - her car parked at the station, the New York trip - so innocent. The only hitch, the snow.

I would remember that it was probably the snow that saved me.

She stopped the car on a shoulder near a barn, switched to the parking lights and left the motor running, the dim dash light etching her face.

"Mrs. Clare, please. I think...I know we should go home. Whatever you have in mind, I'm not interested. This whole thing is not right. Please let's go!"

"Dear, don't be that way. I just want us to - to come closer somehow, to talk and truly be away from things. And don't be so naive. You know that we have a special something that no one else could understand. You know that, don't you, dear?"

"No we don't! Not at all. Why, you're the Headmaster's wife, and I respect that and him. You've been swell to me, and that's wonderful, but really, there's nothing. Mrs. Clare, I could be your son!"

"Wouldn't that be wonderful?!"

"I don't understand. Whatever you're talking about. We're a whole generation different. Oh, God. You know we shouldn't be here. What would your husband think?"

She looked at me, her face aglow, alive. "Henry wouldn't think anything, Timothy. He would understand my feelings."

Now I was thoroughly lost, my thoughts grappling for her meaning. I was trapped in a station wagon, in a snow storm, with a clever woman whose sexual presence so filled the space between us that I tried scrunching against my door, fearful to say more. I had to get out of this, out of the car, back to school. I looked at my low shoes, hoodless fall coat, bare hands, desperately trying to make a decision. Rachel's face hung before me, her words echoing round and round.

"Dear Timothy, don't be afraid. Let me hold your hand - there - like that. I've thought about your hands. Oh, it's all right. Please, don't take it away. For a while, just be my son."

"Like Hamlet to Gertrude. My God!"

She laughed, excited that I'd thought of that. "I hadn't thought of it that way, but it's curious you did. Anyway, you protest too much. I've seen you look at me, at my legs. You like my legs, don't you?"

She steered my reluctant hand to her calf, moving it up and down, from below her knee to her ankle. The only sound was the heater, the car so hot and my hand damp as she moved it from calf to calf. Her stockings enhanced the perfection, heightening the tremble in my fingers. She raised my hand to her mouth, kissed the palm, her tongue wetting it and trailing my fingers. It was terribly quiet, the snow now blocking all the windows as we crouched toward each other as in a tomb, in an awful ecstasy that made me weep inside.

Holding my hand in her right one, she threw back her coat and in a quick motion had her dress unbuttoned at the top. In the soft soundless light her breasts were warm marble, so full they nearly hid the crucifix on its chain around her neck. She kissed the crucifix and

107

moved it to hang down her back. Touring my hand over her breasts, her breathing rasped, her nipples enlarged, protruding.

The words rushed up from my past, from my childhood: Mother, what are those?

Eunice came astride my clothed lap, her dress dropped to her waist, her hands holding the seat back, her breasts in my face.

"Suckle them, dear. Drink, my son. Oh, you are my son, my perfect Jesus. You are my savior, my beautiful Jesus. Good God, you are so perfect."

I didn't move. There was no defense, even if I wanted to find one, her ferocity impaling me to the seat, her senseless words increasingly interrupted with moans until she cried, "Oh, Jesus. I'm almost with you! I'm coming to you! Oh, Jesus, save me! I'm coming to you! I'm coming - to - my Lord! I'm coming again!"

When her hips slowed their hammering to a stop, her chin fallen low, with no motion left, I pushed back her shoulders, my eyes shut tight.

"Please, Mrs. Clare. Get off me. Now! Please move."

I pushed her across the seat, her body languid, her ecstasy spent, but her face triumphant. While she rearranged her dress, I lowered my window to find the snow had stopped, that the land sparkled from the light of a three-quarter moon, still and cold. In seconds the air distilled my daze to the awful reality of what had happened. I could think of nothing to say.

"I don't want you to say anything," she said as if reading my mind. "Ever. You gave me an epiphany that I'll treasure. It had to happen. It's why you're at Ashford, don't you see? It didn't take much to convince Henry. He really needed you - just didn't see it until that night of your interview. Timothy, you will come to see it is right. No need to worry, even though I love you for it."

"Damn it, it isn't right! It's a sin!"

"Not if you're my son."

"That would make it more so. God, this is terrible! Humiliating! I want to get out of here, right now!"

"It's early yet. We're not expected for more than an hour. Remember?"

"That's your problem, Mrs. Clare. Look, you can sit here if you want. I'll walk."

"Don't be ridiculous. You'll freeze to death. It must be four miles. Look at that snow. It's beautiful, isn't it? So clean, so pure."

"I'm going."

I pushed open the door, slammed it, and headed toward the road. I hadn't gone far when I realized I'd made a mistake, but head down, I strode on. Shortly, her car lights shone beyond me, and she came along side, keeping up with me. She leaned out the window.

"Timothy, get in the car. I'll drop you near school and drive around to kill time. I'll work it out."

In the car they didn't speak again. She drove slowly, carefully, and a hundred yards from the south gate, dropped me off. As I got out she said, "Merry Christmas, Timothy. I hope you truly celebrate the birth of Christ. I know I shall."

I stood in the snow, watching the station wagon drive away, tail lights disappearing around the bend past the gate. Cutting across the lawn through the snow, now drifted to three feet in places, I approached my dorm from the rear. I could see Clyde Carlow's apartment lights, so inched up the stairs one at a time, hoping to sneak to my room undetected.

Removing wet shoes, socks, and trousers in the dark, I stood at the window, mind dull, soul cringing. There could be no penance great enough for this. To whom could I confess such weakness? While I had initiated nothing - true most of my life - I was now beginning to realize I let it happen. Could I ever walk anywhere again free of guilt? Could Rachel and I survive this? And how could I continue to serve the Headmaster? Was Jesus ever so full of sin? How could Jesus ever forgive me? Could I ever remove the image of Eunice's breasts? Although I'd not been a participant in any way - she'd not so much as attempted to undress me - I felt I'd been raped.

I didn't move for an hour. Then I saw the lights of her car heading toward East House. I lifted my arm to my face; I could smell her on my sleeve.

I thought of ringing Rachel, but I was sure she had left, and I didn't know what to say anyway. Instead, I decided to call Warren.

"So you're back from the big city," Warren said. "How'd you make out with the boys? Or should I ask how you made out with Eunice?" His laugh was disgusting.

"You're really funny, my friend. The boys did fine. And Mrs. Clare bought a couple bags of stuff. What are you doing?"

"Exams - and a few beers. Come over. Have two left."

"Well, look. I have a favor - a big one. How's your car running?"

"Just put gas in it, and she goes. Why?"

"I need a ride to the train station - in Hudson. I need to get out of here."

"Christ, Jordan. Look outside! And it's ten o'clock. Why not go in the morning - early?"

I hesitated. "All right. How early can you make it?"

"You name it, Coach, and I'll do it."

"How about six o'clock?"

"Christ, Jordan, what's the rush? Let's be civilized. Jesus! Look, be out front at seven. Maybe we can catch come coffee on the way."

Grumbling, Warren was true to his word. I was glum and silent. We stopped in Hillsdale for coffee to go. In the car Warren asked, "Got your exams done?"

"I have them here. I'll call in the grades. I don't have as many as you."

"Why the big escape?"

"Look, Bill, I really appreciate this. I just have to get home, back to Pompey Hollow. It's been a long stretch. Okay?"

"Okay. Just so you come back in a better mood!"

Warren knew not to press me. Warren was a friend.

· · ·

I called the farm from the Syracuse station, and my father was there for me in less than an hour. When we turned down our road, snow piled along the sides from the morning's plowing, some of the tension left me though I was terribly tired.

110

"We need to go find the tree. Your mother's after me. Feel up to it this afternoon?"

"Sounds great, Dad. Do you want to go up in the woods or over to Orie's swamp? There's probably a good cedar in the swamp. They don't shed. And Mother always wants that ground cedar for the wreaths."

"I always feel funny about the swamp. It isn't our land, though Orie says your mother can take all the ground stuff she wants."

"Maybe two trips then. Why don't we go to the woods today? I could walk with Mother tomorrow. She always likes that. Maybe she'd snowshoe."

The trips for the tree had always been a high point - hiking the hill, startling the deer, locating again the maple tree with all the childrens' initials carved in its trunk, walking over and down the hogback to the two converging streams, breaking ground every time, it seemed, like true pioneers. My father's pace was slower that year, the climb more arduous with the foot of snow, and we stopped on the hogback beneath a tall pine. I recalled how as a boy I had trailed my father up that hill. Now it was the father who trailed the son.

By the time we crossed the stream and started up the slope to the pine grove, I was feeling more together, the events of the past hours still at the front of my mind but now in a discernable package of reality rather than nightmare. I felt more ready to deal with it all, even while perplexed about what approach to take. I was back in the known certainty of the woods, of home, of my parents.

We cut the best pine with my father's handsaw, and I dragged it, butt end in my hand, behind my father's track, down through the woods into the yard where we stood it up for my mother to admire. It would be the last time I went to the woods with my father. Years later I was glad I had, and it was likely why I now remembered that ordinary Christmas afternoon after all the years.

The holiday went happily. My father always loved Christmas, more impatient for the presents than anyone else. I had managed to save some money and spent an afternoon exploring Syracuse stores for gifts I could afford. The afternoon of Christmas Eve - traditionally the time for exchanging presents - the family gathered. My brothers and sisters and their spouses and children had all come.

Not to was not only unthinkable, but also everyone wanted to return home to the farm and to parents, and to the valley. I had strayed from my mother's tradition as a Magrill, so I doted on her especially.

So, for a few days and hours, I was able to bury Ashford away. Only at night, softly embraced by my old bed in the north bedroom, behind closed eyes, did I see and feel those fallen moments in Eunice Clare's station wagon. On my last night home, blessedly, finally I slept the night free from that memory.

CHAPTER NINETEEN

Unlike the first semester, the winter term raced by. Though I had the season off from coaching, I found myself attending practices and games of all the sports - hockey, basketball, and swimming. I was relieved there were no more advances by Eunice Clare. In fact, her demeanor was detached though friendly. Even at Sunday suppers, she said nothing about the 'encounter,' staying on the business of school arrangements, and at the end of each Sunday evening, usually standing at the door arm in arm with the Headmaster. It was as though it had all been a dream, and indeed I found comfort in embracing that idea - that I had had a fantasy of sinful pleasure, outrageous and not real. Thus, in denial, I was able to relax on those evenings, enjoying the boys, the Lobster Newburg, and discussions about game results. One evening I led a colloquy with a group about The Red Badge of Courage. The boys seemed to identify with the main character and enjoyed my explanation of the significance of the Tall Soldier. Both Henry and Eunice Clare sat in on the conversation, and I sensed them watching me. Knowing that, they saw I could do more than install the "T" formation.

At the door on that evening, Henry asked, "Timmie, have you thought about graduate school? At some point it will be in the cards for you. Eventually the degree will be a necessary ticket, if you know what I mean - a sign of professional growth. Have you thought about it?"

"Not really, sir - maybe because all of this really wasn't on my mind. Before, I mean."

"You ought to think about it, before your life becomes complicated. You could start off this summer - maybe in New York at Columbia."

"I'd have to start saving some money if I plan to do anything like that, and I'll have to see if my father wants me home this summer."

"Think it over, Timmie. If you decide to go ahead, the school will help all it can. After all, it would be for the school, in a way. We like to see our new people have a Master's degree within five years. So if it's not this summer, it should be next. Anyway, think it over, and get back to me. By the way, the dinners have gone well. Eunice and I appreciate your good help. Good night."

"Thank you, sir. I've enjoyed them myself. I think I know most of the boys now. Good night."

Eunice Clare stood smiling at me, her arm hooked in her husband's.

The final supper was in late February for the last group of Third Formers, and Rachel attended, as well as Mrs. Malley and Warren, who headed the Third Form dorm. It turned out to be the most successful of the suppers, even though by then I had had my fill of lobster, peas, and petit fours. The night was cold, starry, and the snow lay a foot deep, the trees outlined in white ribbons of snow, the walking crunchy in the shoveled paths. My affair with Rachel had resumed, carefully at first, but increasingly through the term we seemed nearly back to our earlier flush. However real it had been, the situation with Eunice was apparently a thing of the past, unspoken between us.

I met Rachel at the Headmaster's door; she was radiant, her hair brushed around her face creating a perfect oval, her eyes sparkling. Before I knocked, she kissed my cheek. "I love you, Tim Jordan," she whispered.

Eunice Clare met us, and at once engaged us warmly. "Oh, Rachel, dear, you look so beautiful. And Timothy, do come in. At last, this is the final one! I'm so happy you two are here. Of course, the boys just adore you, Rachel, especially these young ones tonight. Mrs. Malley is already here. Bill called - will be a little late. Timothy, would you just check the buffet to see if everything's there. I want to speak to Rachel."

A tiny red flag rose in my mind, but I went off to the dining room, looked around at all the food, at the lobster in its steamer. Mrs. Malley was there admiring the perfectly appointed spread.

We chatted until the boys started arriving, clustered in groups, looking around, and I moved about the room, greeting each, followed by the Clares, Mrs. Malley, and Rachel. Her manner captivated them; they seemed not able to take their eyes from her. I marveled at her ease, ability to tease, say the right thing, flatter the

114

most insecure boys. Her wholesomeness was infectious, her genuine spirit appealing, her figure stunning. How I wanted her! Eunice Clare was at her shoulder, a twosome it seemed, her hand every now and then patting Rachel's arm. As I circled the room, their laughter and apparent mutual conviviality followed me, until I ached to know what she had wanted with Rachel. I felt uneasy.

At the end the Clares showed us out, with Warren, who headed off, leaving Rachel and me standing in the drive, gazing up at the moonless sky, our breath defining the frigid, still air.

"Would you like to walk?"

"Where to?"

"Oh, around campus. No one will be looking out. They should be in bed, and it doesn't matter. We'll probably run into the night watchman, but he never talks to anybody - just punches his rounds and leaves at five."

I took her mittened hand, skirted the schoolhouse past the infirmary and angled toward the gymnasium.

"May I ask what Mrs. Clare wanted, or is it women's stuff?"

"It's women's stuff," she said lightly.

"Oh. Okay. None of my business."

"That's right. None of your business," and she sped their steps, swinging my arm in exaggerated cadence to our steps. She clearly was happy, buoyant, a mood much changed from December. We reached the stone athletic building, built of the same stone as the chapel, rising in the night like some citadel, no lights anywhere.

"Would you like to go in? I have a key. We could shoot a basket."

"Would anyone mind?"

"We could warm up for the walk home."

"I'm not sure what you mean by 'warming up.' I know you, Tim Jordan!"

"Don't you ever think about it, about making love?"

"Of course I do, but would you love me if I took off all my clothes and said, 'Screw me right now'?"

I looked at her, amazed and delighted.

"No, I wouldn't love you for that. There will be a time I shall, but not now. I love you, Rachel, and I love your goodness along with all that I know you can give me. Believe me, I don't mean to push, but you're very much under my skin, so delicious, so everything I would want. You wowed everyone tonight. You wowed me."

She moved into my arms, her hands on my face, and kissed my mouth in small relentless forays.

"Oh, Tim. I know, I know. Let's warm up in the gym. It is cold."

Ecstatic, I hurriedly found the key on my key ring, unlocked the heavy door, then slipped inside and locked the door from behind. When our eyes had adjusted to the darkness, we went toward the stairs for the court, but as we passed the door to the pool wing, I stopped.

"Rachel! Why don't we go for a swim? It's even more warm in there. It would be great."

"But we don't have suits."

"Precisely!"

"Timothy Jordan! You said shoot a basket. Shoot a basket, you said."

"I know. I know, but I just thought of it. Look, we're all alone, and there are towels. It's time we had a lark."

She stared at me, a smile of wonder on her face as she shook her head back and forth. She was so "up" tonight - gay, happy.

Then she said, "All right, Tim. But you take one end, and I'll take the other. Only a swim. You have to promise - absolutely."

"I promise. I promise. No fooling around. You take the diving-board end."

She headed down the side of the pool, her shadowy form in the dim light through the pool-door window, but I dared not turn on any lights.

"No one knows we're here," I called softly in encouragement. "Last one in is a Protestant!"

Before I could shuck my clothes, I heard the gentle splashing of water. "Jump in, you Protestant!" she called.

I jumped in, much as I had in the swimming hole in Limestone Creek, feet first, holding my nose. Though a natural athlete in some things, I was no swimmer. I had no buoyancy which meant staying afloat took great energy, so I was glad I had the shallow end.

"Oh, Tim. This is wonderful! The cold night and the warm water. I'm glad you thought of it."

"What if you get a cramp?"

"I'm staying close to the edge - just in case."

"What if I get a cramp - in the middle?"

"Then you'll drown!"

We both saw the flash of light at once - a flashlight beam outside the door to the pool.

"Someone's coming," she hissed. "Oh my God, Tim. What'll we do?"

"Stay down there, under the diving board, and for God's sake be quiet."

"Oh, my God!"

"Rachel, shut up!"

I would brazen it out. It must be the night watchman. At least I hoped it was. The light spilled under the pool door and shone through the glass upper half. Then the door opened.

"Who's in here?"

It was the watchman, bundled against the night, filling the doorway. I answered immediately, to draw the beam to me. "It's me, Mr. Jordan. Timothy Jordan of the faculty. I decided to come take a swim. I do every once in a while. You're Mr. Brachen."

"Yeah. Well, I guess it's you, all right."

The beam bore down on me standing waist deep, my arms wrapped around my torso.

"Thought I heard something - voices or somethin'. You by yourself?"

"Yes. Just a quick swim before bed. Don't you worry, Mr. Brachen. I'll lock up when I'm done."

"Shouldn't swim alone, ya know."

With that he swept his flashlight down the pool, and I sucked in my breath. We were caught!

"Well, stay in the shallow end, Mr. Jordan - and lock up. I have to mosey to make the next stop on time."

He again flashed his light on me and around the pool and then said, "Dress warm. It's cold as hell out there. G'night."

The door closed, and the light disappeared. I waited until I heard the outer door slam.

"Rachel! Rachel! Are you there?"

"Yes, but I think I've drowned. Has he gone?"

"Yes, he's gone."

"I stayed under as long as I could. God, Tim. I held my breath until I just couldn't any more." God, he loved her! "What did you tell him?"

"Just told him I was having a swim. Are you okay? Can I come help you?"

"No. No. I'm fine now. I'm getting out and getting dressed and getting out of here. It was scary, Tim, but kind of fun, you know. I would have just <u>died</u>. I <u>did</u> almost drown."

She walked toward me out of the shadow, her wet hair clinging to her head, arms hugging her body, her whole frame still tingling with excitement. We embraced, shivering, clinging more closely than ever. With the watchman gone, we laughed aloud, rubbed each other's hair with dry towels, and like giggling children, found our way back to the infirmary where we stood in the foyer whispering a recounting of the night.

After I said goodnight, she said, "I won't tell you everything - just one thing Mrs. Clare said to me."

"I don't have to know, Rachel. But if there <u>is</u> one thing..."

"She said I should never let you get away, no matter what!"

"And how do you feel about that?"

"Well, I must say I'm re-assessing Mrs. Clare. If nothing else, she seems a wise woman."

"Does that mean you'll take her advice?"

"It means I am considering seriously what she said. It means you and I are an item again, and for now, that means a great deal. And, Tim, tonight has been exciting - for me, anyway. I feel I can be daring with you, as much as I can. You are my dear, and I trust you."

She kissed me again - a tremendous fervent kiss, and then disappeared through the door.

CHAPTER TWENTY

I had promised my father to return home over Spring Break to prune the apple trees, and Rachel had promised to take her mother to Maine to visit and help nurse her aunt, who had cancer and needed constant bed rest.

A week before school was due to break for two weeks, the Headmaster held me back after a faculty meeting.

"Timmie, I've coached the varsity baseball since I came here. I've enjoyed it thoroughly, and we've done rather well. My problem is that the Board wants me to crank up the fund- raising plan, which means travel, meetings, and I don't like any of it - being away and all that. But it goes with the territory. I was going to have you assist me in coaching, take over when I'm away, but I've now decided you should have it from the start. What do you say? Think you can do it?"

"Sir, I'm thrilled you think I can. Yes, I will, absolutely. I'll do my best."

"Good. Baseball around here is tough in April. We've even played in snow flurries. It's just not a cold-weather sport, but by May we get some good days."

After some discussion, we decided to recruit Bill Warren to assist since he and I worked so well together in the fall.

"Christ, Tim. I don't know anything about baseball," was Warren's response.

"Can you use a fungo bat?"

"What's that?"

"A long thin bat for hitting fly balls and grounders - for practice. It's the best weapon in the game. If the boys can't catch or field the hits, they can't play baseball."

Warren grinned, shrugged acquiescence, and again we were a team. After Rachel, my relationship with Warren had become the most important.

The months of spring found me truly in stride, with classes now simply a challenge to be better, and the ball club progressing well in execution. With no natural hitters, we manufactured runs, and most of the time the pitching kept us close. I had a Sixth Former, Tony Costello, who could throw a curve ball with some control, and two throwers, Byrne and Haskell, who threw medium-fast balls, generally in and around the strike zone. When they walked batters, I threatened to fine all three with extra duty in the dining room. I also had a shortstop, Andy Carey, who could reach everything, it seemed, between third and second. Warren hit hundreds of fungo balls until he was able to hit them just out of reach of the fielders, making them run in every direction. Those who couldn't run well were sent to the Junior Varsity. In the league, we opened the season with four straight wins.

Rachel came to the home games, sometimes shrieking her delight at a hit or a bases-loaded strike out. She thought me simply stellar in my Ashford uniform, directing things, quietly in command. She liked it that I didn't shout. On two occasions, she sat with Eunice Clare on the top row of the bleachers. Usually, she hurried off after a game for dispensary call or to relieve Mrs. Malley. But after the Salisbury home win, she lingered and walked with Warren and me back to the gym.

"Tim, Tony was so good out there. He seems so confident, and he's such a nice boy!"

"He's both of those things. He starts in with that little curve, and then has the batter in his pocket. There isn't much stuff there, but he only walked one. Good job!"

"I hope you noticed no one dropped a fly ball, my friend!" Warren was ecstatically proud of his outfielders and had every right to be.

"Look, you guys, we should celebrate this one. Aren't you off tonight, Tim?"

By the time we reached the gym we had settled it: Warren would come for us at six thirty after the obligatory tea with the Salisbury team, and we'd go to a bar Warren knew in Great Barrington.

By the time I was ready for the night on the town, my phone rang.

"I'm really ticked," Warren exclaimed. "Malley put Denardo in the infirmary. He's really sick, flu or something, 104 temp. There's no one else for the dorm. But look, take my car, and you and that gorgeous nurse go out. It has half a tank, and the keys are in it. Sorry."

I wasn't that disappointed with Warren's fix. When I retrieved Rachel, she wasn't either.

"Denardo's really down and out. I offered Mrs. Malley to stay, but she would have none of it. Guess you and I are just destined to be alone. What a rotten shame!"

By then we no longer cared who saw us together, and we waved to students and faculty who were trooping to dinner. The trees had burst forth with young leaves, and as we drove north in the lush twilight, we could see Mt. Everett to the west, silhouetted by the sun. Renewal was everywhere, and we were in love; her presence seemed to bless the car. I felt capable of anything.

We were laughing the whole way, light, frolicsome, laughing, delighted with ourselves, the day, the time away together.

We found the bar about halfway up Railroad Street tucked in a row of shops. There weren't many patrons, and the high ceiling and muted lighting made conversation easy and private. Once seated in a rear booth, and with our financial resources in mind, we ordered open beef sandwiches and a pitcher of beer.

"What about Maine and your aunt?" I said, pouring out the beer.

"I've been trying to sort it out. It was good - and bad. I'm happy I helped my mother, hopefully making Aunt Bess a little comfortable, and I had you to think about every night. But it's so sad, Tim, so sad that Aunt Bess ... everyone knows she's dying and pretending she isn't. It's breast cancer that's gone everywhere. I found myself dwelling on it, how such a vital person, so full of life, couldn't lift her spoon. Our lives are so precious, so short. I've begun examining my breasts every day. It's so scary."

"You know I minored in medicine, especially diagnosing and examination."

"It isn't funny, Tim. We think we're immortal, but we're not. We're so vulnerable, with so little time. I lay awake up there, thinking about us, how much time we have, whether we should - well, whether every moment shouldn't be treasured. Oh, I hate being so serious, but two weeks living with a dying person, a dear, dear person ... it just made me think about everything, about Aunt Bess. Must everyone suffer, suffer pain? Is it what we all face? Is it needed for us to ... does God test us <u>all</u> this way, to get to Heaven? In training I saw death often, but in Maine it became personal. I guess I wasn't very strong."

"Few of us are, Rachel. You did a wonderful thing in going there. I feel guilty about feeling so annoyed at not seeing you. You did unto your aunt and your mother. They're blessed to have you. But I'm glad you thought about me every night. Let's talk about that."

She eyed me over her beer glass. "Where are we, Tim?"

"Rackum's Bar."

"You know what I mean. It's what I thought about. Are we just going on like this - mind you, it's fine - or is there a next step? Oh, I shouldn't be saying this. I didn't mean to be serious tonight. I just - today, for example, watching you at the game. I was so proud of you, and when you looked back at me and smiled ... Tim, I just melted! Does that mean something?"

"Yeah. It means you're nuts about this sexy brute."

"You don't want to be serious. Okay. I apologize. Let's talk about something else.

I remembered my excitement at that moment. The sense of the shift in attitude, quite unexpected from Rachel, who usually maintained a definable distance from the subject of commitment.

"No, my dear, we should talk about it. It's just that I'm so excited you want to talk about <u>us</u> - or the <u>future</u>. I must say, I can't bear to think of a future without you. How's that for a start?"

"It's beautiful. Oh, Tim, please say you love me."

"I love you, Rachel Mackintire, terribly much."

"I adore you, Tim, terribly much."

So there it was, the two of us holding hands now across the table, speechless, right up to it! I had not thought about a resolution, about marriage or proposing. I was out with the woman I craved - loved - but hadn't ever analyzed just what it meant to say "I love you" sincerely, fully, with no caveats or retreats. Was I ready, truly ready, to move ahead, to take what seemed the next logical step here, and here, at this bar? God, I had nothing. I could barely buy this supper.

"Tim?"

"What?"

"Do you want <u>me</u> to say it?"

"No! Not you. It's for me to say." My mouth was dry, and I looked about, avoiding her eyes, her hands.

"I'm waiting," she whispered.

"Rachel, will you marry me - some time?"

"Yes! Yes! Oh, yes, any time!"

We hurried then, leaving a half pitcher of beer, and found a back road near Sheffield with a pull-off into some woods. Between kisses, while I stroked and kissed her breasts, we decided to keep our troth secret since the next step seemed fraught with problems. I explained the school policy of not retaining first year faculty who married, a policy Henry Clare had brought from Hartfield Academy where it was believed such men not worth the added expense of housing and more salary, regardless of merit or performance. This, of course, infuriated Rachel, knowing me to be finer than even most of the veterans, her fervor in the face of injustice fueled by her longing.

"There's another thing." I said. "The Headmaster wants me to start graduate school, this summer if possible, before what he called any 'complications'."

"So now I'm a 'complication'!" Is that what he meant? Maybe his wife prompted him - she and her sensibilities. Oh, God. What a mess. And I love you so! What's maddening is he's right. You <u>should</u> go."

"He says it's a 'ticket' I should have. The trouble is, I haven't even decided whether all this is what I want. Sure, I like the kids and the coaching, and I'm getting into the classes better. I must say it's fun to be in charge of something, even if it's the dining room! But hell, I don't make any money. My father was right - is right - there's no way I could take care of you - or a family - even if Ashford let us back - married, I mean - or even the next year if we waited."

"There's the housing and the meals in the dining room. That means a lot. And there's my job."

"Yes. There's that."

For a long time we held each other, each thinking of his or her intensified need.

"We are so dumb," she said on the drive back to school. "We should look at the positive - the most important thing - us! Just think, we're on top of the world. You're my love, and I'm yours, and the heck with all the rest. We don't know <u>when</u>, but we know we <u>will</u> always be together. We should be sensible. The Headmaster is right. For a lot of reasons, you should start at Columbia! Even if you don't stay in the school business - if we don't - it can't hurt."

"Yeah. Maybe I'll give it another year, anyway. I'd have to check at home, to see if my father would really need me there. Of course, if I had another kind of job, the kind he wanted me to have, I couldn't be at the farm. Maybe school is just part of this job."

"You're right. If you go, what would you take?"

"English. Columbia has some great people. Hell, I don't even know if I'd be accepted - didn't really start to grade up until the last three or four semesters. Columbia's tough - good standing, though. Michigan's good, but far away."

"Talk to Mr. Clare. I'm sure he'll help. Let's just <u>do</u> it, Tim!"

I had loved the way she said "Let's" - our commitment already oneness - the way she bounced back from the frustration and despair of our love being stymied. Suddenly I felt a responsibility far greater than any before. The feeling subdued me so that my goodnight wasn't a passionate groping but a calm, tender touch ending with both hands cupping her face, kissing eyes, nose, and her sweet mouth.

I parked Warren's car in its usual place, walked up to the room where Warren slouched in his one chair, reading, and in a foul mood.

"Jordan, how the hell do you make out the way you do?" He waved his hand, dismissing his own question - acerbic and uncalled for - but nonetheless describing his trapped night in when he should have been off.

124

"I really hate to tell you what a terrific time we had. Rachel thinks you're a peach - told me to tell you."

"Sure. Sure, I bet she did. Aw, hell, sit down. Tell me about the 'outside'."

After I related our evening at Rackum's, Warren said, "Sometimes I don't see what she sees in you. I mean you're okay and all that, but, Christ, every time I see her when you're not around, all she wants is to know where you are, how you are, what you're doing - all that bullshit. Can you imagine that - all that crap when she could have a veteran, a pro like me? She's one of the few people around here who has class, but she has no judgment."

"I agree about the class. Who else? You said there are a few others."

"Henry. He's got it, and Carlow. Kinney's okay. And Eunice - Mrs. Clare - she may be top of the list. She's smart, all lady, and a woman to boot. You can bet behind that gracious, all-wise creature the world sees is really a bombshell. She's all sex, I'm tellin' ya."

"Hell, Warren, you don't know that. Sounds like part of your misguided philosophy."

"No. No. I'm right. Just look at her. Ever notice the way she walks?"

"No. What's that got to do with it?"

"Everything, my naive friend. Watch her. She walks toed out - not in, not straight, but out. It's the sure sign. That damn Henry. What a time he must have."

"You're nuts! Obviously they sleep together, but you make her sound like a ... like a predator or something."

"Right word, Tim. Right word. Just hope the Head is up to it all. She must be something. Anyway, I'm right. Just watch her walking to Mass - all dressed and devout, toes out, hot as a pistol."

Warren laughed, socking his fist into his hand, delirious over shocking me with his crazy surmise, never guessing that his tormented colleague knew it all.

"Don't mean to shock you, Tim. But I'm right. Of course I shouldn't speculate about the Headmaster's wife."

Feigning disgust, I got up and, over my shoulder, said, "I should have locked your keys in the car."

I had done so well dismissing the episode with Eunice Clare from my mind that I resented Warren's theory - so right and so utterly disquieting on the heels of my proposal to Rachel. During the night I rose from the bed to angrily pace the corridor, and then found myself lying in the dark comparing their breast sizes. Over and over I prayed: Rachel, forgive me.

CHAPTER TWENTY-ONE

In early May, at a faculty hour coffee at the Headmaster's, Henry Clare motioned me toward the study. "Timmie, bring your coffee in here. Look, I wonder if you've thought some more about graduate school."

"Yes, sir, I have. I'd like to try it, to try Columbia, though I don't know whether I can be accepted."

"Fine, fine. I'm pleased. What you can do is sign up for courses beforehand, and then be accepted, depending, of course, on how you do. But you shouldn't worry - with nothing else on your mind, you'll do well, even though Columbia is demanding. Now, when you get set up, the school will pay your tuition, and you'll have to work out the food and room. It shouldn't be that much."

"Well, thank you, Mr. Clare. That's wonderful. I think I can work out the living expenses. Does this mean you will want me back?"

"Of <u>course</u>. Naturally, Timmie. Oh, I thought you knew. If you weren't to return, I would have seen you in March. My oversight. Should have explained. Oh yes, yes. Ashford wants Timmie Jordan here next year. Now let's see, are things worked out at home on the farm?"

"Yes. They understand. One other thing. May I assume my quarters are mine through the summer?"

"No question about that. Only change might be if we should need you another place, but right now everything is set. Now, are we square with school and the summer?"

"We're fine, sir."

"Then there is another thing - down your alley, I'd say. The boss...er...Mr. Leydon at Hartfield called. It seems they have a problem: the school they were to play on their Parents' Weekend - Saturday - had a conflict, so Hartfield has no baseball game lined up. Mr. Leydon called and asked us, as a favor, to play there on the 18th, and I've said we'll be there."

"Mr. Clare, Hartfield! They're 'way out of our league."

"Technically, yes, but you've been doing well."

127

"Against Salisbury, South Kent and those teams. But, sir, I have one so-called pitcher and two medium throwers! We'll get killed!"

"Doesn't matter, Timmie. We're going. I've already asked South Kent to make a change - to free up the day. They didn't like it, but I didn't leave them a choice. Told 'em if they wouldn't play it on Monday, we'd have to forfeit, and that I knew they wouldn't want to win that way. Old Sam Bartlett was furious."

"I should think so. I don't know about this, about Hartfield. Is it really set?"

"It's really set. One of the things I like about you is that you do what you set out to do, and you have a knack for coaching. Like always, the boys will rise to the occasion, win or lose, and what a good experience for them. I wish I could be there, but another New York meeting calls. That's why you're coaching."

"Very well, sir. Wow, I don't know if the boys will be glad or not."

"You'll all be fine. By the way, Mr. Leydon is the head coach. Did you know that?"

"No!"

"Yes. So it would be a real feather if you could win - after doing them a favor. As you would say, Timmie: Wow!"

I had never been on the Hartfield campus, and the prospect of taking my little team up there, against a powerhouse coached by Leydon, drove everything else from my life for the next few days. I had Costello, who might fool them once around, and Byrne and Haskell, who would seem like batting practice to such a group. I had some speed and had Carey at short. Luck and prayer might keep them from a complete blowout.

· · ·

Warren and I talked about plans for the Hartfield trip on Wednesday as we headed back to Ashford from a game with Trinity-Pawling. Half the team slept while the bus headed north.

"What time do we board the bus?" Warren asked.

"It's an early game - one o'clock - so I asked Carlow to have the bus at school at nine, just to be safe. Those old crates don't do much

128

more than fifty. At least the boys will be happy not having classes. I'll tell them to stoke up on breakfast. They won't have any lunch."

"Know anything about Hartfield?"

"Just that Leydon is the coach, that they've lost only once in their league, and that their catcher is a terrific athlete - great arm, great bat. We're like a Junior Varsity to them, a perfect Parents' Day opponent!"

"Well, there's no point worrying about it. We'll throw Tony and see what happens. There have to be a lot more important things going on Saturday than a prep school baseball game."

"I can't think of any."

We were silent for a while. Darkness had descended, and at mid-May the weather had softened. Through the bus window I could smell the fullness of spring - air still warm from the late sun.

. . .

I spent Thursday and Friday going over and over the game plan with the team. Of course, with our own catcher and players it worked often, and the team became enthused with the cleverness of my ideas - all fair, but still with an aura of larceny. Otherwise we spent the time in the batting cage, bunting most of the pitches, hitting with shortened, choked swings. Most of all, there was excitement, the David and Goliath syndrome. The plan even became dinner conversation and infirmary chat, so Friday night when Rachel called, she was well informed.

"You have the boys all excited. Me too! I hope it all works out for you. I'm so proud of you I could burst!"

"Talent will tell. The team has responded well, but some prayers would help. The team goes to Mass in the morning. Want to come?"

"Yes, I do. May I sit with you all?"

"If you don't, we'll certainly lose."

"I love you."

"Me too!"

. . .

For most of the bus ride north to Hartfield I felt nervous, going over details with Warren, wondering about his players, worrying about confronting the myth of the school and its Headmaster/Coach. We'd had the uniforms cleaned so that in appearance, at least, we wouldn't look rag-tag. I composed what to say to the team.

Curiously, as the bus headed down the Hartfield village street to the school, I felt a calm, a confidence, a sort of abandon: we had done everything to prepare, and it was just another game with the same rules for everyone.

When the bus pulled to a stop behind the gym, I stood and turned to the boys.

"Well, gentlemen, we're here. You've chattered and fooled all the way, but when you step off this bus, we have one thing on our minds - to play baseball. Forget the opponent - that doesn't matter to me, and it shouldn't to you. We're here to play baseball as we know how. I'd like to think that this day and this game will be an event you will always remember, and it will be if you will play without worry or concern about <u>where</u> we are or who <u>they</u> are. Mr. Warren and I shall do the worrying if there is any to be done. I believe we can make their Parents' Day really memorable. Whatever happens, we'll conduct ourselves with class. We're from Ashford - we'll carry no one's bat bag - and we'll offend no one, other than to run and play like hell. Good luck! Mr. Warren and I are proud to have each of you here today. Let's go!"

My game plan came to naught when Costello came to me, his uniform top not on, his right arm hanging away from his body somewhat crookedly and said, "Mr. Jordan, my arm. I can't straighten it, and it's stiff. Feels funny."

"Costello! What's the matter? You haven't pitched for a week."

"I know. It was fine this morning, but when I got off the bus, I couldn't straighten it."

"Were you wrestling? Fooling around? Somebody hit you?"

"No. Just rode along, the window open, usually with my arm on the sill. Felt good in the breeze."

Warren said, "Shit". The boy had ridden a hundred miles, arm cocked out the window. Costello was devastated, Warren infuriated. I was stunned.

"All right. You work on it. Exercise it - move it in big circles. Mr. Warren will massage it. Go get your top on. You'll just have to get it going. Send Byrne over here. He'll have to start. And, Costello, no one's arm ever feels perfect. Usually it hurts. Remember that!"

Thinking back, I had forgotten the warm-ups, in-field practice, meeting at the plate with the umpires. I remembered the glorious day, the crowd of parents, and the little man at the end of the Hartfield bench in coat and tie, a fedora, and a light overcoat - the Headmaster and coach. Whatever Costello's condition, we'd decided to attempt the game plan. It had all been perfect. Carey pushed a bunt beyond the pitcher, stole second on the next pitch to Ashford's left-handed hitter, who crossed over for the next pitch, and Carey stole third. Three pitches and we had a man on third with no one out. Surprise, speed, batter obstruction within the rules had all worked. The second out was a weak roller to second, but Carey scored.

My memory blurred much of the rest, except that Byrne managed superb control over his pitches, forcing the Hartfield team to hit their way on. I recalled that Hartfield's wonderful catcher hit a double, a booming triple, and that young Carey made play after play at short to thwart big innings. Our team managed two more runs, bunting and running, and again Carey with a key single. The team played incredibly, led 3-2 into the last of the ninth inning.

"Christ, Tim, does Byrne have anything left?" Warren was eating his knuckles.

"Dunno. Go rub Costello's arm. Make him throw. Get him warmed up, even if he can only toss it. They've got their guns coming up."

The Hartfield side was on its feet, players and parents, even Leydon talking to his 'boys.' Surely, the expected winner would now emerge, they all must have thought.

Byrne struggled, but another play by Carey, whose arm cut off the tying run at the plate, found us with two out, bases loaded, and Hartfield's splendid catcher at the plate - naturally the clean-up batter.

I looked down the right field-line to where Warren had Costello throwing - arcing lobs, but throwing. The yelling and fervor from the other side was thunderous, and Byrne's shoulders drooped as he stood rubbing the ball, looking at me. Byrne threw away outside, hardly daring anything else. On his next pitch the catcher hit a fast foul at third, two feet off the ground, which didn't hit the grass for two hundred feet. He hit the next one four hundred feet down the line, which hooked foul at the last, his timing now near-perfect. At the groans from Hartfield, I jumped to my feet, called to the umpire for time out, and walked slowly out to my courageous player on the mound, who had, in fact, that day graduated from thrower to pitcher, but whose arm truly had nothing left.

I looked over at Costello, still tossing to Warren and said, "Mr. Byrne, you have pitched one helluva baseball game. Do you understand?"

"Thank you, sir."

"But I'm going to try something - and whatever happens, I couldn't be prouder of you. I'm bringing in Costello - show 'em another look. Okay?"

"Fine, sir. Home plate keeps getting farther away."

I took the ball and waved for Costello, who jogged over. Respectfully, the Hartfield side applauded Byrne's exit, but they could taste the happy outcome just moments away.

"How does it feel?" I touched Costello's arm.

"Better. It hurts and it's stiff, but I'll do my best."

"Listen to me: I want you to throw as hard as you can your side-arm curve we've worked on. No fast balls. You couldn't, anyway. I'll tell Billy to give you the signal. We won't show them anything. Do you understand?"

"Yes, sir - the side-arm curve."

"I'm going to tell the umpire no warm-ups, and I'll see our catcher. Make sure you don't throw anything until I get back to the bench."

I walked to home plate, told the umpire my pitcher was ready and to be prepared for curve balls. I did this out of earshot of the big catcher, who stood aside practicing his swing. I told my catcher, Billy Ryan, what to call, and to block or otherwise smother any ball, allowing absolutely no passed balls. Billy Ryan had grinned. "No sweat, sir."

When the umpire called, "Play ball" with no warm-ups from Costello, a high-pitched voice called, "Time out," and I turned to see Leydon at the plate, pointing to Costello with the umpire giving him the palms up, as much as to say, "There's no rule." Wily Leydon wanted his catcher to see Costello's motion, but it wasn't to be.

I turned back to Warren. "Watch this, Bill. It's the game. Say a prayer."

With the big catcher finally crouching at bat, Costello carefully began his wind-up. The whole scene played in slow motion as he dropped his arm and jerked his body off the mound, his wrist snapping just at the end of his motion, his face contorted. He threw everything he had. For the big catcher, the ball indeed came from the direction of third base, appearing so much inside that he bailed out and was nearly out of the batter's box when the ball snapped in a new direction, crossing the plate diagonally and knee-high into Billy's mitt. Nothing stirred for two agonizing seconds until the umpire's right hand shot up. "Strike!" he bellowed.

On his knees, Costello stared, then leaped in the air. Warren and I bounded aloft; the team bounced all over themselves; and we all raced to the mound, a heap of shouting, pounding uniforms in an avalanche over Costello. I stood and saw the Hartfield bunch mute with dismay, but at the plate the small but venerable Headmaster was shouting and pointing at the umpire, then at the Ashford mob, his fedora fallen to the ground. Quickly I grabbed Warren. "Get our guys off the field - now! Get 'em in the locker room before that old guy changes the ump's mind. Now! Go!"

Warren was good at this sort of thing, and in seconds had the team racing from the field, collecting bats and gloves on the way, still doing joy leaps as they ran. I stood alone on the mound, shaking with the emotion I had held in check all day, never so gloriously happy as then. When the umpire finally turned away from the arm-waving curmudgeon, who still stood quivering on home plate, I walked toward him, cautious, but knowing the protocol of shaking hands, of doing the right thing. Leydon's back was to me so I walked around and extended my hand.

"It was a great game, sir. Of course, we were lucky all afternoon. It's been a wonderful day for us just to be here."

Ignoring my hand, the old man looked up at me, his face pinched in fury, his hands gripping and ungripping. "Who the hell are you?" he squeaked.

"Jordan, sir. Timothy Jordan."

"Oh yes, Henry told me about you. Well, you're quite a trickster, aren't you? You fooled everyone, including that stupid umpire - stole the game with your tricks!"

"Sir, it wasn't trickery. It was a side-arm curve ball, right over the plate."

Leydon bent to pick up his hat, stuffed it on his head, turned his back on me, and limped away. I stood there, by myself in the batter's box, my elation fermenting into resentment, anger. The Great One had lost his poise, had handled himself in a manner understandable, perhaps, from a greenhorn coach. I felt insulted, and in an instant decided to take our team away from the place posthaste. I ran to the locker room where Warren was pushing their players to dress quickly.

"Hey, Tim, some clown just dropped off a case of Coke and some cookies to take on the bus. Said they couldn't have a tea, what with Parents' Day. Pretty cheap bastards, I'd say."

"Fine with me. Let's get the hell out of here."

"How was Leydon?"

"I'll tell you on the bus. Let's move it."

∙ ∙ ∙

At Sunday Mass the next morning I found my seat just as Father and two sacristans approached the altar for first prayers. The Clares were in their front pew. It was a glowing May morning, the pungent odor of lilacs inside and out, the altar lush with vases of the purple and white, fresh-cut flowers. Father spoke of courage, the virtue requisite for positive action, and made reference to the

134

Ashford team and its victory - an unusual thing for him to do, since never before had he used an athletic success as an example.

The Clares waited at the door. "Timmie, stop in after breakfast. We had a call from Mr. Leydon last night. Eunice thinks you should tell your side of what happened yesterday. And bring Bill in with you."

It was a grim command, more severe than any I'd yet heard from the Headmaster. When I saw him, Warren said, "God, Tim. What's up? What do you think that old bastard said?"

"We spoiled the day. What happened wasn't in the plan...but I don't know. If the Headmaster asks you, just tell him what happened."

* * *

Eunice Clare brought more coffee to the study and stayed on, sitting in an easy chair, with Warren and me on the sofa, and the Headmaster behind his desk, his mouth set firmly, his voice measured and low.

"Timmie, your win yesterday has had a sour taste since Mr. Leydon called in a rage. I really couldn't make much sense out of it. He was nearly incoherent, but shouted that you stole the game with some treachery - something about talking to the umpire. He said you cheated! Needless to say, it's all very upsetting, and something I didn't expect from you. Before an apology, or whatever there is to do, you can tell me what happened. Mrs. Clare says there are always two sides. So what the hell went on?"

I sat silent, stunned, and looked at Warren, whose nod said, "Go ahead." Eunice Clare sat forward, half smiling, encouraging. Henry was as a stone. I sat forward on the edge of the sofa, and with my voice as even as possible, carefully told my story, from the "plan" to the final pitch, leaving out no detail - of the bus ride, Byrne's performance, Costello's arm, Leydon's frenzy and accusations, the Coke and cookies dumped in the locker room. As the narrative progressed, especially regarding the coaching and baseball tactics, the Headmaster's set face softened until there was almost a trace of a smile.

135

"Finally, sir, Ashford's baseball team played courageously, as Father just said - and daringly, in a way completely honorable. You can be very proud of them. Also, I feel the Ashford baseball team was treated rudely. I would not care to take a team to Hartfield ever again."

Then I sat back. After some silence, the Headmaster asked, "Bill, is Timmie's account the way you saw it?"

"It is exactly, sir. He's left out one big thing, though. I had nothing to do with it; it was all Tim. The fact is that Hartfield was totally, thoroughly out-coached from the first pitch to that incredible last one. They were out-played and out-coached. Ashford showed real class. Hartfield didn't. Their coach lost it."

Another silence. Mrs. Clare was beaming. Henry was a study of conflict, between the old alliance and his own young man, whom he now knew to be in the right and to whom, at last, he turned graciously, warmly. "Timmie, congratulations. You're a wonder, even if I don't know right now how I'll deal with Hartfield. Your story is great, the way you did it, and made it work. I shouldn't have questioned, but the call really caught me off guard. As usual, Mrs. Clare was right about you. Let me shake your hand - and you, too, Bill. A side-arm curve - one pitch!"

When we stood to leave, the Headmaster walked ahead to the door with Warren. Eunice Clare touched my arm. "Timothy, you've done well, again," she said.

"Thank you for interceding - again."

"Always - for you."

We followed the others to the door. It wasn't much, but her "always" caused a stirring, a slight alarm, an intrusion into the relief I felt from the Headmaster's generous mood.

CHAPTER TWENTY-TWO

The end of the season and exams came quickly. Graduation was to be on a Saturday, beginning with Mass, of course, followed by commencement in the gym. All the boys would file in, followed by faculty in gowns and college hoods. Clyde Carlow, the protocol veteran, orchestrated all these moves at rehearsal. The final luncheon would be the last school event of the year.

Prior to rehearsal, I had felt woozy, and by the end, downright ill - hot and clammy at once, weak and even more dizzy. I had to excuse myself from the final drill, managing my way to the infirmary to find Rachel.

I found Mrs. Malley, who pronounced me with a 103 fever and pushed me to an end single room. "Tim," she prattled, "you have the flu, and you're best off here where we can take care of things. Put on these pajamas and get into bed while I get the pills and things you need. Cover up with these blankets. Oh, you poor dear. It's terrible timing, but this is the best place to be - what with graduation and everything. Rachel is at rehearsal, but she'll be back. She'll be so upset, but this is the right thing..."

I remembered giving no argument. In fact, I remembered little of the first hours, in and out of what seemed a coma, an ague I'd never experienced, a rottenness that begged death. I remembered Rachel coming in and out, but felt nothing.

Commencement had proceeded successfully without me. In fact, the entire dismissal of school went forward, the campus emptying completely following Saturday's luncheon. By three o'clock the school was silent, and still I slept. Not until Sunday was I able to really look about with eyes not hurting, to sit up halfway on my elbows without aching too much.

When Rachel came to my room, she smiled, came directly to my bed and kissed my forehead. "Yippee! My Tim is alive, even if he looks awful!"

"What time is it? What day? God, I've never felt like this - ever!"

She sat on the bed, holding my hands, her eyes caressing her weekend hero, her helpless love. I so loved her then.

"You were very sick. None of the boys were ever so ill. But then, good nursing prevailed, and I proclaim you will eventually be your old self - but not right away. You must stay a while. Oh yes, it's Sunday. I said a prayer for you at Mass. Warren said to tell you to quit faking - that he really knows what's going on, but said he'd be by."

"Rachel, I'm so weak. Don't even remember going to the bathroom."

"We helped you. I helped you."

"Oh, God!"

"All very professional, mind. You are heavy, though, heavier than I realized, and you were so incoherent, so silly."

"Really. What did I say?"

"Don't remember. Oh yes, one thing - that you'd love me forever and ever and ever and ..."

"Okay, okay. So what's the deal? Everyone gone? Gee, you guys have been here stuck with me. Look, I'm out of here today. Is Mrs. Malley still around?"

"Of course she is. The faculty picnic is tonight, so we're all around. Besides, there's inventory and things. I don't think we'll be ready to get away until Tuesday. Anyway, you must stay. Doctor's order. Oh yes, Doctor was here for you - said Monday at the earliest. He wants your temp even for twenty-four hours."

She swept off the bed, saying she'd be back, and left me. I lay amazed, pondering this time that I had truly been away from my life - my vulnerability so complete. I recalled that early time as a child when my mother had sat on my bed caressing my forehead, murmuring me to sleep. I lay on my back staring at the ceiling, the hard hospital bed nevertheless comfortable. Then I closed my eyes and slept.

I woke much later, found Warren standing at the foot of the bed, a silly smile on his face, staring at me. "You're really not fooling, are you? Rachel says you're pretty useless."

"Jesus, Bill, I've never had anything like it. So darn weak, but they say I'll live. Where'd you come from?"

"The picnic. It's starting to get sort of messy. Ryan is drunk as hell. He really slopped up the martinis. Big mistake. I stick with beer - probably had too much of that. Henry's trying to move the party over to Carlow's place, but I don't know if old Clyde's buying the plan. Even Henry's pretty loose. He asked me to cook the steak. Never again - all of 'em standing around the grill telling me how they like it. Mrs. Clare was the worst. She wants it black on the outside and raw in the middle. You know how hard <u>that</u> is? She brought it back and made me do another. Said she gave the first one to Ryan, who didn't care."

Warren could always make me laugh. I propped myself up, feeling better, realizing my friend indeed had drunk a few beers.

"It was something having Eunice Clare standing there in her Bermudas, and, God, in a blouse that was cut in front so you could - God, is she ever built! I mean, incredible knockers. I mean, no wonder I couldn't do the damn steak. It wasn't like she meant it or anything - she's so natural. She can't help it, but she shouldn't bend over too far - know what I mean? She's so damn well put together. That old Henry, he's just - well - I dunno - he's in hog heaven, I tell ya. And she's off there talking to Father who's looking her straight in the eye, doesn't dare to look anywhere else!"

I didn't want to hear any more of this. "Was Rachel there?"

"Oh, yeah. She looks great out of her uniform. I mean, she always looks great, but really feminine, you know, not 'nursey.' She came and kept me company for a while at the grill. When I asked her about you, she got all misty. No question, you've got her hoodwinked. Well...guess I'll go back for some free beer."

Father came next. He was out of collar, dressed in an open neck sport shirt over soft slacks, and was sober.

"Rachel says I don't have to give you the last rites," he said. "That there <u>is</u> hope for you."

"Thanks to her. You know, Father, it's awful to feel - to be so helpless. I've never ever been sick like this before. Guess I never understood Christ's message about the sick. Maybe it's growing up. We're not immortal. At one point I knew I was to die, and I think wished it. Have you ever been sick like that, Father?"

"Not physically. But I did once wish to die. I was very depressed, but then God saved me. I don't know why - and it's never happened again."

I didn't want to pry, so commented, "Maybe all this was punishment. If so, then I must say I've purged all my sins. It is humbling. Maybe that's the one good thing about sin - that in the cleansing we become humble. How about that theory, Father?"

"Fair enough. I think there is something to it, that in lowering oneself there's an elevation - of spirit, perhaps. But before all of that, we must avoid occasions of sin. I'm serious this time. When we willingly put ourselves in jeopardy, we err, even if we resist. The human heart can stand only so much, and we must understand that. To take our frailty, our human nature, into battle with sin again and again can be too much, even for the truly faithful."

"Hey, Father. How did we get so serious? I hope you haven't come to see me with a special message."

"Not at all. I really did come to see how you're feeling. Don't know what prompted that little lecture. Maybe it's some kind of residue from a school year of hearing confessions - from a realization that whatever we do, we find ourselves confronting sin. To sin or not to sin, that is the question. Here I go again! Well, I think you'll live, as Rachel said. I'll tell her to bring you a steak. You could use some red meat - the coals are still good."

"Thanks, Father. By the way, how was graduation?"

"It went well. Chapel was full, of course, and the homily brilliant! Clyde Carlow spoke at the ceremony. He was so nervous, you could hardly hear him, but then he braced up. Said the usual things, but there was one thought that impressed me. He said he hoped Ashford had fanned a flame in each of the graduates, a flame he likened to a spirit that united them all, all men, God and man. He hoped that from here, with the flame bright, they would continue to stoke it, never let it flicker, until - and here Clyde looked out across the group, his arms wide and raised, and said 'Until you all, in a glorious burning light, are one, then one with God!' It was startling, and maybe brilliant."

"Good old Carlow. Why, the man is an Emersonian. He's into the Oversoul. I knew he read a lot, but it's pretty heady stuff for the Catholic he is."

Father rose from the chair. "I must go. But I'll be around campus a while. Come by. I'd like to see you before I leave."

When he'd left, I stood, again startled by my shaky knees, found a robe, then the bathroom where I freshened my face, sallow and grayish in the mirror, and then sat in the chair by the window. The sun had set, but the shadowed buildings were slightly orange from the last rays. Faintly, I heard voices, some laughter - the party not yet subsided - and I thought of what I had missed. Strangely, I wasn't disappointed, but instead pleased with vicariously enjoying what might have been, without the necessity for any social amenities, almost like the times I enjoyed loving Rachel without her presence. I wondered if I could make love to her as well as I did in my pleasurable musings... It was then she came in.

"Why aren't you in bed?" Her feigned sternness amused me.

She turned on a bedside lamp. "Come on with you. At least sit in bed. I've brought you something." Ratcheting up the back of the bed, she helped me in and put a bed tray across my thighs. She then uncovered a plate of steak, already cut, and a baked potato, opened and buttered.

"I can make some tea, if you like. What do you think?"

"I think I love you and would much prefer having <u>you</u> for dinner - thoughtful as you are."

"Oh, you! Try it. Bill cooked it when he came back from seeing you. Said you needed something."

I did try the steak, charcoaled and pink in the center. Rachel, rubbing my shoulder, watched me.

When I'd eaten as much as I could, I leaned back. "Warren said Ryan was drunk, that you listened to him."

"Poor Mr. Ryan. Everything's rather passed him by. <u>God</u> couldn't run the school well enough for him. Funny how some men just can't grow up. His wife is so dear, and loyal. She finally got him into the car, to everyone's relief. But really, they shouldn't serve martinis. They're deadly. I must say I'm amazed at how so many drank so much. Are you aware of it, Tim? Does everyone drink like that?"

"End of year highjinks.

"Mr. Clare had too much. He was loud and lurching around. His wife was furious, though not many knew it. But I knew it. Her mouth looks different when she's mad - sort of hard, in a line. I don't think it was just that Mr. Clare was feeling little pain. There was something else." She was clearing the tray away, tightening the covers, fussing lingeringly around my bed.

"Do you have to go?"

"I'm afraid Mrs. Malley might wonder. There's just so much time one can take for comforting."

"I smell like charcoal. Let me freshen up, and I'll come back to say goodnight."

She had lowered the bed, and I lay back, hands behind my head. Father had talked of the occasion for sin. Had it been merely to make converstaion, or had he intended to speak of it? I felt I had never placed myself in the occasion purposely, that my encounters had been passive, unintended, though startlingly real. My rationale was that I had been maneuvered like a pawn, and I felt resentment. With Rachel I had wanted consummation, but I loved and respected her, and certainly she was always my extended conscience. With Eunice Clare I had felt helpless. The gnawing question remained: how helpless was I, or more to the point, how helpless did I want to be? Perhaps the summer at Columbia would expunge the experience with Eunice. I started to pray then, the "Our Father" at first, several times, and then simply "Jesus, help me."

Rachel returned in pajamas and robe, her fragrance ahead of her across the room. She pushed me aside a little and stretched out atop the covers next to me.

"Just for a little, Dear."

Her mouth was near my ear, and for a while we just lay together.

"Tim, this summer - it looks as though I have to go to Maine. Aunt Bess needs someone, and the family expects me to go. I don't want to at all. I dread it - it's so hard, so far, and you way down in New York."

142

"It is rotten. Maybe I could come to see you. I don't know. I don't know what will be involved at Columbia. When are you leaving?"

"Wednesday, probably. That's if you're all right."

"Maybe another little flu attack is in order."

"No, not that again! Guess we just have to be grown up, you know, do grown-up things."

"Rachel, I don't know if I can stand it - a whole summer."

"I know. I love you so, Tim."

She tickled my ear then with her tongue, the shiver running my length. It was all I remembered of her. Astonishingly, with her stretched next to me, I fell asleep.

. . .

I awoke to a glow of light by the window. I didn't know where I was at first and was frightened. Then the glow dimmed slightly to reveal Eunice Clare seated in the chair, lighting a cigarette, her hand cupping the match. Then she blew the match out so that she seemed only a shadow with an orange tip of light moving in front of it.

"God," I almost shrieked, "you scared the hell out of me."

"I'm sorry. You were asleep."

"How long have you been here?"

"An hour, maybe."

"For God's sake, why?"

"Because I'm angry. I went out for a walk - and came here."

We were silent then, the glow of ash bright when she drew on her cigarette. It wasn't the first one smoked since she'd come - the air hung heavily about the bed.

"You mustn't be here. Please go."

"Don't you want to know why I'm angry?"

"Not at all. Please go - and open the window before you leave."

She did raise the window, reaching to stub the cigarette on the outside sill. Then she sat again. "I'm angry that Henry drank too much."

Silence.

"Please, Mrs. Clare, Please leave."

"Dear Tim. Stop telling me to leave. I'll leave when and if I please. If you're unhappy, close your eyes. Go to sleep."

I closed my eyes but heard her strike another match. I hoped the crosscurrent from window to door didn't waft smoke down the hallway, perhaps reaching Mrs. Malley, or upstairs to Rachel's. Moments passed. I lay rigid, expecting anything, praying she'd leave.

"He's never done that before - drink too much."

Silence. I feigned sleep.

"Are you asleep, Timothy?"

Silence. I hoped she thought so. Then I heard her stand, approach the bed. I sensed her gaze, the motion of cigarette to lips. After some moments she returned to the window, paused, and sat down again.

"I know you are awake. You don't have to speak. I know you can hear me. Henry drank too much because he was angry with me. He had come home early this afternoon. An admissions interview hadn't shown up. He was upset with that, and then - then he wanted to make love, go upstairs at two o'clock and - oh, what did he say? Something like 'tear one off!' I just wasn't...it just never seems to work. It's never worked. Today his attitude...as if it was 'the interviewee didn't show, so why not screw my wife?' It hit me wrong. I said 'no', and he was furious...never that way before. And when I relented, said okay, he raged out, saying something about he wasn't into rape...or something like that. He had a bath, had a drink on the tub, so it began early. Then, oh then, at the picnic - I'm so glad you weren't there." I opened my eyes. Her voice had turned plaintive, and I watched her as she stared out the window.

"At first he was all right, but after a couple of drinks, he wasn't, and then was embarrassing in front of snickering faculty - 'our leader, Henry Clare, just a fool!' Finally I got him away and into bed before he finally passed out. All because I didn't jump in bed at two o'clock. It's all so terrible, Timothy, so humiliating. There have been other times I haven't...responded to him but never with such a reaction. He's denied me countless times. But I don't think I'm angry any more. Telling you helps. Maybe I'm simply tired

144

from the year - all the Headmaster 'wifing,' all the longing and pain, all the dreaming..."

She stopped, slumping in the chair. I could see well enough, in the dim light from the open door, and met her look, her distressed, very human look of despair. She shocked me. I was afraid to speak, afraid to extend sympathy, even though feeling it. It was the first time I had looked directly at her in her presence, and for some moments our eyes were locked.

"Mrs. Clare, I can't believe what you've told me, not the part about his attitutde this afternoon. What you described isn't the Headmaster, not to his wife, even in the privacy of his home. It just isn't him."

After a moment, our eyes still locked, she said, "All right, I did exaggerate some. Henry wasn't really crude."

"Look, what you've told me, it can happen to anyone. And tonight - it's like that with booze. And you do recover. Tomorrow the Headmaster will be himself. Forget today. Go home and forget today."

"Did you hear all I said?"

"Yes, I heard. You both had a bad day - on the same day. In the morning you can make it all up - together."

"What do you mean?"

"You know perfectly well what I mean. Now, Mrs. Clare, you're not angry any more. Go, please, before anyone finds you here - or looks for you."

"Timothy, you make it all so simple. You just don't understand."

"In that case, go. Forget what I said - everything - being here, me, everything. Please."

She stood then, not regally but in several movements, until erect. By my bed she took my hand in hers, raised it to her mouth, her lips open on my palm, her tongue touching it. Replacing my hand, she said, "God knows of it all, Timothy, so I shall go. Rest now. Don't worry. He will tell us what to do, and when, and why, and that's what will happen. We are in God's hands. My anger was inexcusable because I forgot the only real truth in our lives - that He will see to us, to Henry, me, you, Timothy, everyone."

145

From the door she looked back at me, and even in the shadows I saw her smile, her maddening smile. I saw it then...and would many hundreds of times to come.

My usual route went nearly into Albany on Western Avenue. I turned north onto Route 90 across the Hudson River and south toward the Thruway Extension to the Massachusetts Turnpike. Over the river I felt the stiffness in my right knee, always there after sitting too long, the old basketball injury worsening as the years passed. I pulled off at a parking stop to walk about. The lights of Albany shone off to my right, a dusty orange in the evening.

CHAPTER TWENTY-THREE

Disconsolate the whole time, I had packed for the summer at Columbia one large suitcase borrowed from Warren. Rachel's mother came for her, which left little time for us, terminated by standing at the car, her mother impatient to leave, neither of us comfortable with our unresolving goodbyes and a proper little kiss. We had concluded the night before that there was nothing but to see the summer through, to bear up, to accept duty's onus, to be stoically unhappy.

Warren commiserated. "Yeah, take the suitcase. I won't need it, and it's a big old bastard. Good straps. Well, Rachel is a trooper. Too bad she's so committed, but she wouldn't be Rachel otherwise. Maybe she can get a weekend to New York, or the other way around."

"Doubt it."

Warren couldn't lessen my determination to be sad.

"Well, at least you look human again - finally. And you know, Tim, it was a good year, for you especially. I must say you pulled off some good deals. Don't know how you've done it, but ol' Henry seems to think you're his boy."

"What's that supposed to mean?"

"It means, my friend, you stand in great favor, and it doesn't hurt that Mrs. C. thinks you're peachy. I think she thinks I'm a weirdo or something, but you're her darlin'."

"Bill, that's a crock. I assure you, I don't please her that much at all."

I stopped at that - I'd never commented on her view of me. It had to be "verboten." I changed the subject to Warren's plans.

"Henry asked me to hang around, help with Admissions. He has meetings and wants to play more golf - and what the hell, he's going to fatten the kitty - not much, but it will help. Besides, it feels kind of good that he would ask. It's really amazing Ashford does so well. Course, no one's paid much."

"God, I know. Rachel and I couldn't afford marriage, even if we wanted that. We all must be nuts. My father just shakes his head."

"We are all nuts, Tim. Crazy to do this. Look, you're off in the morning. How about Rackum's for a few beers and supper?"

So I ended the first year over supper with Warren, bedding down early, and just before falling asleep, deciding to take courses in the Romantic Poets and Hawthorne.

. . .

I worked in the Columbia cafeteria in exchange for food, read for hours, took copious class notes, and sweated out a New York summer on 116th Street, in a third-floor dorm room, a double shared with Walter Bussey, a public high school principal from a small Vermont town. Walter was there on the G.I. bill, taking education courses at Teachers' College for state certification, a man I rarely saw since Walter was either in class, somewhere with a female graduate student called Buffy, or drinking beer nights at the student center. Walter was married, his wife and three children holding the fort at home in Vermont. Walter bedded down late, when he returned at all, and usually was gone before I rose.

Aside from Walter Bussey's shadowy presence, three aspects of that Columbia summer remained in memory: my loneliness and longing for Rachel, the Poetry class and its professor, and the game at the Polo Grounds between the Giants and the Cardinals. Rachel's letters helped not at all, for her grief only exacerbated my own, yet the days with no letter from Maine were even worse. I felt guilt that my prospects were affirmative, stimulating, and generally productive, while hers were, in her isolated circumstance, simply the daily tension from confronting death. The second week I received a letter that seemed illustrative of them all.

148

Dearest Tim,

Your letter today was so nice. I adore you, too, and miss you every minute. I'm so lonely. I count the days. They're so slow! You, too?

The routine here is pretty well set. The visiting nurse comes in three hours a day, a gruff old gal, but very good. Those three hours are precious. Of course, there's the shopping - things like that - but mostly I get down to the shore, walk on the beach. Tim, the water is so cold here! Even the veteran Mainers don't go in, and when you walk in the water, your ankles ache.

Two miles up the beach on a point is a lighthouse, and I walk there and back each time. Usually I think about us - or sometimes Aunt Bess.

Yesterday I found some shells, lots of jellyfish, a stone with a hole in it which I'm keeping for you, and a piece of glass with all the edges rounded. It must have been in the ocean for ages. Wouldn't it be great if we could alight somewhere at the shore? Any schools like that? Well, that's a long way from now. St. John's Church is just north of the lighthouse, and I've gone to Mass there. I said a prayer for us Sunday and lots for Aunt Bess. She's so ill, but won't die. I read to her and tell her stories, some about you.

I don't know why God won't let her escape. Where is His mercy? Should I not pray for her to die? Anyway, the prayers aren't working, yet. I hope my prayers for us work better.

It's strange, but when I walk to the lighthouse, I'm so happy, but the walk back always seems sad. Maybe it's because the walk back means my time is nearly over, or because I'm tired and my ankles ache. Maybe the sea and the sand get to me somehow, that I'm really on the edge of things. And there's Aunt Bess lying in her bed, and I wonder if death has come in my absence. It's terrible, but I almost hope so. And it's those old feelings again, of how short a time we have and of whether things will happen the right way. I realize you are my ring - my only one - to grab onto. There's nothing else for me but you, my Tim. I do love you so much. Put up with me, dearest. I'm so much better with you. When will that be?

Your Love,
Rachel

Darling Rachel,

I wish I were a jellyfish on your beach! You could pick me up any time. I live for your letters. A day without one stinks! These so-called Education courses are a laugh - either that or I'm just not with what I'm doing. Just the reading takes hours. Anyway, I enjoy it - the poetry course most of all because the prof looks and talks the way I imagine Shelley himself. The guy is skinny as a rail and lectures sitting on the arm of a teetery chair. We all think he's going to fall off, but he never does. It keeps our attention. But, God, Rachel, he is terrific! During the regular year he teaches at Michigan. His name is Herman Wagner, and he's a doozy. He reads that poetry as though he wrote it. Poetry hasn't ever really been my favorite, but I'm coming to see the art of it all, and that actually it's realistic. We're into Wordsworth now. Wagner read one of his "Lucy" poems yesterday where he calls her "a violet by a mossy stone, half hidden from the eye." Naturally, I thought of you!

Maybe thinking of you caused my dream last night. We were married! Since everything, anything was okay to do, you were after me all the time, running around everywhere naked, never feeling guilty but ready constantly. What a dream! All I had to do was perform. I guess you can see what I think about most days - and nights! You probably think I'm crazy, but it was all so real. Oh well, I can dream, can't I? Maybe it's unfair to write this.

When you walk back from the lighthouse, think of us, married, and all the great things we have in store. Think about how much I love you. Maybe then you won't be sad. I hate it if you're sad. You are my life!

Back to Wordy Wordsworth, my 'violet by a mossy stone.'

Love you so much -
Tim

. . .

In mid-July I found a message on the door to call Henry.

"Timmie! Is that you? How goes the battle?"

"Very well, sir. There's a lot of work, but the courses are just fine."

"Good, good. I know you'll do very well. Look, I have a meeting in New York tomorrow morning, but best of all, I have two tickets to the Cards and Giants at the Polo Grounds. Ol' Sal Maglie is pitching - the Barber. What do you say? Can you get away for a 1:30 game?"

"Gee, it sounds terrific. Sure! By all means"

Henry Clare was waiting at the appointed gate, more enthused than any boy, bubbling with the afternoon's prospects for "real" baseball.

"You see, Timmie," he enthused, "Sal has made a science of pitching. At his age, he doesn't throw that hard any more, but he puts the ball exactly where he wants - never over the plate, always on the black, nibbling and teasing, every pitch a different speed. And then that curve! There's no other like it in the league! It curves and drops a foot, and he can throw it behind in the count. He's the Barber! Shaves every corner of the strike zone. Hope he's on today. If he is, you're in for a treat."

So the afternoon passed, with Henry bringing up school matters between innings: Smitty had asked that I assist him with the varsity football come fall, while Warren handled the junior varsity, and since it appeared to be a promotion, I embraced the idea on the spot.

151

Mr. Clare's other plans were that I serve on the Discipline Committee, that I would run the bookstore in lieu of the dining room, and that Mrs. Clare insisted I continue to oversee the Sunday night suppers. Neither of us yet knew Kinney's plan for my teaching load.

The top of the ninth inning found the Giants leading 2-1.

Stan Musial stepped to the plate, his body ever moving, corkscrewing arms and legs, his head absolutely still. We sat forward, chins in hands. The whole crowd was curiously quiet. Stan took the first pitch for a strike.

"Watch this, Timmie! Here comes the curve," Clare whispered.

Indeed, it did come, but Maglie was tired, frustrated, and the curve simply hung, a fat melon waist high, slowly turning. Musial's whole body quivered, his eyes saucers. It was as though a spark plug fired in his belly, flashing a swing perfectly torqued, his wrists and forearms propelling the strength from his legs, a monster spring uncoiled, the ball on the bat a doughy crescent before it left the plate area on a four-hundred-foot-plus soar to the reaches of right center field. One poor pitch to one great hitter who saw his chance in a thousandth of a second, and took it.

The Giants lost 3-2.

"Well, Timmie, that's baseball. Amazing, isn't it? One pitch, sometimes, and all is lost."

At Columbia, Henry Clare said, "Timmie, great afternoon. I hope you finish up well here. It should be a good year. We'll look forward to seeing you back on campus. Stay in and pitch."

And then he was gone, the taxi headed for Grand Central. I watched until it was lost in traffic. One thing the Headmaster said was going around in my brain: "One pitch, sometimes, and all is lost."

CHAPTER TWENTY-FOUR

In early August Rachel's Aunt Bess died, and shortly after Rachel was home in Holyoke - tired, relieved, and fully concentrating on the problem of our separation. She wrote persuading me to come by Holyoke right after Columbia, before heading for the farm. The prospect of seeing her spurred a fine finish, with two As and a B. My Emerson essay was "not quite on target" said my professor, but I was accepted to the graduate school.

I caught the now familiar New Haven train for Ashley Falls, triumphant and expectant of heart. Warren picked me up at the station, and in the car, gleefully told me of his admissions successes, that school was full, that Henry Clare had spoken about starting school with "A few bodies stashed in the infirmary."

"God, Tim. We've seen a bunch of good lads. There are two huge guys coming in the Fourth Form, and they're smart, and most of all, they're football nuts. Smitty is delirious!"

"I'm with the varsity, you know. Or did you?"

"Oh yeah. Good and bad. Good for Smitty. Bad for the J.V. Can I pick your brain once in a while?" Then he said, "Well, Mr. Jordan, tell me about Columbia."

. . .

At school I found my room clean to the point of spotlessness, with everything stored away - far from the shape I had left it. Unpacked, I set out to tour the campus. Plentiful summer rain had nurtured lush green lawns, the impatiens lining walkways, and had bolstered heavy foliage everywhere. Each building had been readied, with new paint in several, and like his room, immaculate. In chapel, I knelt at the rear, then saw Father in a front pew, head bowed in prayer. After some moments Father turned to look back, rose and walked toward me.

We shook hands, and he sat beside me. "I was out for a walk and stopped here to say my office. It's too nice to be inside, though, even in chapel. I'm going on retreat tomorrow for a week, up in Pittsfield." He turned to me. "And how's Rachel?

"I don't really know, except we wrote all summer. She's been in Maine taking care of her aunt who just recently died. She's home now, and I want to go see her, but haven't yet figured out how."

"Then I have a plan for you. I'm driving with a friend to retreat, and my car will just sit here. Why don't you take it. Take Rachel to the farm to meet your parents. What do you say? My contribution to the Jordan affair! What is the status of things? Or shouldn't I ask."

"We haven't told anyone, but we're engaged - sort of. I've asked her to marry me, and she's said yes, but you know the rule here. And anyway, we're so poor. But it's a secret, okay?"

"I'm delighted. Frankly, it's a lousy rule. At a certain point it's not healthy to wait. I mean, if two people should be together, there shouldn't be that strain of wanting to be together but not really able to....But look, take the car. I won't need it until I get back."

As we walked from the chapel and along the driveway by East House, the Headmaster's school station wagon approached and stopped. Father veered off to Henry Clare's side and I to Eunice's. Father bent to the driver's window to greet Henry while I looked down at Eunice Clare.

"Timothy," she said quietly, "how wonderful you're back. How are you? Have you lost weight?"

"Probably, but I'm fine. It's good to be here. The campus looks terrific. New York really isn't for me.

"It's been a wonderful summer for the grass and foliage. So are you settled in until school starts?"

"Yes and no. I'm leaving in the morning. Father has let me borrow his car. I'm going to the farm."

"Oh dear, so soon. You've just arrived. How long will you be gone?"

"A week."

"And Rachel?"

"I'll go by Holyoke on the way."

"I see. Well, do say hello to her."

With that she turned toward her husband, who with a wave, pulled away, leaving Father and me to reunite on our walk.

154

●　●　●

Father's Studebaker was a gem - black, of course, tidy, well-kept, unlike Warren's car which reeked of spilled beer, sweat, and cigarettes. A rosary hung in loops from the steering column, its presence rather discomfiting, considering some of the activity it witnessed more than once. I had actually felt guilty, but was resigned that it was my cross to bear.

Rachel had squealed when I called about the car and the week ahead. I smiled with thoughts of her delight as I drove north the next morning, the Studebaker solid and purring.

I was eager, expectant, excited. The summer had been rewarding, but lonely, frustrating, downright abstemious. I hoped Rachel was as ready as I. She had to be. Weren't we engaged, lovers too long apart? I vowed this week must be the time we took each other without any impediment; no more Catholic guilt which I could now easily set aside - nor any Irish pledges "ever a virgin till marriage." No, nothing about being a Magrill, nor anything about sin. While it was all there, we were beyond it, I reasoned, the rosary clinking against the steering column whenever I turned right or left.

I had never warmed to Rachel's mother. I found her grim, so removed from my own Irish mother. She was rigid and unimaginative in both voice and dress, hardly the person I would have expected as Rachel's mother, except for the Catholic adherence to virginal behavior. Perhaps Rachel's usual bonny affirmation of life, even with its sometime lapse into moodiness, was really a rebound from the stolid structure of a home cornered among Sundays and Holy Days. Perhaps her mother's response to me was a natural fear from the threat I posed, lifting her daughter from the Mackintire routine.

My arrival in Holyoke found Mrs. Mackintire just cordial enough that I agreed to lunch, after which I insisted Rachel come with me for a walk. Around a corner, out of sight of the house, I pulled her tight, kissed her mouth firmly. She was fully with me, and it was I who pulled away to take her hand, to say, "Oh Rachel, it's been so long - too long."

"Tim, it's been terrible! Do it again. Kiss me again!"

Finally, her arm around my waist, we walked down the street of ordinary houses where ordinary Holyoke people lived.

"Can you come with me? To the farm? Please come. We can make up for Columbia and Maine. We've earned it - and I want you to see Pompey Hollow."

"Mother won't like it. My father won't mind. I can never displease him. But Mother won't like it."

"Why does she dislike me, Rachel? She obviously wishes I weren't here. God, what have you told her?"

"It isn't you. She doesn't want me to go. Nothing would be the same any more, and she has trouble with that. I think she sees that if I - if we - are married, then her life would be nearly over, or that it would mean the last stage had come. None of us want that. But, dear, it's not you. It's the idea."

"So will you come?"

"Yes! Oh yes, I'll come. Right away, please."

So we escaped Rachel's mother, who stood sternly on the porch as we drove away - not waving, her arms hanging straight down, her hands balled into fists. Rachel soon dismissed her sadness over her mother's demeanor, as well as her parting remark that, if they were going, it was best to leave right away if they were to make the farm by nightfall.

· · ·

For me it would be a week of deepening love and intolerable frustration. It was a re-awakening of family and place that again confirmed my roots, that found me proudly witnessing the loving welcome my parents afforded Rachel. She captured them fully; they adored her from the first moment, especially when she said the first thing she'd seen in their son was his love for them. My mother had readied my sister's room, with its feather bed and collection of miniature porcelain curios, and my father had made ice cream in the hand-cranked wooden tub. There was nothing different there for me, but for Rachel it was a marvel of affection and simplicity which she found irresistible, one she said explained why she loved me so much.

We swam in Limestone Creek in one of the natural pools formed by the water rushing over a log, each of us entering from opposite sides at her direction. But I tugged her to some shallow sand, her wet body wanton and twisting but then slipping away. We walked to the woods beyond the Macintosh orchard, found the tree with my initials, and beneath it I caressed her everywhere, her breasts against my face, in my mouth, but even in that leafy isolation she said she feared prying eyes, and there was no ultimate uniting. There were several times - in the car after a movie, in the barn, alone in the house when my parents went for groceries - when her passion was usually at my level or greater, but she never let me inside her. We knew every part of each other, our hands and mouths exploring to paralyzing climaxes, but she always, often shaking and sobbing, refused intercourse. She kept saying she'd made a promise.

"To whom, your mother?"

"No, not my mother. To Jesus."

"Oh, Christ!"

And that's where it was, my grudging respect for her pledge, unarguable, conflicting with my love and unfulfilled desire because I couldn't marry her. I railed at my poverty, the Ashford rule, the unfairness of love stymied by circumstance, and a woman bound in fealty to her Lord. My odds were unfair, I thought, and my resentment began to move me toward moments of sullenness. She despaired, and despite her attempts to explain and defend, or to jolly me upward, a quiet descended that made the ride back to Holyoke sad beyond measure. We kissed, pledged our love, held each other in Father's car, but when I headed for Ashford, I felt things disrupted - wrongly, of course, but nonetheless the feeling persisted.

Her goodness had baffled me, since her otherwise consummate passion found me everywhere else - on or in her. I felt she denied my ultimate manhood, and I was crazy. She would admit to the sin of fornication, even her ecstasy with it, but never would bend her vow against entry. She had begged me to understand, but all I could see was her mother on the porch, fists clenched, hating me. "Isn't my love enough?" I had asked, too many times, and she would reply, "Isn't _my_ love enough for _you_?"

157

CHAPTER TWENTY-FIVE

I decided that despite my resentment from our flattened relationship, I had best prepare myself for the new school year. I also decided that my introverted life at school must change, so I moved to relieve the insular school world by subscribing to the <u>New York Times</u> to stay somewhat current with the outside one. The inside, now that I felt a veteran, would take care of itself.

Ashford was set to open on Wednesday, September 8th, so I arranged to be on campus on the first, my old room reorganized with my desk facing the window for a view north across the campus, the chapel just in sight to my right. My third-floor perch had visual command of most of the school, except for the Infirmary. To my left, in the distance, Mount Everett punctuated the horizon, the highest point locally in the Berkshires.

Rachel was due back on Saturday. I had tried, unsuccessfully, to persuade her to return earlier, but she felt she owed her family these last days. I fretted over my competition with Rachel's mother and Jesus, unassailable almost, and frustrating at best. Was it the Irish thing, that found a black string in a ball of white yarn?

My somber mood fit the dark sky outside, and I moved to close my window as rain slashed at it from a sudden yellowish darkness. It was only noon, but I needed a lamp to see the paper, with its front-page headline on the McCarthy censure hearings and a story about seventy-five new polio cases in New York State that week, making a total of four hundred and five for the year. Early Wynn had thrown a two-hitter at the Yankees; the Giants led the National League by three and a half games. "Rear Window" and "Duel in the Sun" were box-office hits, and I wondered about going to see the play "Tea and Sympathy" next time in New York.

The storm outside then held me at the window, awed by the bent trees and rain parallel to the ground. The next day I would read that Ashford had been on the sidelines of hurricane Carol, which had devastated Long Island and the northeast coast, even ripping down the spire of Boston's Old North Church.

In the morning I volunteered to help Wilbur and the maintenance staff clean the campus of debris and limbs. Henry Clare, Father, Warren and Kinney all were there, with Joe Ryan pointing out areas for attention. While messy, the campus had actually escaped any real devastation, which Henry Clare noted with relief.

"It could have been much worse, Timmie. The good Lord spared us. Amazing how a storm can come and go so quickly. Look at it now. What a beautiful day! With all of you here, we should be in good shape by noon."

The two of us lifted a large limb from a hedge and set it near the driveway to cut into manageable pieces. Then, his hands resting on his hips, his body stretched upwards to indicate he was done lifting branches, Henry Clare smiled.

"Think I'd better check up at the office," he said. "Seems you men can manage the rest. Good job, everyone. Don't like to tell you this, Timmie, but I've been persuaded by McGrath to go to the Polo Grounds tomorrow! Last chance, he said, before school starts. Only one seat, though. Not even Eunice, but I'll let you know how it goes."

By noon the heavy work was done. Warren, Kinney and I patrolled together, criss-crossing the campus with bags, collecting twigs and smaller debris. We finished a final swath by the river, where we dumped our bags and watched the contents swirl away. It was on the river bank that Kinney made final assignments of class sections, and I was delighted to have a fifth form group for American Literature. My summer with Thoreau and Emerson would find its reward. I felt a lift in my spirit, finally, and in the afternoon started preparing classes, absorbed so fully that I stopped only when darkness forced me to switch on the lamp and then realize I was starved. I decided to walk the three miles to the diner.

The pale afterglow left from the sunset was beginning to reveal the serenity of the school, serenity that would depart after Labor Day when, in one afternoon, two hundred students and parents would descend. As I moved beyond the campus, I began to realize just how much I looked forward to another year, how much I loved this work, this world, and I understood I possessed a facility for achieving success in several areas. That realization buoyed the walk toward town.

And then there was Rachel, my dear Rachel. I loved her; I knew that. I must assure her, protect her, possess her if she would but have me. How could I wait, when we both hungered for communion? How could I handle Jesus?

And then...the other. I must destroy the other - for myself, for Rachel, for my job, the school. I must pray for strength to repulse and resist Eunice Clare, to cleanse my mind and soul, to never again see in my mind's eye her amazing breasts, or the perfect union of calf and ankle. I must somehow construct a defense stronger than before. There could be no more rationalizing, or blaming my innocence, or thinking myself a victim. I knew the adversary, her moments of madness, the monumental sin, the overwhelming treachery. Prayer and goodness were not enough any more. My resolution grew until, on the walk back, I was a knight, Sir Galahad, a fortress of virtue, fearless and unafraid. I felt even stronger when I found a note on the door: "Mass at 7. Want to serve? Father."

I slept well and arrived early in the sacristy to find Father already vested.

"Good, Tim. You found the note. A few asked why Mass is this early, but I've a golf thing at eight with Clyde Carlow, Kinney and someone else. We won't dally. God will understand."

As we processed to the altar, the few in the pews stood, Eunice Clare in the front row. The morning had been cool, and she was in a long tan coat buttoned high, her hair hanging straight down beneath a tan straw hat, her hands clasped in a steeple between her breasts. I had noticed Kinney, Carlow, and Mrs. Malley halfway back, and some at the rear I couldn't identify before turning to face the altar. Father did move apace, and I stayed alert to make the responses. Shortly I rang the bells for the consecration and held the plate under the chins of those who received. Eunice Clare's eyes were nearly closed in adoration when Father placed the host on her tongue.

After Father had rushed away, I hung the surplice in the closet and had turned to fold the others when, framed in the doorway to

161

the altar stood Eunice Clare. She smiled and started toward me, her hands at her throat as though to unbutton her coat.

"Father told us he thought you would serve. Henry left early for the ball game, so I decided to come to Mass."

She was near me then. Her hands had stopped moving and were clasped beneath her chin as she gazed directly at me, her lips parted. There was no noise or movement; everyone had left. In that moment the silence seemed to roar. I would remember the sacristy smell of past incense, and then her smell as she took the white alb from my hands, placed it atop its drawer, and stood just in front of me. In a moment so swift I couldn't protest, she undid the coat buttons to her waist, and stunned, I saw she wore nothing beneath the coat. She took my hands and cupped each to a breast. This was, I realized, no sudden impulse, but rather a plan, perhaps begun the evening before, and determined as she saw the Headmaster off to see the Giants play baseball. Feeling a mute fool, I stood there, unable to remove my hands from the magnificence I held in them, my mother's words - "they are me" - spinning in my brain so that at first I had hardly sensed Eunice's dexterous success with my belt and trousers. No Galahad he, no knight at all, even no incredulity as I heard her almost chant:

"Dear Jesus, my son, now we will consecrate your being and blood. My God, what perfection you are. I will have your body and blood, over and over, forever and forever."

"My God, Mrs. Clare, this is the sacristy!"

That had been all - the faintest of protests. I remembered that my head tilted up slightly, jammed against a bottom drawer, and that as she moved, I would see the fullness of her left breast, then through the door, the tabernacle on the altar, then the breast, then the tabernacle, faster and faster until it was a blur of flesh and silvery gold. In all, the rise and fall of Timothy Jordan on the floor of the sacristy in the Ashford School chapel, took less than five minutes.

Eunice Clare was a thorough, tidy lover. Before she rose from her knees, she had deftly put me back together. When I opened my eyes, she stood over me calmly buttoning the top of her coat, clearly elated, a woman at that moment so fully beautiful that even in my

162

despair, she appeared as though a halo bathed her. She gazed down at me, still on my back.

"Timothy, are you all right?"

"Hardly. This is..."

"This is what?"

"This is the most terrible thing - and here in the chapel. My God, after <u>Mass</u>."

She stooped over me then, her face directly above mine, her expression transported. The quietness seemed awful; her large eyes searched my face.

"Timothy, don't despair. You are so perfect, my dear, so perfect - and we are connected together. It's all so pure, so don't be afraid. Right here we've come in perfect communion."

I remembered staring up at her. She straightened, stepped to the door to the altar, looked about, turned to smile at my prostrate form and disappeared into the chapel.

Finally, I pulled myself to a sitting position, my head in my hands, moaning softly and slightly swaying. The violation - horrible, damning, outrageous! No guilt could ever be enough. I knew myself a fake, weak, and I almost laughed hysterically when recalling the iron resolve with which I'd armed myself just hours before.

· · ·

This detail of my egregious fall forced me to turn back from the long, vacant stare at the lights of Albany. I shuddered. The evening had become damp, and I was stiff from standing a long time in one place. I walked about, whipping my arms around, squatting several times, until my bones and joints were operative again. My watch said I had stopped for more than an hour. I had miles to go, I thought, "miles to go before I could sleep." My ignition keys were in my hand. As I approached the car, I realized I didn't remember getting out of it. "Come on, Tim. Get with it" I thought. In a moment I swung back onto Route 90 and back into the recall, one I had to finish.

CHAPTER TWENTY-SIX

My depravity, its detail, its roots, meant I couldn't confess to Father, who though priest and bound, was an Ashford teacher and a close Clare friend. On Saturday I borrowed Warren's car to drive to Sheffield for confession at Our Lady of the Valley. I'd practiced what to say and realized that confessing fornication just didn't cover it all. Should I divulge all the connections, places, relationships, positions? Or could I escape with just one fornication? Whom would I fool? What solace would come? Would forgiveness be real, duly discharged? Wouldn't Rachel's Jesus know?

I still anguished as I walked into the small white church, situated just west of the Housatonic River, where it flowed east of the village of Sheffield. It was 4:30 and already eight people stood along the wall, waiting their turn at the confessional. I knelt in a front pew, fixed my eyes on the tabernacle, and begged for help. Instead, my confusion increased, my thoughts a vortex, and at its eye, Rachel's face, my true love. But concentrate as I might, her visage would fade and then return, and in the faded moments, in the eddy's eye, was Eunice Clare's breast, fleeting and fading, returning and pressing; my prayer lost ground.

Turning, I saw the line for confession down to one. I stood and strode from the church, past the car to the river bank, where try as I might, I couldn't stop the tears. My shoulders shook in torment as I confronted this exquisiteness of sin, the exhilaration and the terrible remorse. My weakness terrified me, that I had not the strength to love God, to seek Jesus, to choose goodness.

In the car driving back to school, I still cried, wiping the tears and my nose with the back of my hand. Fortunately, Warren was not in his room. I scribbled a note of thanks and hurried away to the river log, to sit sadly until dark when, unseen, I found the way to my room. I knew Rachel would have returned to Ashford by then, but for so many reasons I decided not to check. In the dark I sat by the window for a long time. The telephone rang twice, on and on both times, but I didn't touch it. Finally, I rose, out of habit prepared for bed, and lay down. Near dawn I slept, through Father's Sunday Mass, until midday sunlight said "enough."

Remarkably, I felt ready to cope, almost as though I were the same person as before, and though I knew it a lie, prepared to move on. My Sunday <u>Times</u> distracted me at first. I learned the Headmaster had seen his Giants lose on Friday to a Gil Hodges homer. I read of the Nazi U-boat moved into the Chicago Museum of Science and Industry, of a remarkable performance by Marlon Brando in "On The Waterfront," that Eisenhower signed a bill to increase Social Security, and in an interesting article regarding polio, that officials believed the peak had passed, with fewer cases than in the epidemic of 1949. A report from Chicago said gamma globulin offered more protection than previously thought - as stated in the Journal of the American Medical Association - that it was gleaned from human blood and contained disease-fighting antibodies. The report noted that one study said gamma globulin helped, but another one didn't conclude whether it helped or not. However, public health officials advised it be used in families or groups when someone had been infected with polio.

When the telephone rang, I glanced at the clock. It was 11:00. I had to answer this time.

"Timmie? Hope I didn't wake you," the Headmaster said evenly.

"Oh no, sir. No. I'm just reading the <u>Times</u>.

"Look, if you are about, would you come by the office in a few minutes? I want you here."

"Of course, sir. I'll be there."

I was sure it was the end of it all. Henry Clare knew. The tone of the Headmaster's voice - I had heard it before. Never had I felt such fear or shame. The walk to the office was Golgotha. Perhaps I should just walk to the train station, never stop - but I had been summoned by the person I admired and respected as I did my father, by the man I had betrayed in God's house.

Outside in the waiting area, I encountered Clyde Carlow and Joe Ryan. My God, must they be included in such humiliation?

Shortly, the Headmaster motioned us all into his office, Carlow and Ryan on the sofa, I alone on a chair. Henry Clare leaned forward, hands clasped on his desk.

"I know it's Sunday morning," he said, "but a call this morning from Walter Abernathy I think ought to be discussed... You remember his son Bill, third former last year from Philadelphia. Walter called to say Bill has been diagnosed with polio and won't return. He's very ill - in the hospital."

I exhaled, stood and turned to the window, exhilaration and relief combining so that I had to hide my expression.

"Timmie, I know you knew him well, but the odds that one of our boys would get it were high. That's all. It's very disturbing, but everyone must cope." The Headmaster's voice was indulgent, but he was clearly ready to move on.

I turned back to my chair.

"Yes - yes, of course. We...Is Bill paralyzed?"

"Too early to tell. They'll know more in forty-eight hours, but there's a high temperature and stiffness. They're all very upset. The father also called because Bill had seen two other Ashford boys over the summer, one time just last week. He thought we should know."

"God, who were the two?" Joe Ryan asked.

"Wiggins and Conroy." Quick glances and shaking heads; resignation. "They stopped at the Abernathys' and Bill's mother urged them to stay overnight, so the contact was for some hours. Certainly they've been exposed, but of course, they will be back to school, as they should. It's certain many others have been exposed to some extent. And anyway, there's so little anyone knows about it all - how it is spread. I do know we better be ready for some problems. Right now it's off campus, but we should think about it. Any thoughts, Clyde?"

"I'm so sorry about Abernathy. The polio is all about us, but now it's close to home. I'm afraid I don't know enough about it - you know, what precautions, if any, we should think about. What is our responsibility to the rest, to the families and boys? Are we any different than an ordinary community?"

Everyone thought about what Carlow's said. Clearly the questions were disturbing. Did the concentration of students, from all over New England and beyond, pose a special problem?

Joe Ryan said, "It certainly isn't like measles or flu. I mean, you know, when we get them it's all over the place. God, if this polio spreads like that - God, I just don't know."

Their problem was that no one knew that much about polio, except that it was a fearful thing that had lately reached epidemic levels in other places, that research from the March of Dimes had as yet found no cure nor inoculation.

"I read in the Times that officials think the peak of the epidemic has passed," I offered.

"Perhaps," Clare said, "but it hasn't disappeared. We just don't know enough. Even though knowing more may not help, it is best we be well informed. Timmie, I want you to find out as much as you can and be ready to fill us all in at faculty meeting. The parents will want us to know. Meanwhile, we should just go forward, get on with opening school."

"Do you think, sir, that Wiggins and Conroy should be asked to stay home for a while, two weeks maybe?" Carlow's question lay in the air for some moments.

"I hadn't thought of that. Of course, who's to know? We only know of their exposure, even though others are likely in the same situation. Who's to know? Maybe it's a question of fairness."

"Yes," Carlow said, "but the fairness has to be for all. We must be fair to the school - all the boys, the faculty. It's hard. Where to start or end."

I knew from Carlow's words why he was Senior Master. His wisdom pervaded the session, even if leading to indecision by exposing every consideration, one of which was my suggestion that Wiggins and Conroy return, but to the infirmary for some isolation, with homework and food sent in, for a period to be determined by the doctor. After some discussion, Henry Clare said, "Look. Putting the boys in the infirmary will only bring attention to it all, and we don't want that. If anything, we downplay it all. Besides, it wouldn't be fair to Wiggins and Conroy."

After a pause, he went on. "Yes, we'll just simply open school as usual. Timothy will give us his report. We'll get on with things. We'll have a very good football team, so morale should be just fine. And we will pray to God young Abernathy gets well and that his case will be the only one. Eunice says we shouldn't worry. I've never seen her so up about the start of a year. We all should be, I think, especially in the light of things. Look, thank you for coming on in on a Sunday morning with so little holiday left. Any other thoughts, just give me a call."

We dispersed then, Henry Clare striding back home, Joe Ryan squeezing into his small Ford, Carlow and I walking to the dormitory.

"Mr. Carlow, do you think it will go well?"

"I don't know, Tim. The Headmaster made his decision - not easy. It's likely best to be optimistic. He is right so often and after all, what else is there? Close school? Of course not. And whenever Mrs. Clare is 'up and at 'em', he surely is."

I said nothing else. Back in my room I sat on the bed for some time, my senses awhirl with relief, worry, guilt, and wonder. On the third ring, I heard the phone.

It was Rachel, back at last, driven in that morning by her father who had lugged in all of her things, had coffee and just left.

"God, I thought you'd never come," I said.

"Oh, I know. I know. It's been so - so, well, hectic, you know, at home. I'll tell you about it, but not now. I have all this stuff to organize, but it can wait. What are you doing?"

"Sitting, just back from the Headmaster's office. Bit of a problem. I have a job that you can help with. Want to do our river walk?"

"Oh yes, Tim. Right away. I've missed you so!"

Her voice had its old gay ring, and her response in the infirmary foyer was maddeningly sensual, her tongue erotically long and lingering. Our river walk became a tour of violent hunger, abetted at last, manually, out of sight. Then, breathless, we sat on Rachel's log, hands clasped, staring at each other.

"Tim, we must get married! We must make our love a sacrament! I mean, I'm so full of feeling, my skin is bursting, and

I love you so, and I want you, and I want us together to be good and true."

"You are wonderful, Rachel Mackintire. You're the sexiest lady in the world!"

"Stop that! Well - no - don't stop, but you know. Have you thought about it - about us - about getting married? We know all about the rule, but what about a secret no one knows?"

Astounded, I looked at her. "Do you mean that? Do you know what you are saying? What about your parents?"

"I don't know. Actually, I've just thought of it today - this morning. It was something my father said - that I shouldn't be like him, that I should never hold back on an opportunity, to be aggressive, to stop weighing the consequences. He's never talked to me that way before, and there's something there he wouldn't tell me."

"About your mother?"

"I don't know. Anyway, after he left I thought about what he said and about us - where we are, and how hard things are for us, and what I believe, and then I called you."

"God, Rachel. I don't know. You know damn well how much I want you and love you - and how frustrated I get. It's just that it seems we shouldn't have to hide anything. I'm so proud of you. And then, what if you should become pregnant? It could happen, you know. We haven't talked about that, but I suppose you are up on all the rules."

She had laughed then, saying of course she was, and that she would just, at certain times, wear an iron corset. I could remember our good humor and light hearts prompted by the discussion, the exhilarating prospect, the inner glow of such an immense secret at Ashford. More soberly I had asked aloud: "I wonder what the Headmaster would say if we went to him to plead our case. He knows about us - I mean that we go out and all that. Everyone knows. I'm sure Mrs. Malley confirms it with the community."

"That's true. She thinks we should elope!"

There was no resolution. However, the prospect was exciting, and confirmation of our relationship became most secure. It had been amazing that there had never been any dent in my devotion, my love for Rachel because of Eunice, who was a dark, shadowy figure in the everyday school life. There had never been a comparison, a measuring, or any attempt to balance two experiences, for I had rationalized the other out of any concept of truth, certainly out of the confessional, and into a subconscious realm that I could, for the most part, confine to my dreams.

CHAPTER TWENTY-SEVEN

After Henry Clare opened the first faculty meeting of the year with his usual welcome, he explained about Abernathy and then turned to me for my report, a partial research of poliomyelitis, or infantile paralysis, gleaned in substantial part from <u>New York Times</u> files. The disease had reached epidemic levels between 1942 and 1953, but 1954 saw a decline. Clearly, there seemed a lack of certainty regarding the disease, but the virus appeared to enter through the throat, and symptoms included headache, fever, sore throat, nausea, vomiting, diarrhea and drowsiness. Eighty percent of the cases recovered in three to four days; severe cases found a stiff neck, pain in the back and legs, and muscle tenderness.

The faculty had sat quietly, attentively, as I had talked. I said that paralytic polio resulted from the destruction of anterior horn or motor nerve cells of the spinal cord, that destroyed cells do not regenerate because nerve cells cannot regenerate, that paralysis progresses from transient weakness to complete paralysis and atrophy of unused muscles. I explained the theory that in an epidemic, for every paralytic case there are dozens of non-paralytic cases which can infect; they are unrecognized virus carriers. The best guess appeared that the incubation period was possibly three to thirty-five days, but probably a week.

I paused, looked around the long table of faces, all staring at me, and asked for questions.

"Tim," Kinney said, "a friend of ours has an uncle, an adult, who has what he calls bulbar polio. Is that what you've described here?"

"Yes and no. Bulbar polio attacks the bulb or brain stem just above the spinal cord. It affects swallowing and talking. There are cases where secretions in the throat led to suffocation. Usually, serious cases mean an iron lung. It can affect children and young adults - sometimes older adults. Predisposing factors can be strenuous exercise, sudden chilling, pregnancy."

Kinney smiled. "Well, we wouldn't have to worry about the latter condition."

There was some unenthusiastic tittering.

"Is there anything else you would add, Timmie?" Henry Clare said.

"Just that there is a Doctor Jonas Salk who has done some good work toward a vaccine. It isn't ready yet, but he is conducting field trials as we speak with a vaccine that induced antibody formations in monkeys without instilling the disease. It will be a year before the testing is done."

After the meeting while everyone was standing about, Rachel came near me and whispered, "You were wonderful - so cool, so competent. I love you."

Warren reminded them it was faculty picnic that night, that he was head steak chef but could use any help available.

"We'll be there, aiding and abetting," Rachel said.

"You needn't bring Timmie, dear. Dump him, and you and I shall charcoal together, just smoke the night away while he wanders through the faculty wives checking on stiff necks."

"Isn't funny, Warren," I said.

"I know," Warren, misunderstanding, said, "polio is nothing to be flip over. But do we have to be serious tonight, Mr. Jordan? Can't we wait until the morrow?"

"You're right," I said. "Tomorrow is business. Tonight is play. C'mon, Rachel, I'll walk you to the infirmary."

School opened on September 8th, 1954 for its thirty-eighth year of full operation. Except for Abernathy, everyone arrived, healthy and in good spirits. This time around I appreciated the professional skill, from the Clares to all the faculty, in competently reassuring, soothing, welcoming over two hundred young men with their parents - effortlessly registering and housing the invasion in not much more than two hours. No one asked about Abernathy, not even his roommate, nor did any mention arise about polio. Clearly, Abernathy had been the only Ashford casualty of the disease, so that, for the moment, my report, indeed the whole subject, could be put aside.

The first days of school were always memorable: the boys looked so sharp in coat and tie, the usual dress, of course, but neat and creased - before the routine drifted toward a casualness that saw

174

tie knots lowered and shirt-tails loose. No one was tardy those first days; class attention was keen; and no one yet felt overwhelmed by the work. Most were out of shape, and they limped and creaked from the practices from which no one was exempt. Even the managers had to do calisthenics. Aside from preparing them physically for the games, most schoolmen subscribed to the notion that physical exhaustion made for a more comfortable resident operation, sleep capturing them all at a reasonable hour, as long as they could remain awake for their studies.

With real regrets of the part of Warren and the JV, I moved to the varsity football with Smitty, who wanted my T formation ideas, along with my rapport with Donnelli, in all likelihood the classiest quarterback in the league, if not in New England.

With no games that first Saturday, Smitty planned an extensive practice for the afternoon. During the Saturday morning classes, he and I had a free period together, and in the faculty room we discussed the drills for the team. Joe Ryan was there, as usual, smoking his Chesterfields and listening from behind his newspaper.

During a pause, he said, "It says here that polio signs may be mistaken for other diseases in the early stages, like meningitis, or just a cold or fever - says the polio virus can be in well people - says one of the signs is neck pain, a stiff neck."

"God, Joe," Smitty said, "half the squad has stiff necks! Course, they're sore all over. It's amazing how out of shape they are. Only a handful, like Donnelli, did anything to get ready. Tony is a marvelous athlete. He came back ready to play."

"Maybe we ought to go a little easy," I said, "not tire everybody out too much."

The suggestion came from two sources: one, naturally, my brief research of polio, the other from the unusually hot weather which found faculty permitting the boys to remove jackets in class. Even Carlow announced the previous night at dinner that they could hang their jackets on the back of their chairs - truly an incredible concession from a man whose roots in the protocol of dress never wavered. The discomfort from the sultry conditions found spirits lagging when ordinarily the enthusiasm of a new year held on well into the term - at least to the first defeat in football.

175

"Here's another thing on your polio stuff, Jordan," said Ryan. "Says gamma globulin gives high protection against paralytic polio. I hope that scientist, Jonas Salk, is onto the right thing. Too late for poor Abernathy, though."

We were quiet then until the bell sent us to their next stations. That afternoon Smitty nursed his squad through their drills with ample water breaks. In the locker room the squad was checked for injury or aches; aside from expected soreness, the players appeared in good fettle, encouraged by the general ease and brevity of the practice.

CHAPTER TWENTY-EIGHT

Eunice Clare was not at Mass on Sunday. Henry chose to stand at the rear of Chapel, looking over the full group of his boys, twice stepping to the open door to look out, or catch some cool breeze. Even at eight o'clock it had been unseasonably warm. Rachel sat near the front.

I knelt in the last pew, praying hard - as though to obliterate the sacristy horror by sitting at the furthest remove, to pave some path toward forgiveness, or at least toward a state that could bring me to penance. Coincidentally, Father's homily was of penance, as he reviewed a schedule for confessions, communion, procedures - convincing with compelling assertion that Jesus loves everyone, each person, and that no transgression could keep them from Him if they but prayed and sought forgiveness. Father walked down the aisle as he spoke, stopped at my pew, and then retreated, stepping slowly backward to the altar. He was very good, the boys' eyes following him, eyes fixed on his rich robes and voice, heads craning as he passed.

I sat, head bowed. During the previous week I had managed, at least during the day, not to think of what had happened with Eunice, aided by the business of the beginning of school. At night I had fallen asleep quickly, and only once in a dream had the image returned, and then as a kind of wondrous glory, haloed and shimmering, a fully sensual experience that found me floating on a sea of perfect large breasts, a glorious contralto singing, "We shall come in perfect communion." Here, in chapel, at Mass, prayer and dream conflicted until I lost all reason. Distraught, nearly helpless as Father began the consecration, I rose, stumbled past a startled Headmaster and ran for refuge. My emotion was inexplicable, never felt before. I had trouble breathing; my eyes bleared; my nose ran. Slowly, I took a long route to my room; again I had not received communion.

Sitting on the bed, head in hands, I felt hollow despair made worse when I asked Jesus to help me, even having denied Him twice so fully, and knowing my prayer not sincere. I felt I could no longer

177

cope, and I knew returning to Ashford had been a terrible mistake. It would lose me my soul, for I had not only denied my Saviour, but also my Headmaster, my mother, my love, myself. My life was wreckage. My self-pity was like a fungus, embracing, oddly satisfyingly, so that when the phone rang, I felt better.

"Timmie, you all right?"

"Yes, sir. I just felt nauseous - thought I'd better get out for some air. I'm okay now, but didn't feel like breakfast."

"Well, all right then. Mrs. Clare was off her feed this morning. Maybe there's a bug. If you don't feel better, see Mrs. Malley. Better yet, see Rachel. Okay?"

"Yes, sir. Thank you for calling. I'll be fine."

The next school week was a downhill blur. I felt I was sliding, that I had no hand-holds on anything, re-active, never assertive. One night I kept falling from the top of the barn at home, teetering off its peak in a free fall, never landing, but over and over back at the peak, each time something nudging me off, each time my mother looking up, horrified, mouth agape in a silent scream, arm raised toward me. At last, on the hundredth fall, I awoke. I lay on my back, arms folded on my chest, like a mummy, very frightened. It was five AM.

Sitting up, I feared sleeping again, so dressed and left the room, descending to the drive. First light made silhouettes of the buildings. Shivering, I hunched up the chapel path, eventually making two full tours of the campus, near six o'clock circling beneath Father's apartment window. The light meant Father was up for Mass. I strode away, then stopped to look back at the window. Mass was out of the question - I could not take communion. Beneath a tree I debated the dilemma of desperately needing the sacrament while unable to confess, at least not now. I watched as Father left the building and walked toward chapel, stopping once to survey the eastern sky as sunlight had by then touched the top of the chapel tower. Finally, I retreated to my room, prepared for the day by thorough cleansing and shaving, clean clothes, from socks to shirt, even wiping my shoes - so that Thursday, September 16th, 1954, I headed for breakfast as purged as I could be, without confronting my sin or my Saviour.

Things were working well enough on the surface. I impressed with a lecture on Hawthorne and The House of the Seven Gables. I held the attention of another class to the degree that, when I diagrammed a complex sentence, I actually believed some of them understood dependent clauses. I knew before the Headmaster that the Dodgers had won six in a row, were only three and a half behind the Giants; I had chatted with Kinney about Democrat Edward Muskie becoming Governor of Maine and heard Warren describe Miss America, nineteen year old Lee Ann Meriwether as a hundred and twenty-four pounds of absolute fun, her legs exceeded only by Eunice Clare's - this in Warren's room after lunch.

"I'm tellin' ya, Tim, like before. Our Eunice has 'em. Don't you ever see her walking around?"

"I never notice, Warren. We've discussed all this before."

"My, my - very touchy. Okay. I think we'll win three games and I've got the best classes ever. It's also too damn hot to practice football, or go to school, for that matter. Everybody's draggin' - even Carlow. He didn't jog to chapel last night." He paused, looking at me. "You don't look so hot either, my friend. Anyway, Henry wanted to know how the boys were in the dorm - if I thought everyone seemed okay, felt all right. I think he has your polio thing on his mind! Told me to not push them too hard at practice, to make sure they got their sleep. He seemed - what's the word? - he seemed pensive, sort of sad."

. . .

Sleep was an on-going nightmare, picking up from the night before. In this episode, each time I fell from the peak of the barn, two women watched from below - Mother and Rachel - each with arms upraised, mouths stretched open in silent shrieks, almost but never catching me, then the return to the barn roof, and a small push toppling me off again. In this dream the earth and sky went round and round as I spun toward the women, yet slowly enough that I identified familiar things: the oak tree planted at age eight, the Spy trees on the hill, my father's truck, Limestone Creek, Pompey Hollow Road, and the North Star near the sun. I felt the women's shrieks more deeply than if I had heard them, continuous, so terrible, so mad, that this time I woke sitting up, hands clasped over my mouth, in a tremor so violent that perspiration dropped and ran on my hands, down my arms. Minutes passed before I stilled, before I dared open my eyes.

Finally, I put feet to the floor. Again it was five o'clock. My eyes adjusted to a dim light, and I touched my head, legs, arms, for assurance that all was there, was awake, was alive. Stiffly I arose, disrobed, and stood for several minutes in a cool shower. I shaved, dressed for the day, took my book bag and headed for chapel.

The dream of the two women I loved brought resolve and enough courage that I strode directly to the sacristy where Father stood, half robed, looking out the rear door, open to the early sun.

"Good morning," Father said. "You're up and about early."

"Is there a Sacristan coming?"

"Yes, Evans. But he won't make it until a couple of minutes before Mass, in fifteen or so minutes."

"Father, if there's time - if you can - I need to make confession."

"Sure thing, Tim. Here, or down in back in the box?"

"I think in the confessional would be better."

We walked out to the altar and down the north aisle where Father entered the center alcove, motioning me to the altar-side booth. When I knelt, Father had the voice slot open. I closed my eyes hard and began.

"Bless me Father, for I have sinned..."

I thought of the fornication with Eunice Clare, simply saying, "I have committed the sin of fornication."

It was all I said, and Father only asked, "Are you truly sorry?"

"I am very sorry, Father."

"Then say the rosary and try, even though it can be hard, to stay away from the occasion of sin. Now say the Act of Contrition."

Father closed the slot and left, leaving me kneeling there, relieved, grateful, spent. There had been no lecture - just a kind of knowing acceptance. Would one rosary take care of it all? Was I really back? Absolution couldn't be so painless, or penance so rote, or sin so little grievous.

After communion, while I watched and listened to Father's finish, I thought about the sin and where it ranked in the large picture of evil. Perhaps the fornication itself, while a sin, wasn't the great evil I had supposed. I had never told Father of the betrayal - of both Rachel and Henry Clare - the broken trust, the terrible stain of a love dishonored. So while technically re-instated, I walked to breakfast far short of the elation I'd sought, or the honest forgiveness I had first thought my due. However, it was a start. I had gone to Father, confronted the issue, so that hopefully next time I could brace for a total reconciliation. With God's help, with a spirit newly armored, perhaps there would be no "next time," at least on the same subject.

. . .

When the phone rang in the faculty room at recess, I picked up. It was Henry Clare.

"I'm off to New York," he said. "There's a family, the Schumachers, twin sons, who seek a school. At this late date! They'd be fourth formers, are reasonable students, like sports, and they can certainly pay their way. Two more boys wouldn't hurt, if they're good lads. We have Abernathy's place and can squeeze in another for a while. Coming this late, the Schumachers should be happy with anything."

"Is there anything we should attend while you are gone?"

"I left Eunice a note. There'll probably be dinner tonight to meet the boys and Mrs. Schumacher. Odds are heavy I'll stay on and catch the ten o'clock in the morning. I think making tonight's train would be pushing it. No, I think everything is fine. I've talked with Clyde. Why don't you check with him at dinner - keep an eye on chapel."

At evening chapel I stood with Clyde Carlow outside the entry, checking the boys by, the last ones racing up the path while Carlow counted down: "Ten, nine, eight..."

This night the boys had sung rather well, either because the hymn selections were familiar, or it was the final chapel of the week, or perhaps because they felt good after Father's talk, which

181

said they were a special group of young men because they had been selected for Ashford, and more important, because they were creations of God, in His image, and that each one sitting in the chapel that night had in a sense a divine mission, and that whatever that mission might be, it would honor his school.

"Remember," Father had said, "God loves you each and every one. In our closing hymn sing praise to Him." And they did, as though they truly believed.

Following dinner, at faculty coffee, Clyde Carlow commented to one circle of faculty and wives that it had been a fine week, that the mood and morale spoke well for how things were going. All those present were ebullient, a mood usually prevalent early in the first term, and if otherwise, often worrisome.

Eunice Clare came up to me, who with quaking heart, could hardly look at her.

"Henry called," she said. "He's at dinner with the Schumachers. He hopes to have good news."

"Good. Well...if you'll excuse me, I must check in at the infirmary about any dispensary problems, to see Mrs. Malley." And I moved away awkwardly.

"Rachel's upstairs," Mrs Malley said when I got to the infirmary. "We had so few boys come in, and she seemed flushed, so I sent her up. Go say hello."

"Okay. For a minute."

So I could do that now. No one questioned me or wondered about my visiting Rachel in her apartment during the day or regular hours. I never went there otherwise, because I knew it inappropriate and because she would never permit it. The school code and the apartment occupant red-lighted any thought of a nocturnal visit, even though I had choreographed several plans of how to achieve one.

She was sitting in her easy chair in a yellow cotton robe, barefoot, a tray on her lap - milk and crackers with jelly.

"Come in, come in. My, you look handsome."

I stepped to her, leaned down to kiss her cheek. "Hi. You okay? Your cheek is warm. Feel okay?"

"Sort of yucky. Might have a little temp, and my head feels thick. Know what that's like? Like a soccer ball full of sawdust."

She laughed at her simile, and I sat on the sofa facing her. "Should you take something? Aspirin?'

"Already have. I'm fine. Just gonna go to bed. Feel sorry for myself, but it will all pass. Kinda been off kilter for a week or so, going back to Holyoke, but it's nothing to keep me down."

Concerned, I stared at her. Not feeling good wasn't Rachel's way.

"Maybe what you need is a thorough massage."

"Tim, you are dear, and I love you, and think you are just marvelous, but I don't think this old skin would hold up. You can bring me some water, though."

I did, held her hand for five minutes, and then left to check on the corridor for evening study.

CHAPTER TWENTY-NINE

After my final good-night room check at 10:30, I stepped outside to look at a sky - mostly clouds, only two or three breaks revealing the stars. With no moon and not many lights from the dormitories still on, the night was indeed dark. Driveway coach lamps dispelled only patches of darkness. It was mid-September, but the evening remained warm. I walked around the dormitory once, looking up for anyone sneaking late lights. Amazingly, all windows were dark.

. . .

I was frightened awake by a hand against my cheek.

"Don't be afraid. It's Eunice. Don't move - no noise."

The voice was a whisper, close to my ear. "Don't be afraid. It's Eunice. Don't move - no noise."

I lay frozen, every danger of her presence suddenly terrifying as I became aware I wasn't dreaming, knowing I wasn't because of her scent, so soft, and so erotic.

She knelt by the bed, her head bowed to mine. Even in the near darkness, I could see that her shoulders were bare.

"My God, how in hell did you get in here?"

"I waited for the night watchman to head for his round at the gym and slipped through the shadows."

"Jesus, you're in the <u>dorm</u>. There are twenty-four boys out there!"

"I've locked your door. We're safe, Timothy. But make no noise. Don't move. Do nothing, and please don't be silly and protest because I won't leave - not yet."

With that she lay her head on my chest, just below my chin, her left hand wandering over my belly.

"Mrs. Clare, please don't do this. It's insanity, madness. It's so wrong, sinful. Please, I just went to confession and communion. Please leave. Please!"

185

"Confession - but why? We've done nothing wrong or sinful. Dear Timothy, you are my Saviour. It's no sin. You've set me free. You're my son, and I love you. You're my pure love, my perfect lover. Don't you understand? Your coming to Ashford was for us, for me. You're here because of me. Don't you know that?"

Her hand kept circling until she held all of me. "Dear God, you are so perfect, magnificent."

She lifted her head then, knelt erect on her knees, her breasts full above my chest. I jerked to sit up, to get free, but she was incredibly strong moving on me, breasts pushing down my chest. Our brief struggle was suddenly frozen by a noise, steps in the stairwell which both heard. I listened carefully, now back flat on the bed, Eunice Clare's upper torso across me, her left hand stilled, but still clenched there.

"It's the night watchman," I whispered.

We tried to breathe slowly. As the steps came closer, I held my breath, her grip still a vice. For an eternity, it seemed, we could hear the old man breathing outside the door, winded by his climb. Then there was the shuffle of steps, down the hall, stopping, then a sound like a chair scraping the floor.

"Is he still out there?" she whispered.

"Yeah. There's a chair down the hall. Sometimes he rests there. God, that's what he's doing - sittin' in the hall. My God!"

Slowly she lifted her head and whispered, "You must make not a sound, not a move, and do as I say."

My eyes, accustomed now to the dim light, saw a mischievous smile as she turned her face, her forefinger to her mouth to signal silence. Then she rose slowly, silently, like Venus from a deep pool, swung her leg across me in an effortless, agile arc, never letting go her grip. Her perfectly formed, hungry body pinioned me, so deeply riveted that she controlled the night. She made no sound, with only imperceptible movements outwardly, though milkily rippling inside, her breasts inviting silent agonized adoration. During it all, we listened for the watchman's footfall until, at last, beneath her power I was helplessly at the last extremity, we heard his steps headed for the stairwell, the fire door open and close, and then his steps on the driveway beneath the window.

186

When Eunice Clare heard the fire door close, she slammed forward, her belly and breasts hitting hard, until I gave up any control, and as both erupted, she growled in a terrible whisper, "Dear Jesus, you are mine. Dear Jesus, you are mine,..." I grabbed her face and yanked to mash her mouth in near equal fury. Complete madness.

It was many minutes before both of us stopped shaking, before we ceased sobbing, she in unrestricted joy, I in limitless despair. In time she lay quietly beside me, her mouth near my ear. I was dumb, helplessly stricken between despairing remorse and ecstacy never ever previously felt. I wondered if I should hold her close or kill her. Could I ever again face anyone - Henry Clare, my boss; Father, my confessor; Rachel, my fiancee?

She asked, "What time is it?"

"Three. Three-fifteen."

"Will he come around again tonight?"

"Every hour until six."

She put her arm across my chest.

"Don't start that again," I said.

"But your bed is so narrow."

"You have to go."

"Right away?"

"You have to get out of here before it gets light."

"But getting out is tricky. Outside I could always be out for a walk. I do that, you know, sometimes on the sleepless nights. I've met the watchman several times in the past."

Oddly, for I certainly didn't want to prolong this debacle, I asked, "Why sleepless nights?"

After a few moments, she said, "I suppose there are several reasons. I've never slept well, except when Henry and I were first married - the first couple of years. When I was younger, I didn't need much sleep. Now it seems I can only sleep when thoroughly exhausted. Mostly, I'm awake because I'm trying to figure out the future, and I'm having little success."

"The first couple years - they were okay?"

"No problems then. The sex was so great, so non-stop. Free periods, lunch time, before and after practice - not all in one day,

187

of course, but we were insatiable. I slept just fine. And I'll sleep tonight just fine."

"Mrs. Clare, is getting a night's sleep what <u>this</u> is all about?"

"Please! Call me Eunice. Mrs. Clare is so - so distant."

"It's meant to be. I shouldn't call you by your first name. Your husband is my boss. By position and age, you are Mr. and Mrs. Clare. And this, whatever it is, doesn't make any difference."

"In answer to your question, sleeping is not what '<u>this</u>' is all about. The great sex in the beginning was also about being happy, fulfilled, about achievement. But in time we weren't achieving anything."

"You mean children?"

After a pause she said, "Timothy, I don't think this discussion is for now. Please?"

"Okay. What <u>is</u> for now, though, is your solemn promise, your pledge, to never do this again - with me. You take advantage, and I admit I can't cope. Please stay away from me this way. I have a job to do, and I'm in love with Rachel."

"I haven't finished my story."

"If you'll pledge to stop, I'll promise to hear your story - but not like this."

"I promise."

She said the words looking me straight in my eyes. Then she glanced down the length of my body and smiled. "But before I go..."

They heard hurried footsteps in the stairwell, then loud knocking at Timothy's door and the night watchman calling, "Mr. Jordan! Mr. Jordan! Wake up, Mr. Jordan! There's something you should know - somebody should know!"

Desperately, we looked at each other, for the first time Eunice Clare without her confidence. I attempted to call back sleepily, "Mr. Trumbull, is that you?"

"Yes. Yes, it is. I saw a boy running. Are you awake?"

"Now I am. Look, whatever it is, go to the office. Keep an eye out from there. I'll be along as soon as I can."

"All right. See you there."

We listened to his retreating steps, and then Eunice said, "My, Mr. Jordan, you are clever."

"Listen, we don't know who he's awakened - including Carlow, although they all sleep like logs. Maybe even some boys. I'll go over and keep him there. Just wait to make sure no one is wandering around the building. Use the other entryway, away from Carlow's place."

We were both dressing. Despite the frantic hurry, I noticed red marks on her breasts, from my hands and teeth, I later remembered. She tied a black kerchief on her head, sat on the bed and smiled up at me.

"Be off, Galahad!"

I looked at her there on the bed, still devastatingly erotic, her ankles visible beneath the hems of her slacks, sweatshirt rounded to perfection, and I cursed myself for feeling the excitement of our conspiring allegiance at that moment. Unlocking the door, I peeked out. All seemed silent.

"Timothy," she whispered.

"What!" I whispered back, irritated and anxious.

"Button your fly!"

190

CHAPTER THIRTY

The watchman stood on the patio against the outer office wall. He stepped out of the shadow as I jogged to a stop.

"Sorry, Mr. Jordan, but you were the first person I thought of tellin'. Maybe it's nothin', but Mr. Clare always said for me to let him know if I saw boys out of their buildings, and I know he's not around. I tried Mr. Carlow before but couldn't raise him"

"That's fine - fine, Mr. Trumbull. You've done the right thing. Now tell me, you saw someone?"

"Right over there" - pointing halfway between Warren's dormitory and the chapel - "Like he was runnin' from the dorm up the hill. Had to be a boy. He was fast, and his size - looked like one of the young ones. He had a sack over his shoulder. Course it was too dark to really see him. I'd just come out of the office."

"Did you see where he went?"

"Right past the chapel over that rise. Looked like he was hell bent to get outta here, right toward the main road."

We both looked to the chapel and past to the lighter eastern sky. It was after five.

"Mr. Trumbull, I'll take care of it. You have another round. Go on your way, and let me know if you see anything. Good work. You've been most alert."

"Just doin' my job. Good luck, Mr. Jordan."

Trumbull headed away and I took out my master key, let myself in the office and stood at Henry Clare's office window. My last two hours had apparently gone undetected, but I wondered, nervously, if Eunice had made it safely back to her house. And now this boy, likely running from Warren's dormitory in the middle of the night, carrying a bundle. I could only conclude that one of the young, new lads had decided to run away, go home, and had made his escape while the school slept.

A light from the Clare's caught my eye - likely a hall light, for in seconds it went out. She was back and now upstairs. I waited for her to make the bedroom, turned to the Headmaster's desk, and dialed. It rang once, and she answered.

191

"This is Mrs. Clare."

"I'm in the office. Apparently a boy has run away, probably from Warren's house - at least that's what I think. By now he's likely out on Route 7 trying for a ride. I'd like to get the school wagon. Can I come 'round to your back door? Just leave the keys on the kitchen counter."

"Of course."

In the short time it took me to walk swiftly to the Clares, she had found the keys, changed into the sheerest nightgown she had, and stood by the kitchen counter, keys in hand. When I reached for them, she wrapped her arms around me, and kissed my mouth deeply, her body adhering to mine in an unbreakable weld.

When she did pull her mouth away, she said, "There, now you can go. Drive carefully. If you find him, bring him here. Now go, Timothy. God be with you."

First I drove to the Canaan Diner, just to make sure the lad hadn't decided just to stoke up, but there was only a truck driver at the counter. I didn't know who the runaway was, so didn't know where was home. I sat in the car in the diner parking lot debating whether to head south or north on Route 7. On a hunch, I turned left, heading north toward Sheffield, Great Barrington, maybe beyond. My chances were not very good; the boy might have caught a ride with a truck, a farmer, someone off to an early job in Pittsfield. There was no traffic, so I turned the lights to high beam to better scan the shoulders on each side.

I felt wide awake - amazing after the incredible events, the tension, the unfettered passion, the horror brought on by realizing the ecstatic pleasure I had felt in the midst of such danger - with an older woman, too complex to understand, whose husband I respected deeply, a man who trusted me, had given me much responsibility, a man cuckolded by a feckless, greenhorn fake!

In Sheffield the main street ran parallel to Route 7, separated by a narrow green, so I circled around the green checking store fronts. No one stirred, and I headed north again from the village, beams high, toward Great Barrington. About two miles north of Sheffield I saw the boy, far ahead, slouching along the right side of the road, his pace marked by a limp. As I approached, the boy turned toward the oncoming car, thumb out, a green book-bag slung over his shoulder, a hopeful face squinting at my lights, a face streaked with dry tear runs. I pulled past him, onto the shoulder, and in the mirror, watched the youngster limp to the passenger side and open the door.

"Hop in, young fella! Where ya headed?"

The boy jumped in, slammed the door, stuffed the bag at his feet and turned. "Pittsfield."

When he recognized me, he slumped, his chin to his chest. "Oh, Mr. Jordan, it's you."

"That's my name. And let's see, you're Fitzgerald. Patrick Fitzgerald. Am I right? And you're in Mr. Warren's dorm."

"Yeah. Yes, sir. I'm Fitzgerald."

I had pulled back onto the road and continued in the same direction, driving as before, glancing at the forlorn figure next to me - dressed in grey flannels, white shirt, dark jacket, but no tie. He was average size for a Third Former but athletic looking, handsome, his angular face topped by short, curly blond hair. The boy sat cracking his knuckles, nervous, no bravado left.

It had been coincidence that I had met Patrick's parents at the tea on opening day, had introduced them to their son's housemaster, Bill Warren, and had in turn met Patrick's two sisters. All of them had Boston accents. A splendid family, I had thought, proud to have their youngest attending Ashford, an opportunity denied his sisters because Ashford was for boys and because the girls refused to leave home. Up until opening day, at least, Patrick couldn't wait to escape his sisters and start a new adventure at Ashford. His parents clearly had large plans for this only son, plans that would take him into a professional world quite beyond the successful restaurant/ bar his father ran in South Boston.

"Well, Patrick, what was your plan? Boston is a long way. You were heading home?"

"Yes. I'm going home. It isn't that the school isn't good. You know...well...it's just not for me."

"Sort of homesick. Nothing wrong with that, Patrick. If you weren't homesick, then I'm not certain we'd want you at Ashford. Being homesick is a good thing - says a lot about your family, how you love them and miss them. You know something? I'm homesick

193

a lot, still, and I've been to college and away for a long time, but it's a good feeling, really. Of course, it doesn't mean you should abandon what you're doing."

Fitzgerald looked at him then, confused but relaxing a bit. With some probing I learned the boy limped from a hit in football on Warren's squad, that his stomach had been upset for two days, and that the previous evening he had not been able to reach home on the phone. Then when Mr. Warren barked at him about having a messy room at lights out, he had made his decision. Ashford was no place to be. If he could make it to Pittsfield, he had enough money for the train to Boston.

I heard the boy's saga with sympathy. I had long since learned from other boys that what Fitzgerald related was a not insignificant reality fot a young, self-pitying teenager whose ties to Mama remained very firm. The boy's pain was clear, its causes obvious. Listening, I'd decided on a tack.

"Look, Patrick, I'm going to take you back to school. It's still early. No one will know you were ever gone. What we'll do is go to the infirmary. Mrs. Malley will be up, and we'll check out your stomach. If you're okay, we'll have some breakfast there. It will explain why you are not at breakfast. Then we'll talk about going home to Boston. We can call your parents, and I don't see why you couldn't go home for the weekend, if that seems to be a good plan. Then you could talk things over with your family. You seem like a young man who could make a good decision - when you've had time to look at everything, and talk about it. Then, if you decide to stay on, no one need ever know about this little nocturnal jaunt you took. What do you think?"

The boy had intently listened, his gaze fixed on me until I turned and smiled, and Patrick Fitzgerald smiled in return.

"Mr Jordan, it sounds like a very good plan. Thank you."

At the infirmary I drew Mrs. Malley aside, quickly told her what had happened and the plan, prompting the first steps to recovery - the Malley hug to the motherly bosom, the several, "Oh, you poor dear," the kind hands to the face, a massage for the sore leg, followed by toast, eggs, and milk at the kitchen table. During these ministrations, I learned Rachel was sleeping in; just as well, since I wasn't ready in any way to face her. I called Eunice Clare to report on Patrick, that my plan was to have no one, at least for the moment, know about the boy's defection, that some minor problems meant the infirmary was where he belonged now - and could she look at the Headmaster's parent list in his den for the Fitzgerald number in Boston.

"My, it appears you have everything worked out," she responded. "I'll have to go downstairs for the number. Will you wait?"

"Yes."

I thought she took much more time than necessary, but I held the phone patiently until her voice said, "Timothy?"

"I'm here."

I wrote the number and thanked her, but before I could hang up she said, "When will you hear the rest of my story?"

"Mrs. Clare, I am...look..."

"You'll drop off the car keys?"

"I'm on the way to the office. I'll leave them at the switchboard."

"That's a poor plan."

"Sorry, but that's the plan."

I asked Mrs. Malley to keep Patrick until I returned. At the office I called Patrick's parents, who explained they and the girls had been at an uncle's for dinner, had stayed later than planned, had tried to call school for Patrick, but by that time the school switchboard had closed.

Back at the infirmary I arranged for the boy to call his parents from Mrs. Malley's quarters, while Mrs. Malley and the now arisen Rachel and I sat waiting until Fitzgerald returned, awkwardly scanning the room and the three adults seated there.

"Sir, I've talked with my parents and - well, everything seems better now. I think I'd like to stay on here. My dad said to give it a chance, and they're going to drive here tomorrow if they can."

I stood to wrap an arm around the boy's shoulders. "Pat, sounds to me you've got a handle on things. Let's just chalk up last night to an experience we should all forget. Think you can go to class?"

"Yes, sir. I have to get a tie on, get my books."

"Good. You do that. If anyone says anything, tell them Mr. Jordan wanted Mrs. Malley to check your leg."

I shook his hand saying, "You'll be fine, Pat. Next time you have an urge to get out, give me a call. We'll talk."

I watched young Fitzgerald walk away, somehow feeling connected to him, and thought how each man has demons he must escape.

CHAPTER THIRTY-ONE

That afternoon Ashford opened the football season at Salisbury. By game time I wondered if I could stay awake, but Donnelli's performance, with two perfect touchdown passes, insured full attention. At the end of the first quarter Ashford led 20-0, and by game's end had overwhelmed Salisbury 42-6.

Rachel hadn't come, still feeling achy and generally unfit for sitting on a bleacher. I barely remembered the bus ride back to school or the victorious entry to the dining room to standing applause, so tired that I, too, felt I had flushy aches to go with a dull headache. I did manage a visit to Rachel, again to her upstairs quarters, both of us dull and slouched in a dual malaise, Rachel because she had some kind of persistent virus, I because the last twenty hours had been sleepless, sexually exhausting, with the further drain of decision-making and the final burden of a guilt so great I couldn't yet determine if survival were possible.

The guilt became even more acute when I realized how grateful I was that Rachel had no interest in being with me, and that I did not have to deal directly that night with the woman I loved so deeply - the woman I continued to betray again and again. As I sat on her sofa, slumped, head lolling, she seemed to understand my lethargy. I closed my eyes, too shamed to face hers as she commiserated over my long night and day, and wasn't I so dear to come see her when I felt so rotten.

"Rachel, no more, please. I should go."

"I don't know if I should kiss you. This bug hangs on."

"Shouldn't you see the doctor?"

"If things aren't better, I'll see him Monday."

"Good. Sick or not, you're still so beautiful!"

I hugged her to me for several moments, so that after some time she pushed back to look at my face, to ask, "Tim, are you all right? I know you are tired, but you seem sad."

I stood, looked down at her, placed my hand on the top of her head and said, "I'm fine - just sort of exhausted. You take care.

Nurse, heal thyself!" At the door I turned back. "You do know I love you, that I shall always love you, no matter what."

"Yes, yes. Of course I do. And I you, Tim, always."

"Good. Good night then."

In bed with just the clock lamp on, not dozing, not even thinking, hands under head, I stared at the ceiling crack that in outline resembled my father's Ford Forty-niner. I had come to that conclusion about the crack nearly a year before, before any of the weird amalgam of events of the ensuing twelve months, before love and betrayal, success and failure, ecstasy and agony.

My phone rang. I reached without moving from the bed, laying the receiver against my neck and shoulder.

"Timmie, glad you're there. Didn't know if you'd be at the movie." It was Henry Clare. "Just got off the horn with Pat Fitzgerald's father. Of course, Eunice knew much of the story, but he filled me in, and they are so pleased with what you managed and pleased with the school. I must say, Timmie, you handled the whole affair like a pro, using great judgment - you weren't punitive, just understanding - and without it known all over school. I had to call to thank you for stepping in."

"We're lucky no one else picked him up."

. . .

Not far now, I thought, heading south on the Taconic Parkway, a road which invited speed but whose construction confined any real increase in pace. In fact, it was a rather dangerous road, too narrow, hilly and windy. I drove with both hands on the wheel, carefully at a steady fifty, my headlights now in full effect. I drove at a pace I calculated would provide enough time to finish, finally, the whole memory, in disturbing sections before, never linked, indeed never real. I saw that my mother's death fostered the need to clarify the visions, connect the sections, see myself in full dimension, no matter how devastating, how cathartic it all might be. Jaw set, I forced my mind back over the years to that Sunday, September 19th, 1954.

198

A mild morning, "summery", I thought, as I left the dorm for the walk to Mass that mid-September day. The walkway was a line of dark jackets moving unhurriedly. From the lefthand path came Mrs. Malley and Rachel in their whites, and Eunice Clare in a flowing blue dress, stunning even from several yards away, the three women clearly conversing, a hand gesticulating, a head turning, Rachel's rippling laugh which made me smile. She sounds better, I thought, and then wondered what Eunice Clare had said to provoke her laugh - or was it a Malley sally? I slowed my pace so not to meet them where the paths intersected - I'd become increasingly uneasy whenever I saw Rachel and Eunice Clare near one another, or talking by themselves - but Rachel saw me and sent a half wave as Eunice Clare talked, head bent to Mrs. Malley. The Headmaster and Carlow stood at the chapel door, looking everyone in. I lagged with them, waving in the stragglers.

I hadn't been a participant in Sunday Mass since I'd begun wrestling with whether or not to receive communion. Every facet of my faith said no, the mortal sin of my transgressions with Eunice a terrible, hideous fact. Why, then, any debate? Why now did it all now seem less than damning, especially since the rescue of Fitzgerald and then the call from Henry Clare, so that from a dark wanton night grew a kind of satisfaction with myself that made life seem somehow well-formed, guilt-free, safe. Could I rationalize all of it out of my soul, out of my heart? Could I walk that aisle to have Father put Christ's body in my mouth, where only hours before I had devoured Eunice's breast? I sat and heard again the ripple of Rachel's laugh - felt a deep ague. More than Father's words, or my mother's admonition to remember I was a Magrill, or any agonized conscience, the memory of Rachel's laugh across the campus, on a Sunday morning on the way to Mass, contorted the hours between then and Eunice's night visit, into the deadly sin, the overwhelming fall from grace, the destruction of any integrity - that I knew had to be faced.

The first pew of boys knelt in a line at the first step to the altar, and lines a third of the way from the front had formed in the aisle. At the rear I knelt, still undecided, heart and mind in awful conflict, until I heard some commotion from the altar. Father stood, a host in

199

hand, looking to the congregation, then back toward me, and I saw Rachel and Mrs. Malley run from their pew to the front. I started up the aisle until I saw a boy lying face down on the carpet in front of Father, with Rachel now kneeling next to him. Fainted, I thought. It wasn't unusual for a boy now and then to feel light-headed at Mass after a night's sleep and the long fast. Father had spoken to them about being free to leave should anyone feel faint, to go out for some air, to lower one's head between the knees. "It can happen to anyone," he had said.

However, this lad had truly fainted; it took some moments for the two nurses to navigate him to the sacristy and out its exit door, with me leading the way. Indeed, outside the boy remained staggery and said he was nauseous. Rachel looked at me. "You'd better help us with him - to the infirmary. He needs to lie down. What's your name?" she said gently.

"Paul - Smith," he said, his voice betraying fear.

We trooped down the grassy slope, the boy mostly sliding along, I bearing nearly all the weight, Rachel helping. Mrs. Malley kept abreast, cooing "Don't you worry"'s and "There, there"'s.

For some time I waited in the dispensary until Rachel appeared, frowning, to phone Dr. Haley. She caught him as he was leaving for the golf course. He would swing by school on his way to the club.

Hanging up she said, "Paul fainted, and he still doesn't feel well. He has a temperature - 102 degrees - and a terrible headache."

I had left then. Mass was over, and I joined my table for breakfast. After a second cup of coffee with the Carlows, I left to check the dormitory, expecting the corridor to have especially neat rooms on Sunday mornings since the boys weren't pressed for time to make classes.

Sunday mornings were still favorite escapes to the New York Times, and today, September 19, I read that Rocky Marciano had knocked out Ezzard Charles in the eighth round in Yankee Stadium, that the Cleveland Indians won to clinch the American League title, and one across in the crossword puzzle was "City on Cayuga Lake." Agnes DeMille had choreographed a new dance for a film version of "Oklahoma." Nixon was campaigning against "Trumanism" and

Truman was quoted as saying "Republicans haven't learned anything since 1896!"

In the late morning Carlow knocked at his door. "Mr. Clare wants us at the office."

Already at the office were Dr. Haley, Mrs. Malley and the Headmaster.

"Doctor," Henry said, "tell Timmie and Clyde what you've just been telling us."

"Paul Smith has every symptom of polio. I have talked to his parents, and we're sending him to New Haven Hospital for confirmation, but there isn't any question."

"God save us, poor Paul," Mrs Malley moaned. "God save us."

"He'll go in an ambulance - from Barrington," Haley said. "Its the best thing. His parents agreed. They're coming up to New Haven."

"How were they, Doctor?" Carlow said.

"Devastated, Clyde. Mother was hysterical. Father was bitter, but wanted to know if any other boys were ill."

Then all five of them sat, already past poor Paul, quietly projecting in their minds the implications, what nightmare might now descend on their school.

"Well, Doctor, what to do now? What are we looking at? Timmie has already told us that it's likely others have the virus, are carrying it, even if they don't come down with it. Is that right - as you see it?"

"He's right, Henry. But Paul likely was exposed before returning to school, and just perhaps we're looking at an isolated case."

"But, Doctor, Paul has exposed others already! God, he was at Mass with the whole damn school - and there are teammates, classmates, and the entire dormitory. It doesn't take long at school for one person to contact nearly everyone!"

Haley stared at my outburst, and my chagrin deepened when the Headmaster reminded everyone that calm, cool heads were needed, and that together they must thoughtfully adhere to Doctor Haley's recommendations, whatever they might be, at the appropriate time. Meanwhile, perhaps they should discuss what approaches were best in presenting the situation to the school community - surely the boys and faculty would soon know. Smith had collapsed on the altar!

After some minutes the fact of Paul Smith's polio became set, accepted, and we talked of what to do. With only the one case at the moment, Haley said there was obviously no epidemic - yet - and that notification of anyone outside Ashford was not yet necessary. So we concentrated on dealing internally with the issue, one about which all, to ourselves, realized we knew nothing. Haley urged that the coaches go easy at practices, for the present, considering the unusual warm, even hot, September weather. Faculty should watch for signs of fatigue, stiffness, especially in the neck area, and temperature or any nausea complaints. Everyone gradually came to the conclusion the biggest challenge could be morale, sagging spirits, likely induced by the dreadful fear of a paralyzing specter in their midst. Henry Clare decided to meet with the school that evening.

"I dread a meeting like this. I have no idea right now what to say, but if rumors are to be quelled, the boys have to know and understand. Even then, the call will come from parents. What to say, what to say?"

No one there could have imagined the terror-filled days that lay ahead for Ashford. Certainly, no one envied or aspired to Henry Clare's job that September Sunday afternoon. The ambulance came soon after lunch, quietly, yet obviously, departing for New Haven more a vehicle of death than life. Though attendants were present, Rachel chose to go in the ambulance with young Smith, to comfort him, his parents, and then rode back on the evening train, which I met.

"Oh, Tim. Paul is so sick and frightened. His parents were waiting, frantic. I'm glad I went, but I'm afraid I wasn't much help. What can you say? No one really knows what to do."

"You did all you could. You were wonderful to go. Who knows? He may come out of it just fine. Many do, you know. Not everyone is affected forever."

"Pray to God you are right. Can we go by chapel? I feel like that, for Paul, for the whole thing."

We knelt and prayed. Soon she slipped her hand in mine, and then lay her head on my shoulder, and after a while said, "Dear, take me back. I'm so tired."

CHAPTER-THIRTY-TWO

It was with a sense of urgency that I went to Mass on Monday, to pray for the school's safety, and for Paul Smith's. Later the <u>Times</u> informed me that Pope Pius XII was ill, very weak, and I worried that it was an omen. However, the school day went smoothly, perhaps because of the Headmaster's speech, perhaps because any really good school can shake off a problem and get on with things. No patient lay abed in the infirmary to remind them, so Paul Smith's crisis receded, as when water fills a rocky tidal pool until the surface smoothes again.

It seemed that only those of us in the office on Sunday remained concerned, so that when called together that evening in Henry Clare's study, we were all indeed saddened when Dr. Haley confirmed that young Smith had polio, that he was unable to move his legs, and that he would not return to school. Struggling in her pain to find some source to blame, the boy's mother was convinced he'd caught the disease at Ashford, that it had been a ghastly mistake to have sent him to "that school."

Behind his desk the Headmaster pushed back in his chair, partially slumped, the fatigue gray on his face.

"She was so distraught that finally Paul's father came on to relay details about the boy, but he, too, had trouble. Paul is their oldest, and their only son. Great hopes for him, of course. He has no idea of any exposure, contact, except if here at school. It just happened. The father struggled to be rational and all - doesn't blame anyone, but the mother wants to connect it with us. It's unfair, of course, but they are terribly upset - and it's understandable."

No one commented, each looking at his shoes. I caught myself rubbing my neck and pushed the hand into a trouser pocket.

Henry Clare continued, "Two calls came in this afternoon from fathers, ostensibly just friendly inquiries - 'anything they could do' sort of things, but the worry was there."

Still no one spoke, but everyone now looked at him as he stared at his hands clasped on his lap, forefingers extended into a steeple.

Muted faculty conversation could be heard beyond the door, ripples of laughter, before he spoke again.

"Well, we must pray for Paul and his family. We must also be prepared to handle any problems. Let's face it. Word will get back about Paul. Indeed, we must inform the community on the state of things - meet with the faculty first, maybe, and talk to the boys. Eunice, is Father here tonight?"

She nodded.

"Ask Father to join us. He should should have been in on this from the start."

Eunice rose, moved behind me and left the room.

"Any thoughts - anyone - while we wait?' asked the Headmaster.

"What about our games? The young lads on Wednesday and then the varsity football on Saturday against South Kent."

"What do you mean, Clyde?"

"Sir, I just wonder, with what's happened here, if we aren't obligated to tell the other schools - you know - that we have this case, just so they know about it when we play. Is there an appropriate thing to do? It just crossed my mind."

The Headmaster stared at Carlow, his face immobile, then grimacing, head nodding up and down, then side to side, then leaning back to stare at the ceiling.

"My God, Clyde, that never crossed my mind. Oh God, what a mess. Of course, we have to let the schools know! I can't imagine it will affect anything, the games I mean. You know, everyone's outside and this could happen to anyone, but we have to tell them. I know all the Heads. I'll call myself and explain."

The door opened and Eunice showed Father to a chair, resuming her spot on the sofa.

"Father," Henry said, we wanted you here. It's about Paul Smith, who is very ill - paralysis. We're mulling what's to be done. Could we have Mass for him tomorrow?"

"Of course. Certainly his own dorm will want to come. I wouldn't have it required for the whole school - let's see how many choose to come on their own."

"Good. It's ten minutes to full faculty meeting. At the end I'll explain about Paul and Mass in the morning. Any last thing - for now?"

"With what's happened," I said, we might want to repeat the boys coming together at Sunday night suppers. Maybe not right away, but it might help morale. If not that way, then in the dorms we might have food at break, or have different routines. We don't want them dwelling on this problem too much."

"Good thinking, Timmie. We'll all think about the situation and your idea. Until things settle, morale is key, and the faculty must do its part."

As events developed from that meeting on, Ashford would not be the same, at least for many, many months.

. . .

At Mass the next morning - September 22 - nearly every pew was filled. Father spoke briefly about the Mass for Paul Smith, about prayers for his recovery, and also about praying for the school community. It was a somber start to the day, but again the boys were chatting and animated by the time they reached breakfast, almost as though Mass had inured them, but more likely because they were boys and young, many high with anticipation about that day.

In the faculty room at recess, Joe Ryan answered the phone. "Yes, sir. They're here. We'll be right along."

He gestured to Timothy, Carlow, and Smitty, and they headed for the Headmaster's office. Henry Clare was looking out his window, his back to them as they trooped in. Turning, he motioned them to sit.

"Sam Hartnett just called from South Kent. I talked to him last night about our problem, and he seemed fine. But he talked to his Board Chair this morning, to check things out, and I'll be damned if they're not sending their teams today - or on Saturday. Says they have to think about their boys - and parents - and maybe they should wait to see how things go. I was stunned, but, gentlemen, I honestly don't know what I'd do if the situation were reversed. We can't

<u>make</u> them come. Jesus! He said it right out to me - they're scared - he can't take the chance."

Everyone sat, still and silent, until Joe Ryan said, "Oh, shit!" And then, "Excuse me, Sir, but this is bad. I mean, having no games will really get to the boys. God, we can't not play! Hell, they're not going to spread any germs out on the field, and Smith isn't here. What the hell is wrong with old Hartnett?"

"Joe, he hated calling me today - feels terrible. But he's under the gun. And the terrible thing is he's probably right. It's what I mean - what would <u>we</u> do? Clyde, what do you think?"

"About what we would do? It's hard. It's all different, not like anything before. Sam Hartnett knows what it means to a school - his <u>or</u> ours - to have the games. I'm sure he hasn't taken it lightly."

Smitty was shaking his head. "Mr. Clare, there's no question about this? It isn't just the Junior Varsity and Midget teams today, but also the Varsity on Saturday?"

"No question, Smitty. I'm terribly sorry."

"What's your thought about the other schools? I mean, once they hear about Hartnett's decision, what are we looking at?"

"I've called Doctor Haley to come here. I don't know how long we would have to determine if Paul is an isolated case. Maybe two weeks. I didn't ask Sam Harnett about that - just said we'd keep him posted. There were all those boys at Mass - and in the dorm..."

"<u>And</u> on the field, in the shower, in the dining room," Ryan said.

"<u>And</u> with the faculty."

"Yes, Clyde, the faculty, too." And with that Henry Clare started rubbing his face, his hands covering it all, except his nose, while the rest were silent again.

• • •

After hearing about South Kent's decision, Dr. Haley said, "Henry, I'm sorry to say it, but Sam Hartnett is right. He had to do it. It's just that we don't know, not for sure. The lousy thing is, we're not far from a vaccine. Jonas Salk has one in field trials, but there have been problems. The word is that he's really onto something. Meanwhile, it goes on, not as severe as two years ago, but it still goes on. The fact is, a whole group of our boys has been exposed, but exactly how the virus is carried remains unanswered."

Henry Clare stared at Haley. "And there's nothing else - no shot or pill ar anything?"

"Apparently, there will be something -it's called gamma globulin - available in about a week. It's the only proven weapon available to physicians for prophylaxis against paralytic polio. It can provide a temporary immunity of five to eight weeks. But it's tough to get. Has to be an epidemic situation."

"Hell, Doc, we're not an epidemic."

"No - not yet. But we're on hold. I recommend every effort be made to ensure as much rest as possible - light workouts, no huge homework assignments, plenty of sleep. One thing we do know is that germs and viruses like weakness, low immunities, tired, run-down people - so without making a big deal of it, takc it casy on the boys."

"Damn it, Doctor," Henry said, "won't the changes just underline the situation - make the boys really nervous, scared?"

"They already are - but you are right. The changes will define the problem, but I feel it's important. As for the worry, the morale - the faculty has to come up with a lot of strength for these kids. I recommend you insure the resolute posture of your faculty first - before you go to the lads. We don't want faculty shivery and quaking, or wondering aloud about anything."

CHAPTER-THIRTY-THREE

The next days were excruciating for the school, a period when Henry Clare's strength and greatness held Ashford together in a climate of fear among boys, parents, and faculty. He stood solidly as the leader, in manner and voice providing assurance for everyone. Calmly, he first met with the faculty, securing and defining their role for the days ahead, and then with the boys, explaining, asking for patience, encouraging strength, allaying trepidation, until, except for canceled games, the school seemed to function, for a while at least, much as usual. Calls from parents, several at first, diminished, and then ceased after a week.

Of course, news of the polio case spread to other schools when South Kent canceled. The irrelevance of practice as games were canceled made worse the already dense curtain of fear, that though unspoken, draped itself everywhere on campus. Morale kept declining when additional schools called to regretfully pull out of the scheduled games, so that indeed Ashford became all but quarantined, except for unsuspecting deliverymen and vendors. On the weekend that South Kent didn't come, Smitty had an intra-squad scrimmage which the rest of the school attended, but there were no cheers for anyone, a depressing, sad time with no future in sight for Donnelli and his teammates. I would remember that the Saturday nignt movie had been especially hilarious, but there had been few laughs, and from the rear of the room I saw many rubbing the backs of their necks. Bed check, usually a boisterous challenge on Saturday nights, was subdued, each boy under his covers when I came by, a few in prayer. All across the campus few lights were on, even at an early hour, nearly everyone retreating to bed, for quiet, perhaps yearning for dreams to dispel the reality of day.

The next morning was Sunday, September 26, 1954. I would remember each date that fall, at least until near the end of everything, both for what had happened each day, and for what the elapsing time and days had meant - incubation, days free of crisis, days full of crisis, days of passion and sin, and love and remorse, counting the time since the last seduction, facing Christ at all, or never.

The lines of boys heading for Mass moved quietly ahead of me; Henry Clare and Carlow stood at the entry looking down the paths, watching their school move toward them, smiling and welcoming, anything to lift the spirits of a frightened school.

As I approached, the Headmaster was talking to Mrs. Malley and Rachel, who were assuring him that nobody was ill, and only one was in the infirmary - with a severely sprained ankle.

I had a clear view down the aisle to where Donnelli knelt in prayer, stood when Father came to the altar, and collapsed during the Kyrie.

I reached him in an instant, followed by Mrs. Malley and Rachel. Together we assisted Donelli outside, where he sat on the short wall, head between his knees, surrounded by Carlow, the Headmaster, the nurses and me. In moments he seemed recovered, but Mrs. Malley insisted on the infirmary, and the three men watched Donnelli trudge off, assisted on each side by a nurse, his walk somehow atilt and not steady.

Henry Clare said, "Gentlemen, pray Donnelli just fainted. If he has polio...Look, let's not guess. Tony isn't the first boy to faint at Mass."

· · ·

Ashford waited, poised, all knowing what had happened at Mass, and who it was. After breakfast boys hung about their rooms and dorms, knowing the doctor's car stayed long, and when the ambulance came - no siren but red light flashing - the grim scene was set. I watched the red and white vehicle pull slowly out the drive and wondered if Rachel were in it, too. It wasn't long then that Carlow, quiet and somber, stood at my door.

"The Headmaster asked me to tell you that Donnelli...he's on his way to New Haven, and Rachel has gone along. Dr. Haley says Donnelli is...very ill, that he doesn't like some of the signs - whatever that means. He wants us over at four o'clock, at the house,'

"Yes, sir. I'm devastated, for Tony - for everyone."

"I know. Look, I'll see you there."

I remembered that Sunday, that the weather was still summer hot, that Mount Everett appeared hazy as the heat hung heavy, pressing down on everything, on everyone. My anguish over Donnelli had me near tears through the afternoon as I kept setting aside the Times to rub my eyes and forehead, to stare from the window. I read, dully, that Colgate had beaten Cornell. None of that mattered, nor the rising stock market, at a twenty-five year high. "Tea and Sympathy" still played in New York - I'd never had a chance to see it - so much meaning, so far off and unreal.

As I neared Henry Clare's, I saw Dr. Haley's car in the drive.

As I went in, the Headmaster turned and gestured everyone to sit: Dr. Haley, Father Delaney, Mrs. Malley, Joe Ryan, Clyde Carlow and me.

The Headmaster sat, rubbed his forehead, crossed his legs, and folding his hands in his lap said, "Thanks for coming. I'm certain you all know about Tony Donnelli and can guess our school faces uncharted seas at the moment. We've managed, to date, to...well, to manage, but it isn't easy. Until today we've been in a holding pattern, but now it's anybody's guess."

"What is the situation with young Donnelli?" Carlow asked. "Not certain, Clyde. Rachel called to say they made it to New Haven, that he was very stout, but very sick. Doctor, what about it? What do you think?"

"Henry, Tony has it...has polio. All the signals are there. His shivers, his difficulty talking and swallowing were distressing. I've talked to Dr.Larry Peterson down there - he's tops, best we have in the East, and he's on it. Said he'd call when he had something more definite, but I can confirm here and now that there isn't any question about what's wrong with our wonderful quarterback."

Our silence, while everyone stared straight ahead, bespoke concern for Donnelli and fear for the days ahead at Ashford, of the unknown, of events even Clyde Carlow had never experienced.

Then the Headmaster spoke, slowly and carefully, but remarkably sure. "Eunice - She's upstairs, queasy stomach this morning, but when she heard of Tony, she said that I must call the

213

schools today, that they must know that future games will have to wait. She's right, of course, but it is a rotten thing, all around. I'll hold an all school meeting after supper tonight, and we better have maintenance and the kitchen staff there, too. By that time, Dr. Haley will have heard more on Tony?" - Haley nodded - "and we will have had time to form some approach. We must assume this virus is still with us, and we must be sure the boys and their parents also understand that. Right now, I can't foresee our course, but I do know that you people sitting here must help lead us through it. Father, before we talk about what to do, would you lead us in a prayer?"

We prayed, Father improvising, the last peaceful moment most would have for weeks, myself, for months. Then we talked at length, Dr. Haley saying he now felt he could justify acquisition of enough gamma globulin serum for the school. What he did not tell them was that Dr. Larry Peterson had reported to him that Tony Donnelli appeared to have bulbar polio, and that if his diagnosis proved correct come Tuesday, Donnelli faced a future in an iron lung. Everyone agreed that administering the gamma globulin as soon as possible would be a positive action, not only for the health of the school, but more significantly, for the morale of the whole community.

Student resilience remained admirable, though the nurses saw growing numbers complaining of various symptoms that, while scary, proved mostly figments induced by imaginations. The parents were another matter, as they started calling with feelings and concerns ranging from sympathy to outright threats to withdraw their sons. For the most part the Headmaster was able to explain that their children were likely safer at Ashford than at home, since the number of cases were growing everywhere in the East, especially in cities. He explained the gamma globulin plan for the school, an approach not available to individual families. By Wednesday the calls had subsided, and as nearly as possible, the school moved in its rather monotonous routine, a monotony now cherished. There was even time for the Headmaster to inform me that Ted Williams had announced his retirement, and after lunch on that Wednesday, several faculty slipped into the Headmaster's to catch the beginning of the World Series, the Giants against the Indians.

CHAPTER THIRTY-FOUR

On the last afternoon of September Henry Clare called a faculty meeting, rather recklessly giving the boys the afternoon off, free time previously unheard of for Ashford; he had concluded that this change of pace would promote no more trouble into which any students could thrust themselves than that which already prevailed. To great cheers he made this announcement after lunch, challenging them to enjoy the change, but to behave responsibly, as he knew they would, and announcing that he would meet them all at the door for evening chapel. He had Carlow spread the word privately to faculty of the afternoon meeting, a slight precaution so that the boys wouldn't know that no faculty were around in mid-afternoon.

At the meeting Dr. Haley explained the procedure for administering gamma globulin to "every member" of the school community the next day - every member to include all students, staff, and faculty children and wives. A project for the infirmary, of course, he explained the process involved an inoculation in both cheeks of the behind, that the discomfort in sitting would increase throughout the day so that standing was best, and that a sense of humor would help. He was convinced the procedure could deter the polio virus, which, he admitted, had to be present, and was optimistic that despite any discomfort, the positive effect on morale would lift school spirits all around.

"All right," Henry Clare said, "you have all heard the program. I'm appointing Timmie to schedule the school for it all to happen, to work with Dr. Haley, Mrs. Malley and Rachel. Bill, if Timmie needs help, give him a hand. Clyde, we'll detain the school at breakfast to explain the day. We won't tell them tonight - let them think it's classes as usual. Joe, tell maintenance and the kitchen staff about it in the morning. Timmie will have a schedule worked up so everyone will know when to be there. Guess that's it. Any questions?"

There weren't any, so the Headmaster stood and said, "Well, in the midst of the events of recent days, other things have happened - besides the Giants, of course. Mrs. Clare had good reason to be

217

feeling out of sorts. After all this time, God has blessed us. You should know Eunice is pregnant!"

He paused, emotion seizing him, then said, "In all this difficult, dark time, there has come this marvelous light. Please pray for us - for her."

Another pause and then Carlow stood and began to clap, followed by the rest. The meeting was over, and faculty crowded around the Headmaster. I sat stunned, uneasy, and then slipped outside by myself. I, despite the weather, felt cold.

That night I created a schedule for the gamma globulin shots - students first, proceeding from dormitory to dormitory so that there could be solace in community suffering, followed by faculty and their families, and then by the rest of the staff. When the boys were in bed, I went to the schoolhouse to make copies which in the morning I could pass strategically around school. Then I went to see Warren, to ask for his help in maintaining order among the boys as they waited in line - weather permitting - a line outside the infirmary.

"No sweat, Tim. It should be some day, but we need to do something. Tony Donnelli's situation has really been terrible. I mean, God, Tim, he's such a terrific athlete. With him it just seems worse than if it were - well, you know what I mean."

"Yes. It hasn't sunk in with me yet. Rachel told me they have him in an iron lung - to keep him alive. She said the doctors reported it was a good thing he was in such good shape."

"But Tim, he may never throw another football!"

After a moment, Warren asked, "What about the meeting today?"

"What do you mean?"

"Well, aside from your getting stuck with this whole infirmary deal tomorrow - of course, you're the guru of nurses anyway - what about the big announcement! In the midst of all this nightmare, we hear that Henry did it! Isn't that something?"

"Yes - yes. It's wonderful news." I couldn't summon so much as a smile.

"What's the matter with you?" Warren said.

"I'm sorry - sorry. I guess this medical emergency has me down. Of course, it's great."

"You're right. And it's a hard time for Henry - his great achievement in the midst of a polio epidemic - a crisis no school ever faced before."

I didn't recall the rest of what was said, only going back to deposit the schedules in my room, and then a slow walk around campus to stand outside the infirmary with thoughts of sneaking to Rachel's room, then retreating to wander back, remembering that, as Eunice Clare in the sacristy reached to pull back her coat, she said twice, "It is the perfect time. It is the perfect time."

. . .

I slept fitfully, arising at six to shower and dress. It still wasn't Fall; the walk to breakfast felt like a July morning. At the top of the schedules I had written the date, Friday, October 1, 1954, and underneath in capital letters, GAMMA GLOBULIN DAY! I posted one outside the dining room and gave one to each Housemaster and other key people, including Henry Clare and Eunice, who rarely attended breakfast, but this morning sat at the head table, glowing and radiant.

Though the nurses might have helped administer the shots, Dr. Haley had decided to give them all himself - with Rachel and Mrs. Malley assisting, checking off names, loading phials and needles, and humoring everyone. Consequently, the procedure moved steadily, but slowly. Warren and I otherwise kept order, kidding nervous boys as they waited in line and as they left. One lad described the feeling as like having a softball in each cheek. So that many could hear, he said, "My ass hurts like hell!"

Curiously, they could walk more easily backwards than frontwards, but sitting was out of the question. Standing or lying on one's stomach were the positions of the day.

By four o'clock only Mrs. Malley, Rachel and I had not received the injections. Haley came into the reception room where they sagged. "I'm sorry," he said, "but that last boy got the last shot I have. We're out, but I'll come back in the morning. You three

219

must have it, but you can wait a day. Okay? You all were superb. It went just as well as possible, and I think we took their minds off contemplating their own navels - or should I say rear ends! But I must say, they're a great bunch." He thanked us as he left, reminding us to be on tap the next morning for our shots.

Mrs. Malley stood. "I hardly think anyone will be back here tonight. Rachel, let's clean up a bit together. Then I'm going to settle in my apartment, have supper on a tray, answer any phone calls. It would be a great night for you and Tim to get out, away from this place. Please go, or do whatever. I shall do what I like. So should you."

And it was settled. I would go check the dining room - I was off dormitory duty - see about Father's car, and pick Rachel up around seven o'clock.

On my way back to the room for a shower and change of clothes, the Headmaster intercepted me by the office path.

"Dr. Haley stopped by. Said it went as well as possible. Many thanks, Timmie. I know it's been a long day."

"Thank you, sir."

"And the boys - look at these four on the drive - walking backwards! At least they're laughing."

"You would have been proud of the boys. There were a few dopes, but most were amazing."

"Good, good. Well, you may like to know that Johnny Antonelli did it today - beat Cleveland 3-1, and Dusty Rhodes hit a real homer in the seventh. Beat Early Wynn. He's just amazing."

As I continued on, I mused on the Headmaster's devotion to baseball and the Giants, unflagging in the face of crisis. He seemed to gather strength from his allegiance, which gave deeper meaning to his oft-used directive, "Stay in and pitch."

This energy proved limitless when he phoned me later to say he planned to drive to New Haven to visit Tony Donnelli. When I had offered to drive him, he said he would be fine, that if he were too tired he would stay over, drive back in the morning, but that Donnelli's parents would be there, that he must go.

As I showered, my fatigue faded in anticipation of the hours ahead alone with Rachel. Father had tossed over the keys, so I had a car, my love, and enough money. Perhaps tonight would be the night Rachel and I....

In the years following, I had decided more than once that it was my preoccupation that evening - one that found me in heady anticipation of having Rachel all to myself that triggered at least the beginnings of the next fateful events. But hours, even days, were so compacted then that they obscured reality, less intense only in the analysis that reflection permitted.

I slowed down as I passed the sign that said Route 23, a road which would take me through Hillsdale to Route 41 to head south toward Ashley Falls. Not much traffic tonight, I noted, and only about twenty-five miles to school. Rather grimly I calculated that I could finish all that needed finishing if I drove carefully - at the speed limit. I had taken this road so often, several times a year since 1954, that I now knew each turn, nearly every house. I determined I had come this way at least forty times during the nine years. How often from now on? - to visit the farm, the graves, but less and less, in all likelihood. As I stared ahead now, each event stood clear in memory.

As I was about to leave the room for the dining room, the phone rang. It was Rachel.

"Tim, dear, do you have a plan?"

Her voice had sounded distant, both in measure and tone.

"Not really. I have Father's car, a few bucks, some great ambitions, a beautiful woman - so I thought we could plan as we go. Why? Do you have a plan?"

"Well, not really. I guess I wondered, after the day you've had, whether you felt like anything."

"Rachel, you know that no day would mean I wouldn't feel like anything!"

There was a pause, more than a pause, and I said, "Rachel, are you tired? Rather stay in?"

"It's not that, not that at all. Look, go do your dining-room check and come here as we planned. We'll go from there. See you soon."

And she had hung up, leaving me wondering, on the way to the dining hall, whether there had been some message I missed. I had decided not, but after we headed for Rackum's, I knew something was amiss. Her usual fun, jollity, spirit were absent, replaced by monosyllabic replies or silence. I tried to make light of things, determined to rescue the evening and continue my pursuit of her - now an intense urging, perhaps made more compelling by her sulky mood. But when we had two beers in front of us, I confronted her.

"Okay, Rachel. I know you are tired, but what's wrong?"

"My mother called."

"She can be difficult, but just her call didn't put you in this mood."

"No. She called because my father isn't there and hasn't been for two days."

Tears now came, and I grabbed her hands.

"Go on. Where is he?"

"She doesn't know. He did call to say he was all right, not to worry, but he didn't know when he'd be home. Oh, Tim, she's so - so desolate. I don't know what to do. I said I'd come home, but she said absolutely no. She almost didn't call me, but then thought she'd better, in case anything should happen - bad, I mean."

This last came out between deep sniffles. I remembered feeling helpless.

"Why, Rachel. Why did he leave?"

"I don't know. Mother doesn't know - at least she won't say."

"Have they not been getting on?"

"I don't know. I think they have. It's just - well, they just aren't very warm toward each other."

"Either of them?"

"Yes. Well, maybe Mother more than my father. She seems cold at times."

I would remember thinking Rachel's father probably had just cause to bust and run, but I said nothing. I was not able to help her; indeed, I had mostly felt baffled, so turned to her trip to New Haven with Donnelli. It was another unhappy topic, one I shouldn't have broached, though I was curious about her reaction. She described Donnelli's bravery, and fear, as well as her own, and though knowing he was in good hands, seeing a ward with patients in iron lungs confirmed that Tony's condition was truly one of life or death.

The humor surrounding their day with boys with aching asses helped little. It was an evening whose downhill slide never bottomed out. Nevertheless, I had fought the slide, determined against all odds to have my delight in her tired but breathtaking body.

I had parked in their usual spot, but she allowed me little, remaining stiff, preoccupied, unresponsive, until finally I suggested her apartment might be better and cozier. Looking back, I knew her assent then was merely to end the grappling, to get closer to home and safety, to her own privacy of place and thought. By now, however, my frustration had driven me to a kind of mad determination. I would not suffer her father's fate, not this night. I had, of course, totally blinded myself with complete insensitivity, unlike my usual behavior, not recognizing there are wrong times to force the issue, that persuasion doesn't always succeed, that indeed defenses can become impregnable; even when love is there, it can be pushed aside.

Like an elephant I stomped her fragility, and in her apartment where she maintained I didn't belong, she fought back, not slyly or with her practiced aplomb, but fiercely. I did manage half undressing her, half on and off the sofa, but she crossed her legs, folded her arms across her breasts, refused to open her mouth, except to repeat between clenched teeth her refusal to have intercourse, nor even to satisfy me.

"Damn you, Tim," she growled, "you know very well my promise. Stop this now! What are you doing? Can't you see you're hurting me."

Her eyes were wide, frightened, but I was out of control. Finally, I pulled my trousers back on, sat against the sofa and said, "I don't care any more. I've had it."

I turned toward her as she sat in a ball, shivering on the sofa.

"You can forget me. No more. You can take your promise to Jesus, be like your mother, and die for all I care. I've begged you for the last time. I may love you, but I won't suffer you. Goodbye, Rachel. Call your mother to ask about your father!"

Disheveled, still violently angry, I slammed out of the room, the infirmary, and at that moment, her life, I hoped.

I had never been so angry, nor ever would be, and it didn't dissipate soon. Seething, I sat on my bed, wishing for a beer, wishing I smoked, wishing for release. It was 11:30 when the phone rang.

"Where have you been? I've been calling all evening." Eunice Clare's voice was impatient but seductive.

"Out. Why?"

"Henry called to say he's staying in New Haven to be with the Donnellis, and for me to be in touch with you about Tony."

"Well, thank you. I just came in. Tell me about Tony."

"Out with Rachel?"

"Yes. About Tony?"

"He said to be in touch. He didn't say by phone."

The pause lasted until finally, incredibly, I heard myself say, "What do you suggest?"

"To come here, of course."

"Where are you?"

"Upstairs - in bed."

After another pause I said, "All right. I'll use the fire escape to your terrace. Unlock the door."

"Come through the garden. Soon!"

By the time I replaced the phone and was dressed in dark trousers and sweatshirt, my anger had coalesced to a driven conviction that my next move was a natural consequence of rejection on the one hand and my given right on the other to achieve satisfaction. All of it was madness, of course, which would be recognized too late, after the consequences had formed an awful substance in my soul. At that moment, however, I was a cunning predator, both cautious and swift in movements down along the river, to approach the Clares' garden from its rear.

When I reached the back fence, the rich scents of Eunice Clare's roses came fully to my senses. I easily vaulted the top rail, and once in the garden, feet firmly set, I looked about before running toward the lower ladder of the fire escape. My dash across the garden was unimpeded - so that I didn't notice the faint form sitting on a bench in the dark by the south hedge.

Once on the ladder, I clambered to the terrace in seconds. Through the glass door I saw her, the bedside lamp casting a pinkish glow about the bedroom and about Eunice Clare who sat upright, back against the headboard, legs tucked up, naked, gazing at him, smiling. In a moment I was inside the room, inside her in every possible place, our lust coursing every bedded and carpeted surface, I in a relentless pursuit of her heated ivory skin, connecting one final time mid-bed, my head in the crook of her right arm, my eyes staring across her swollen, raw nipples, my gaze leveling to the French doors, and directly at a round face pressed against the glass, a shadowy hand on either side, eyes wide, mouth stretched to a wide circle, aghast in a silent scream. I saw it only for a moment, looked away, and then back, but Rachel's face was gone. Eunice Clare never knew.

Incredibly, I had lain back, devastated, done, exhausted, and had slept. Much later I awoke, disoriented, but then realized where I was and that this insatiable woman was having me again, for breakfast she had said. I had fallen so far, I accepted it. Before dawn she sent me away, down the ladder, complaining that my rough manner had given her a headache, and that her back and legs even ached. Unbelievably, I never asked about Donnelli nor thought of her pregnancy.

CHAPTER THIRTY-FIVE

I would never remember that next day well. I did recall lying as low as possible, especially away from the infirmary. Warren hadn't been on campus anywhere. Someone else ran things. Carlow called to ask me to cover the Saturday- night movie. But mostly I suffered, and wondered. How had Rachel known? She must have seen me. I could hardly bear any of it, especially since I loved her so much - and yet literally ran to the pregnant wife of my Headmaster. I was without any shred of decency. I was both mad and evil.

No one called; no one came by. Apparently, no one cared. I made it through the movie, through check-in and hunkered down in the room, staring at the phone, but not daring to call, Rachel or anyone else. I turned on my small radio. The Giants had crushed the Indians in Cleveland 6-2. I listened to Jimmy Durante on the Texaco Star Theater. On late sports I heard the college football scores: Colgate had beaten Holy Cross 18-0. I started to cry then, quietly sobbing until, still dressed, I collapsed on my bed, knees drawn up, falling asleep at last in the fetal position, not to dream - just bleakness, nothingness, until dawn.

. . .

I prepared carefully for Sunday Mass, wondering what to do when I encountered Rachel, even as my thoughts seemed like echoes, disjointed, sere. I moved mechanically, like Dorothy's Tin Man, no tears left to ease my soul. Then I realized I'd lost it, thrown it away, that indeed my heart was dust, and wondered whether attending Mass would be yet another sacrilege.

Nevertheless, habit found me walking to the chapel along with everyone else - except that Rachel wasn't there, nor Eunice Clare, nor the Headmaster, who certainly must have been back from New Haven. I knelt in the last pew, behind Warren, who twice turned to look at me, expressionless, eyes searching, grim. We fell into stride at the end, turning for the dining room, no words for fifty yards.

Then Warren asked, "Has Rachel called?"

"No. Why?"

"All the way there she never talked."

"All the way there? What do you mean? Where?"

Warren looked at me then, shaking his head. "You don't know, do you? She came to my room before light yesterday, knocking on the door - scared the Hell out of me - wanting me to drive her home. Christ. She had a suitcase, looked like hell, could hardly talk, and she never did. I mean, tell me or anything. Never occurred to me yesterday you wouldn't know. She just sat in a ball while I drove her home. Thought something happened to her parents. God, Tim. She got out of the car and ran into her house. Never said thanks - nothin'! She never called you?"

"No. I didn't know all this. I'm sorry, Bill. You were great to do that. I just don't know what to say."

"Well, I just assumed - well, you know - and since I was up and all, I went home yesterday. Didn't get back until late. Was going to call, but your light was out. Anyway, it was a weird thing. I felt so sad for her. I'm sure you know I really like Rachel!"

Fortunately, arrival at the dining room precluded further comments, even if he had any. I had felt myself crumbling, having no sensations, for her departure had nothing to do with her father, and everything to do with her so beautiful face pressed to that window, recognizing me.

At table I served eggs to the boys wordlessly, all of them eyeing me, wondering about this mood from Mr. Jordan, ordinarily so effusive and friendly. I felt the uncontrollable tears begin to well and had to leave, to go I knew not where, but finally back to the room, door locked, standing but bent over, hands on knees, my body racked in an ague that erupted from a deep terror, terrible recriminations, my spiritual worthlessness an emission of physical devastation.

At last, the telephone's insistent ringing caused me to lurch to the bed, slowly pick up the receiver and whisper, "Hello."

"Tim? Is that you? You okay?"

"Yes."

"You have a cold. You sound hoarse. Sure you're all right?"

"No - yes. I'm fine. Who is this?"

"Tim, it's Father. Would you please go downstairs to Clyde Carlow's, and I'll be right over. We have a situation. Could you be there right away - a couple of minutes?"

"Of course - of course. What is it?"

"I'll be right over."

After Father hung up, I stretched and shook my arms, attempting to collect myself, and went to the bathroom to wash my face. I saw there someone I didn't know, so I scrubbed my face hard, passed my fingers through my hair, cinched my belt and descended the two flights to Carlow's. Father was already at the door.

Clyde Carlow showed us into his study.

"Gentlemen, I'm afraid I have some very disquieting news. An ambulance is at the Headmaster's now to take Eunice Clare to New Haven. Dr. Haley has been there all morning. He is certain, I'm afraid, she has polio. She's very ill. Her symptoms are much like Tony's."

"Oh God, Father," Carlow uttered, hands flat on his desk, head bowed, the first time during the recent days he revealed the latent tension that certainly gripped nearly everyone.

"Henry asked me to see you two men, to tell you, and for us to determine the immediate course - whatever it might be - for the school. He said he could go with her, knowing he left with things in the best hands. No one else, as yet, is aware of the situation. In fact, I'm sure they've left by now." Father paused, then said, "Perhaps we should pray first."

We did pray, each blessing himself, silently looking to the floor. I would remember I had not being able to think anything, the shock landing so heavily on my already tortured soul.

In some moments Father looked up, said, "May Jesus's healing power come now, for Tony, for Eunice Clare. Dear Jesus, her goodness has earned your saving grace. Amen."

We are doomed, I thought.

Over the years, that moment in Clyde Carlow's study had always remained a succinctly final, awful prophecy.

Despite the powerful eddy that sucked me downward, and despite the harrowing prospect both Father and Carlow faced, the

229

three of us braced, accepted coffee from Mrs. Carlow, and turned to the business of administering Ashford, a school besieged in a fearful epidemic, one whose leader was tragically distracted.

"I'm convinced," Carlow said, "this weather is part of it. It's October 3rd and so <u>hot</u>. We haven't had any Fall, no frost to kill the germs. Did Mr. Clare leave any directions, Father? I know his mind and heart were elsewhere."

"No - just for us to meet. Said he would call, but for now we should handle things. People know something's amiss, with the ambulance. Henry thought first to use a car, just because of the message an ambulance might send, but Dr. Haley would have no part of that. One problem is, there's no nurse on campus. Mrs. Malley went in the ambulance, and apparently Rachel's gone home. She left a note for Mrs. Malley but didn't see anyone. Tim, what's up with her?"

"Father, all I know is that she asked Bill to take her home early yesterday, and he doesn't know why. It may be something about her father. Apparently he left home the other day."

"Good Heavens! Well, she'll likely call you. Anyway, until Mrs. Malley is back, Tim, why don't you camp at the infirmary. Any real problem, you can call Haley. Damn it. We could sure use Rachel. There really must be something major - leaving like that is so unlike her."

Both Father and Carlow sat looking at me, but I could not respond, so I said, "Yes. Well, I'll go to the infirmary. But what is the next thing?"

"The school will be at Benediction tonight, Father. Something will have to be said."

"I've thought of that. Perhaps it would be the right and natural setting for someone to speak of it, and perhaps by then we will know more. I'm not certain it should be I, however, since I preside at the ritual. Clyde, you are Senior Master. Shouldn't you speak to the boys?"

"Father, as you know by now, I'm just not good at that sort of thing - speaking, I mean."

I couldn't believe that they both turned to me, eyebrows slightly raised.

"Tim," Father said, "I've heard you speak - they could well take all of this better from you than anyone."

"Father - not me - I couldn't, really..."

"Nonsense. It's settled. It need not be long. Just tell the boys what has happened, and where we are."

Much of that day I no longer recalled, except for my attempt to compose remarks suitable for chapel, to tell the school, in essence, they were all gripped in an epidemic that had stricken the Headmaster's wife, the Headmaster's pregnant wife, the school's most incredible lover, all the while fearfully contemplating my true love's disappearance - and silence.

CHAPTER THIRTY-SIX

It was a somber Sunday Chapel; even the organ sonorously set a purple tone as I walked slowly to the first altar step and turned to look back at that crowd of frightened faces.

"Gentlemen of Ashford. I must report to you tonight that Mrs. Clare, our Headmaster's gracious wife, has been taken to the New Haven Hospital. Our Dr. Haley and Dr. Patterson of that hospital have confirmed that Mrs. Clare has poliomyelitis, very similar to the strain from which Tony Donnelli suffers. At present she is resting as comfortably as possible and, of course, receives the ultimate in care. I know this is difficult news, but you have all shown great strength with the problems we have faced, aided, I'm sure, by your prayers and your faith that in God's hands we can place our trust - that this evening at Benediction all of us can renew our spiritual commitment to Christ, the Supreme Healer, who made men walk, the blind see, the dumb talk. In our prayers we should remember our Headmaster in his difficult travail; he is with Mrs. Clare now, along with Mrs. Malley.

"I speak for the Headmaster and the faculty to ask that you continue on with your tasks, cooperate with any proposal, behave as you have, as Ashford young men of fiber and resolve. Do that and God will care for us all. What better place could any of us be right now than here, in the chapel, at Ashford where faith forges strength, where Christ's love is present.

"We plan no changes but to go forward as usual. The Headmaster will return tomorrow and will bring all of us up to date. You should also know that Tony Donnelli holds his own. Tomorrow afternoon or evening Mr. Clare will meet with us all."

They sang well that night, and when Father elevated the monstrance, the reverence was palpable.

Father complimented me, and even Joe Ryan said, "Tim, that was a tough thing to do. Glad it wasn't me."

I had prevailed well, I thought, and had spoken in an eerie detachment that belied the verity of having consumed and been consumed only hours earlier by this indescribably passionate woman who now lay stricken. No intimacy could have been greater; I must have ingested her virus, and yet I coolly confronted the irrefutable fact that the odds I'd contracted polio seemed absolute, overwhelming. I knew it and accepted it, for I deserved it.

· · ·

Sunday night the dormitories lights were always out early, the theory being that the boys had a whole day to prepare for Monday, and that a good night's sleep was the proper way to prepare for the week. Despite the appalling events, I found himself at my desk, after the last bed check, to prepare for Monday's class, so much was I into the habit and routine. I had hardly opened the grammar handbook when the phone rang.

"Tim. It's Mrs. Malley at the station - just in from New Haven. Could you come for me?"

"Of course, of course. Don't fret. I'll be along. I'll get Father's car. Won't be long."

In the car I explained how we had covered the infirmary, that Warren was there now, but it didn't seem to matter much to her. She was very tired.

"Tim," she said, "Mrs. Clare is not good. It's almost certain she will be in the lung by tomorrow, if not sooner. Mr. Clare, that poor dear, is a wreck, and he's such a strong man, too. I only wonder if he can survive all this, what with her pregnant, too. Of course, I'm sure that won't work out now. Oh, Tim. What are we to do?"

When I didn't answer right away, she said, "And Tim, what about our dear Rachel? Have you heard from her?"

"No. Nothing. Father said she left you a note."

"Yes - and it's odd, too. I'm so upset, her leaving like that. It isn't our Rachel - without speaking to me. I can't imagine what happened. She already knew about her father. She had told me that, and if it was about him, why didn't she say so? And no word from her! Have you called her, Tim?"

"Well...no. I.... It's been crazy at school."

At the infirmary I asked, "Mrs. Malley, what did Rachel's note say?"

"I have it here." She handed it to me.

"Mrs. Malley, I am terribly sorry, but I must leave. It is awful to leave you in such a lurch, but I have no choice. Pray for me. Rachel"

I read the note several times.

"Tim, you're trembling. Are you all right?"

"No, I'm not. Like you, I find it very upsetting."

After some moments, I showed her to the door.

"Tim, please let me know when you hear."

"Yes, yes. When I hear."

Rachel hadn't written that she'd left for home, nor did she indicate any time of return. I returned Father's car, slipped the keys under the door, and while walking to my own place, realized Rachel would not return to Ashford, not as long as I was there.

I had cried often in that period, but never more wrenchingly than during that long, sleepless night.

At the stop light in Hillsdale where Route 22 and 23 intersected, I decided on a beer, which I'd find at the Catamount Inn up by the ski area on the way to Egremont. I drove at ease now, only three miles from the Massachusetts border, and only the final events left to finish it all.

On Monday Henry Clare did return, not because he was abandoning Eunice, but because he was driven by that compulsion always present in any true schoolman: to tend to the daily tasks of his school with all force. Not even the gravity of his wife's condition could keep him from at least checking in. He would say, of course, that it was something Eunice wanted him to do, and the fact was that his presence on campus was a welcome sight indeed, even if he looked haggard and immeasurably exhausted. He thought his men had done well, thanked "Timmie" for his chapel talk, told the school after lunch that both Mrs. Clare and Donelli sent them all their greetings, that he knew the students would continue their normal high level of attention to their studies, and that he could see that soon all things would be back on an even keel. He said it all so movingly, with just the right levels of seriousness and good humor, that it seemed nearly everyone believed him.

235

In his office after the meeting, Henry Clare smiled wanly at me, Father, and Clyde Carlow.

"What do you think, Timmie? Will that talk see them through until tomorrow?"

"Yes, sir. You were just what we all needed."

"We..." and he sobered quickly, "It wasn't easy. I must return to the hospital. Some decisions there ... it seems ... well, there's so much they just don't know, and she doesn't seem to stabilize, one way or the other, but they have her in the lung - you know, the iron lung - Otherwise, she...she just couldn't...."

He stood then, his back to them, his arm reaching back for the handkerchief in his rear pocket.

"Sir," Carlow said, "why don't we just go?"

"No, no Clyde!"

He turned back, wiping his eyes, and with a wave of his hand, directed us, half out of our chairs, to be seated.

"Sorry. No. We have to talk some here. Anyway, it is best we get it out. Eunice is very, very ill. She will lose the baby, of course. Right now, gentlemen, it is a matter of her survival, but she is a strong, determined person. My bet is we'll be back on the golf course next summer."

"Henry, our prayers are for just that. Please tell Eunice how we all feel, starting with last night's chapel."

"I shall, Father. Thank you. Now, my secretary tells me I have many calls, and I'm sure most are not about Eunice, but about taking sons home. Donnelli's situation is well out, and by now so is Eunice's. You can be certain we'll see a lot leave. What do you think, Clyde?"

"Sir, I don't know. We've never experienced this before. But if you expect even one such request, we might well have a plan in place."

"What sort of plan?"

"A plan to close school on a moment's notice, for a week or two, until everything quiets - so perhaps we're not seen as the culprits. I think it would be better to take the initiative, rather than be forced into it."

"I think you're right, Clyde - very wise, very good. Father? Timmie? Any comment?"

Father nodded agreement. "I think we could do it quickly - phone calls to parents and send the usual boys on the train to New York - someone with them to help with connections."

Henry Clare smiled. "Timmie, guess who that would be?"

We planned it then, the closing of Ashford, should it come to that. The Headmaster had said for us to execute the plan if the moment came, whether he was on campus or in New Haven, and the odds were good he could well be absent. It would, of course, be the Head's decision to make.

When we'd gone over the finer points, Henry Clare reached into a middle desk drawer and removed an envelope. "This last thing is very disquieting, as well as a major problem. This morning some man my secretary had never seen before brought this letter to the office - addressed to me. It's from Rachel Mackintire, whom I guess you all know left school the other night."

He took out a single sheet of off-white writing paper:

"Dear Mr. Clare,

It is with deep regret I must resign immediately from Ashford. I realize it is a very unprofessional thing to do, and that it comes at a very difficult time for the school.

Please know I cherish Ashford and am so grateful to you for giving me the job, and to Mrs. Malley for her wonderful guidance. I can only pray that you would forgive me if you knew the circumstances.

Sincerely,
Rachel Mackintire"

After a brief pause, during which I was sure they could hear my heart, Henry Clare said, "Well, Timmie, I think you would understand if we look to you for some explanation. There is nothing here to explain her action, at least not the Rachel Mackintire I know. What's going on?"

I had somewhat anticipated this. Even though I had no idea where she was, I knew perfectly well why she had resigned, but I obviously could never say it. So I fell back on the disappearance of her father, concluding, "Beyond that, sir, I just don't know."

"But haven't you called her at home?"

"Well...no I haven't. It's been very busy here, and ...well, I guess I have been waiting for her to call."

"Sir," Father said, "do we know if Rachel is at her home?"

"Well, not really. I guess you are right, Father. We...I think we shall see for ourselves."

He looked at me and reached for the phone, his faculty telephone list, and dialed. Everyone watched and waited, until he hung up.

"Guess no one is home. I'll have the switchboard keep trying until we make some contact. Something's wrong. Rachel's too solid to just take off without compelling reason. First, we have to make sure she's safe. Well, I'll let you know. Think that's it. We're set. Despite everything, don't hesitate to be in touch. And get your rest - we all will need it."

CHAPTER THIRTY-SEVEN

The next day - Tuesday, October 5th, I would remember - I read Arthur Daly's column on Willie Mays, the twenty-three year old wonder player. There was, as well, the account of Marilyn Monroe's divorce from Joltin' Joe DiMaggio after nine months, and an advertisement for a round-trip ticket to London on TWA for $290.00. I had remembered the ad because in my circumstance I had thought London would be an excellent, immediate destination, but also in my circumstance, I couldn't possibly afford it.

I read the <u>Times</u> in the Faculty Room. It was during a free period at midmorning, with only me and Joe Ryan present.

"Wilbur took the Headmaster to New Haven this mornin," Joe said. "Left real early - around six o'clock. What do ya' think, Tim. Think that globulin stuff will work?"

"It can't hurt, but some people might be too far along, already have polio. It may not have been in time. Everyone seems all right this morning, but we know that doesn't mean anything. I do know another case means the school's had it." I felt like a prophet when Warren entered the room, to quickly say he had Tyler Parker in tow, sick like Donnelli was sick, that they were headed for the infirmary and for someone to call Dr. Haley. Joe Ryan went to the phone, and Warren and I helped young Parker, a fourth former, stumble to Mrs. Malley's dispensary where a temperature of 102 degrees and a terrible headache sent him to Room 3, Donnelli's old room, to await the doctor. By noon Haley knew Parker had polio, without any confirming tests, but this time Parker's parents elected to have their son transported home to Worcester. A special limousine came for the boy at 3:00 PM, and as Dr. Haley later reported, the parents expressed a concern that apparently many families shared, so that when Carlow, Father, Dr. Haley, Joe Ryan and I gathered in the Headmaster's study an hour later, all that remained was the Headmaster's approval to close, and working out the details of how to send home an entire school by the next morning. A call to the Headmaster's hotel in New Haven resulted in the return message that Wilbur would have him on campus by early evening.

Back in his study at seven, the Headmaster quickly took charge, assigning people to call parents so that, if possible, each family would be notified that evening. At seven thirty Henry Clare met the school to explain the plan and the reasoning behind the decision, causing a much needed lightening of spirits, a buzzing and bustle not felt nor seen in days, so the hard-pressed faculty knew the direction taken was best. Some parents who lived close enough came for their sons that evening, and as red taillights exited campus, I remembered that I had felt the relief from seeing the departure of all those potential victims, removed to some other person's aegis. Naturally, I had received the train assignment - the first train the next morning.

After breakfast, Harry brought the school truck to the parking lot in center campus where boys loaded their bags and then climbed into faculty cars to be shuttled to the station.

Henry Clare gave me five hundred dollars in small bills. "Don't try to be frugal," he said. "Just get them on the trains and planes and buses safely. You're on your own with this one, Timmie. Dr. Haley wants the faculty off and gone, too, away from the bugs - but I don't worry about you." Clare smiled at him, cocking his head. "Timmie, that isn't true. I worry much about you, more than anyone. It's just that if one person is to do it, I've picked my best man."

We stood in the office awkwardly, both electrically sensitive, until the Headmaster turned back to his desk and said evenly, "Timmie, I talked to Rachel's mother. Funny woman, I think. Anyway, Rachel was out - at least that's what she said. Said Rachel was fine, tired, but they hadn't talked much, that she knew Rachel would call me, but she didn't know when." After some moments, he went on. "Did you two fight - have a falling out?"

"No, sir. No fight. No falling out."

"Then why hasn't she called you?"

"Mr. Clare, I'm terribly upset with this whole thing - and disappointed - and worried, but I can't help you. Not yet."

"I won't press - and we have so much else. Save enough of that money to get yourself back. After things have cleared out, Wilbur will drive me back to the hospital in New Haven. Clyde will watch the school till you're back tonight. Call me when you get in, whatever the time."

We shook hands then, the Headmaster placing his left hand atop our grip, pumping up and down three times, and then pushing me away with a light touch on the shoulder.

I had ninety-one boys on the train, and it was crowded, since we had not had time to notify the line of the need for an extra car.

I told everyone I would be stationed at the information booth at Grand Central if anyone needed help, directions, counsel, or money. Several had little or no money in their school accounts, so that within minutes of their arrival I had given away over three hundred dollars. But by one o'clock most were on their way or waiting for a train. One lad from Chicago needed one hundred dollars. I gave him the money and counted twenty-five dollars left to take me back to school after an early supper at the Oyster Bar.

The Catamount Inn was dimly lit, quiet, just one couple at the bar and another couple at a table. I took a seat apart from anyone, went to the bar and asked for a bottle of beer, noting that the clock over the bartender's shoulder said nine PM. My watch had stopped. With a beer and some chips I returned to the table, musing that perhaps my life, too, had stopped, or at least until the recall was finished - over - collected at last into one reel which might be put away somewhere, or even erased.

The train ride back to Ashford that night offered a sound sleep, my physical exhaustion overwhelming even my spiritual turmoil.

I remembered calling Warren, who came for me at the station and who said the campus was dead. He had thought it likely only he, I, and Father would be on campus that night. Once in my room, I called Henry Clare at the New Haven hotel at 10:00 PM, but there was no answer. Nor did the number answer at 11:00, nor midnight. Then I fell asleep.

Father Delaney's call the next morning - it was 10:00, Thursday, October 7th - didn't seem distressing - at first.

"Did I wake you, Tim?"

"It's okay."

Father had paused until Timothy had said, "Father, you there?"

241

"Yes... yes. Look, Tim. I'd like you to come over - after you're well up. I've got some coffee."

"Fine. Good. See you in half an hour."

I had felt better after a shower. On the way to Father's I felt more together, though I had not yet brought my attention to Rachel, to that fearful cloud that now shrouded my whole existence, to that ball of agony, of leaden remorse, inside me.

Father handed me a mug of coffee. "Tim, Eunice Clare's condition remains grievous. It was a bad night, and Henry has asked me to come down today, and Eunice has asked that you come, too." Father said it looking directly at me and paused until each had drunk from his cup. "I'm leaving in an hour. Can you be ready?"

"Yes...yes. Of course. Is she truly so ill? I never thought that she'd ... well, not...<u>beat</u> it, you know."

"Henry's been up all night at the hospital."

"And you're sure she asked for me? I really don't understand..."

"Tim, you must know by now that for her you were...well, family. For Henry, too. Well, look, finish your coffee, do what you have to, and I'll see you at the car at 11:45."

I couldn't remember the ride to New Haven other than that there were some references to the Giants, the still-hot weather, and I had told Father about my day at Grand Central. Mostly I had looked out the window, dreading the arrival, and terrified of seeing Eunice Clare at all, in any circumstance, fearing that some final denouement could strip me naked so all could see who I truly was. What must the Headmaster think, she wanting to see me? Father's presence was a clear thing, as a close personal friend and spiritual advisor, and sadly, perhaps more than that on this trip. But I, Timothy Jordan, to be included? I shut my eyes as if to block out a collapsing world.

Henry Clare met us in the hospital lobby and suggested the cafeteria for coffee. His exhaustion marked his walk and speech, moving now mostly on nerves, but he managed a smile at the table, insisting on an account of the train trip to New York and the dissemination of the ninety plus students. Then he looked away, head downward, his fists clenched.

"Henry," Father said, "tell us about Eunice, and what the doctors say."

Henry's strength was incredible. He straightened, shoulders back, steadily looking at Father and calmly said, "They're very cautious. Eunice needs the lung to breathe. She is so weak, in all respects. She just can't seem to muster to any challenge, to resist, and there isn't any medication or serum or injection. What she needs is resolve, her old self, so we thought you two coming could cheer her. She didn't ask, but last night wondered out loud if you might come, Father, and I'm ready to seize anything. She's so tired - she needs a lift, a burst of something. Of course, her helplessness overwhelms her, and being in that machine in itself would frighten anyone. Be warned. She's in a ward of four of them - all pumping - all overwhelming - young Donnelli is one of them. The doctors seem positive about his condition, that he will escape, but apparently things complicate with adults."

After another pause he said, "As Timmie reported back at that faculty meeting, it appears that pregnancy can be a predisposing factor. God, Father, it all seems so wrong, when it all did seem so right."

"We know God is with Eunice, that His will is in this.

"And the baby?" I asked.

"Gone. Lost. Yesterday. She truly lost ground after that. Her will seems to have gone, too. Is that God's will?"

"We can't judge. We can pray and hope for God's miracle of science and medicine that will sustain her."

Then, in the silence that ensued, I understood I could never cope, that Timothy Jordan had no reserve left, that the measure of my guilt truly had no measure, that if God's will were truly done, then that day, Thursday, Oct 7th, 1954, would be my last....

"Tim - Tim. Are you with us?"

"Oh, yes, Father. I'm sorry. In a daze, I guess."

"Henry suggests we go up now, with him. Come along."

I trailed Henry Clare and Father Delaney down the hall to the elevator. I considered feigning illness. In fact, I did feel nausea, and certainly a reluctance I always felt visiting the sick. But in this circumstance it seemed to be a restraining force that actually slowed

243

me, until the two looked back at me, the Headmaster motioning to stay up. I could hear the noise of the iron lungs, muffled whooshing sounds from coffinlike machines, in which lay victims stricken with bulbar polio. The sounds were of death, not life, or at least of life at the last extremity, the sound forcing one to look about, fearful it might cease, all of it frightening, ghastly, terrible. We stopped before a large, plate-glass partition through which I could see four machines, each enveloping a patient, so that only the head lay outside, on a pallet, above which was a small mirror, allowing the patient to see who came - doctor, nurse, visitor. I didn't recognize the face closest to the partition.

"Eunice is on the far side along with Tony Donnelli. I hope you both will visit him, too. Let me ask the nurse if now is a good time. They only allow one at a time, and then only briefly. I'll be right back."

As the Headmaster checked at the nurses' station, Father and I stared into the ward.

"Father, I find this very difficult. I'm sorry, but I don't know if I'm up to it."

"There isn't any choice. Henry needs us here, now, to do this, so we will. You'll be fine. You always are. For both of them."

A nurse came to lead us in. The Headmaster stayed outside at the window. She led me to Donnelli and Father to Eunice Clare. The boy saw me in his mirror and smiled, saying quietly, "Mr. Jordan! This is great, you coming here."

"How goes the battle, Tony?"

"Pretty tough, sir, getting used to this tank. But I do feel better than before."

"I hear you're doing very well - that you're going to get out of this thing."

"Yeah, I think so. So how about school?"

I remembered that Donnelli, though ill, had good color and a sparkle in his eye, that if it weren't for that steel constriction, he'd throw for a touchdown. The boy had said the main thing that bothered him was the sound of the lung and the problems of going to the bathroom. I hadn't lifted Donnelli's spirits - Donnelli had lifted mine.

Shortly, Father was standing beside me saying, "Tim, Mrs. Clare will see you now. She's tired, so don't be long."

I said goodbye to the boy and went to the fourth machine by a window. Her lovely hair fell loose from the pallet; her face appeared thin, her high cheek-bones prominent, only a tint of pink on them. Our eyes caught in the mirror as I pulled a chair closer, and her voice, just above a whisper, said, "You're wonderful to come, Timothy. It's so far."

"Not at all. I was Father's co-pilot."

She smiled as though it hurt a little. "Timothy."

"Yes."

"The baby's gone. Oh, Timothy, I'm so sorry, but our baby's gone."

"Please. I know, but God will have his way." I looked quickly around, afraid someone was near enough to hear.

"Everything was so perfect. Oh, Timothy, you came here, to me, even though it's over. Listen to me, Timothy. Henry needs you so. He has come to depend on you. Please stay with him. Promise me, you will stay with him."

"Mrs. Clare, you will always be his right hand."

"Perhaps. But promise me - please - you will stay at Ashford with Henry."

I had no choice. I knew that.

"Yes. I promise."

"Thank you, Timothy. You've always made me so happy.'

She closed her eyes and some moments went by. I thought she had fallen asleep, and I looked around, then stood up. When I looked at her face again in the mirror, her eyes opened, and she slowly formed her lips in a kiss.

"You must go now. Timothy, will you promise to remember one more thing?"

"Yes, of course."

"I love you."

She closed her eyes.

. . .

Standing at Father's car, Henry said to us, "Thank you both for coming. I can't tell you how much it means. I think the Donnellis will be coming, and I expect my brother and his wife, along with Eunice's mother, but your being here was the most important. So anyway, I'll be in touch. Drive carefully.'

And he wheeled and strode back toward the hospital, not inquiring about their opinions on either patient.

The ride home found us avoiding the subject of how each felt about Eunice Clare's future. I thought about her final words, about my promise, one which I sensed I would have to keep.

CHAPTER THIRTY-EIGHT

The next day, Friday, October 8th, I was up at eight, having slept surprisingly well. Today I would resolve my problem about Rachel. I was, in fact, no longer sure that I <u>had</u> seen her at that window, that perhaps I'd had a hallucination, summoned by what I had all along worried about: discovery. Perhaps the face existed only in my mind. My facile rationalizations had become more prevalent, and they made me feel better. After collecting the <u>Times</u>, I headed for the diner on foot since, finally, the weather said Fall - the air bracing, refreshing, some leaves afoot.

I read over eggs and bacon, incredulous that a Giant player raked in more than five times my own annual salary! Mrs. Roosevelt would turn seventy on Monday, and I recalled her regal speech at Colgate my sophomore year. I could buy a Plymouth for $1,595.00 - not much less than my annual salary. The French had withdrawn from Hanoi, and the Communists had the North. The English teacher, Richard Dadier, was hero of "Blackboard Jungle," a violent book according to Orville Prescott. Ashford had no such problems - only a polio epidemic.

So I was distracted, unprepared, when passing Father's place on my walk back, the priest leaned out his window to motion me to his quarters.

Seated, Father told him, "Eunice Clare died early this morning. Henry called just now. I'm on my way, and I was going to leave a note, but I'm glad I saw you."

"My God, Father. She certainly didn't look good, but I could never believe...."

"I know. Henry said the doctors are perplexed because she was a strong woman. It is as though she just gave up. It's not my business, but did she say anything to you that indicated she knew - or anything?"

I wondered whether to tell Father anything and decided not to. Father was simply too close to Henry Clare.

I pretended to muse on Father's question and said, "No. Not really. She did seem down, but what do you expect? No - she just thanked me for coming. But, Father, what now?"

"I've no idea. Stay close. I'll call when there's a plan. And, Tim, say some prayers - for all of us."

That day did pass, somehow. Eunice Clare's death had stopped my plan to resolve things with Rachel. Handling the information that the woman with whom he had shared such frantic sexuality just days before had today been extracted from that steel vault - dead - overwhelmed my conscious thought, so that most of the day I just sat on the bed, staring, seeing nothing, my mind turning over and over again her last words to me: 'I love you." I grew hungry but still didn't move, rooted it seemed, as immobile as Rodin's "Thinker," naked, stripped, defenseless, emotions marbleized.

In this state, as dusk made much of the room indistinct, I heard my phone ring - once, twice, three times, until I jerked upright and reached for it.

"Mr. Jordan...er...is this Tim Jordan?"

"Yes. I'm Tim Jordan."

"This is George Mackintire, Rachel's father."

A prescient chill passed through me. "Oh, yes, Mr. Mackintire. What can I do for you?"

"Well...Mr. Jordan...Tim, I mean..."

There was a coughing and some other sound.

"Yes - yes. What is it?

"There's been a terrible accident. Rachel borrowed my car this mornin'...and, well...Jesus, Jordan. She ran into a semi truck, and, well, it was direct, head on - way up on Route 7, north of Williamstown. God knows why she was up there - but, Mr. Jordan, Rachel is dead! Instant. State Police talked to us, and the people at Williamstown hospital. We're goin' up there in a minute, but the Missus thought the school should know - and you."

Mackintire was nearly incoherent, sobbing over the phone. Frozen at the window, phone to ear, I noted the last orange glow of the setting sun behind Mt. Everett, that even in the lowering gloom I could see the cool autumn wind curling leaves along the drive below my window, that with everyone gone from Ashford, no light shone anywhere.

"Mr. Mackintire, you are thoughtful to call. Please tell Rachel's mother how terribly sorry I am - how we all will be. Will you call me if I can help?"

"Okay. Well, then - Tim - we have to go."

"Goodby, Mr. Mackintire."

. . .

I caught the evening train for Pittsfield, and from there a milk train to Syracuse, eventually to be retrieved by my mother the next morning. I hid at the farm for several days, during which funeral services for Eunice Clare took place in Ashford's chapel, mourners so profuse many stood outside.

Since her body had been destroyed in the collision and subsequent fire, a memorial service went forward for Rachel in Holyoke. Henry Clare likely forgave me for not attending his wife's burial since he could understand the grief surrounding Rachel's tragic death, and Mrs. Mackintire was likely more comfortable with me not at the memorial service. All the while, my absolute grief, coupled with a tangle of guilt, made for a desolate homecoming.

I was able to help my father in the orchard. It was peak season to pick Northern Spies, the staple crop, and cider season was in full flow. Lifting and tugging and picking made sleep possible, so, though my heart and soul suffered continuously, my body shortly became fit and hard. My mother truly mourned for Rachel. At night I thought I would die - wished for it, ached to join her. I knew she had no valid business on Route 7 north of Williamstown; I knew her to have been a superb driver. I did not know how I could survive without her in the full knowledge that I never - ever - deserved her.

On Wednesday, Oct. 27th, I was unloading the apple wagon by the barn when from the side porch Mother called me to the phone.

"It's your Headmaster, Mr. Clare," she said.

"Timmie. I knew you would be at the farm. You all right?"

"I think so, sir."

"Of course we haven't talked, and the phone is not the place, but Rachel's death was tragic - and I'm so sorry."

"Sir, thank you. She was....I want to apologize for not coming to Ashford, to Mrs. Clare's funeral. I was in shock, but not to have responded was - well, totally thoughtless. You deserved better from me. I do apologize."

"Timmie, we were both devastated. We'll talk of it all. But now, we have Ashford. We're bringing everyone back on Sunday, Timmie. Could you come back tomorrow - at least by Friday - to give us a hand - give me a hand?"

"All right. Yes, sir. I promise."

"Timmie, you don't have to promise. Your word is good enough."

"Thank you. Nevertheless, I promise."

I returned Thursday afternoon. Thereafter, no polio cases came to the fore at Ashford - ever.

• • •

Just before Christmas break I found a long envelope in my mail box, inside of which was a brief letter from Mrs. Mackintire and a small envelope, sealed, with my name, "For Tim" on the outside.

"Dear Tim,

As we finally came to sort out Rachel's things, I found this note with your name in a stationery box in her desk. Please know I have been strong and did not open it.

Our lives will never be the same without her. I've come to understand now how much it could have meant to us all to still have her - with you. She loved you so much.

Mrs. George Mackintire"

My tears made me fumble in opening the small envelope, tears through which I read:

"My Dearest Tim -

I know I made you so angry that Friday night, and after you left, I just had to get out. I wanted to go to your room and decided to sit on the bench in the garden, to calm down, plan how to sneak to you. I saw you then, run through to the fire escape - climb up. I don't know what made me follow, but I did - what happened was all my fault. You tried so hard, and I failed you.

Now I'm so sad. Even Jesus seems so far away. It was wrong to run away, but the only thing is to keep on running.

Should you ever read this, dearest Tim, know that I always loved you. Pray for me.

Rachel"

CHAPTER THIRTY-NINE

Folded four times, her note had been in my wallet ever since. I refolded it now, inserted it in my wallet, drained the last of the beer, rose from the table, and in the parking lot of the Catamount Inn, breathed deeply several times. It was clear now, the sharpness of spring bending to the warmer May time, and I could feel the renewal all about me, perhaps because I had done it all this time, start to finish, and perhaps because the ensuing years since did just what time often does - not heal fully, perhaps, but enough so that the scars don't start nightmares, but rather suggest the softness of love and loyalty.

I had no recall of that Christmas break, for I had taken a "personal holiday"; it was what Dr. Leipowitz had called my breakdown. She had been a fiftyish psychiatrist from Austria whose handsome face I first recalled seeing across a desk from me in March of 1955, three months after Warren found me, late at night, prostrate on the river log, my arms around it, hands locked so tightly it took Warren and Henry Clare minutes to unclasp them, finger by finger, and then carry me between them back to school.

I had seen the woman for some days before I fully sensed my surroundings, a comfortable room at St. Anthony's Hospital in Hartford. In pajamas and a robe, I sat on a straight chair, my hands flat on a desk. She smiled at me, touched my hand -

"Hello, Timothy. How do you feel?"

"Okay...I guess...funny."

She explained how I had essentially retreated from everything, a long way, she had said, so that to return required, among other treatments, electric shock. I had revealed much to her that she understood, and together we had made my way back.

"Your recovery will be complete," she had said. "In fact, you can be stronger than before. Your progress has been remarkable."

She knew all about Eunice, Rachel, my mother, the betrayals, the fixation, the faith - everything. Dr. Leipowitz had been gentle, firm, as confident as one can be with the near complete deterioration of a man's psyche.

"Doctor, did I go insane?"

"No, you turned your back on reality and took a holiday. You couldn't stand any more events - or yourself. You're fortunate. Not all who take such a holiday return." After a pause she said, "You can leave soon - in a few days. Henry Clare wants you at his house, or you may prefer going home to the farm. We can discuss what to do....There is one thing I couldn't fit in. Nurse Bromley, at Colgate - that you weren't her son - you repeated that over and over. Can you tell me about it?"

Embarrased, I summed up for her that long-ago night. As I managed to get it out, I realized the significance of that all-but-primal scene.

She nodded. "It's the piece that fits - finishes the puzzle. You just carried on after that night, built a callus over it all - but it was there."

We later decided I would go home where I could rest, grow in strength, help with the spring farm work, and by summer be ready to return to Columbia for another session.

The day I left the hospital Dr. Leipowitz checked me out. I tried to thank her, and couldn't enough....

"It's all right, Timothy. You are my success story. That's thanks enough."

"Doctor, I've a question. If there were one thing you could do to stop - or cure - this sort of mental illness, what would it be?"

Promptly, she siad, "I would buy a shot gun and go out and shoot all the mothers in this world."

We looked at each other a long moment. When I turned to go, she put out her hand. "Timothy, don't be afraid when you feel things - because now you will, much more than before. It will be good. You are a fine man, and you will become stronger than ever. God be with you."

I walked away, not looking back.

I drove into Egremont, down a back road through Sheffield, and at last onto Ashford's campus. It was ablaze still - break time, I guessed, from evening study - and as I slowed by the flagpole, a boy waved me to a stop and bent to look in my window.

"Mr. Jordan?"

"Yes. Oh, Smith, of course. What's up?"

"Mr. Clare thought you'd be along any time and asked me to flag you, to tell you he'd like you to stop at his place. Okay?"

"Okay. Thank you, Smith."

I parked where I was and walked to the Headmaster's, who lived by himself in the same duplex apartment. It was Mr. Jordan, Assistant Headmaster now, the first such position in Ashford's history. When the Carlows had moved to a retirement home at the edge of campus, Henry Clare gave me their apartment, unusual for a single man, but with it I was named Athletic Director and two years later, Assistant Headmaster. When Mr. Black, the organist, retired, Henry Clare was at last rid of the "old guard" and had his "own" faculty, so to speak, which meant he could utilize Timmie Jordan in responsible ways despite my youth and relative inexperience. In the years since the "awful time," I had learned the school craft well, with Henry Clare as mentor. I knew the Headmaster counted on me heavily, especially during the intense time of the school's fund-raising campaign.

The Headmaster greeted me at the door. As a widower he had aged well, just as tall and erect, more gray than before, but still blessed with a wonderful golf swing. He had become a tower among Headmasters and headed or had headed every important association in independent education in New England, indeed, in America. A marvelous speaker, he was always in demand, so that I had had many opportunities to run Ashford on my own and usually well.

We settled into the study, Jack Daniels on the rocks in hand, and at Clare's bidding I told of my mother's funeral.

"My mother always reminded me never to forget I was a Magrill. As to its precise meaning, I don't know. I just knew I'd better do the right thing."

"Well, have you?"

I swallowed, then said, "Of course not - but the standard, vague as it was - was always out there."

The Headmaster smiled, nodded, and took a sip from his glass. "I got a call today from a Robert O'Toole from Chicago. He and some others think they want to start a school, patterned after Ashford. Seems he heard of us from an alumnus, Bobbie Stafford

255

- here before your time - when they met on a Florida tennis court. O'Toole asked Stafford where he'd gone to school, and Stafford filled him in. The people he talked about are Catholic, and they don't want to send their sons all the way east to New England. He admitted they're crazy, but they want to start a school. They even have some beautiful property in mind, and it sounds like there's money. Anyway, he asked me what to do first."

"Well, Mr. Clare, what did you say?"

"I said that the first thing would be to find a Headmaster, someone who knew the business and who was nuts enough to cross the Hudson into that Wild West on a whim and a crazy idea."

"So what did he say to that?"

"He asked me if I knew anyone with those qualifications."

"Do you?"

"I said yes, that his name was Timothy Jordan."

Clare raised his glass again, looking at me, lowered the glass, turning it in his hand.

"You know, Timmie - no wait, it shall be Timothy - Timothy Jordan. Eunice called you Timothy. Do you remember? She told me not to call you Timmie, but back then it seemed fine. Since then I guess I couldn't change, but now I feel it should be different. You just aren't Timmie any more. Not now. So, what do you think of all this, Timothy?"

"Do you think it's real, sir - O'Toole's idea?"

"I think it's worth checking out. He left his number for you to call by tomorrow if you have an interest. He doesn't sound as though he's fooling around - sounds like a mover, which such a project would take these days. He said he'd fly you out there - look at the property, meet the others."

"God, it's so far away. I mean - out in the Midwest. Do they have independent schools out there?"

"Of course. Not as many, but some good ones. It's probably the area with the get-up to try such a thing."

We had another "touch" as Clare called it, at ease with each other in conversing about the prospect of a new school, our years of work together creating a professional comfort, a warm mutuality of thought, a confidential rapport often rare among schoolmen - the mentor and the protege, the father and son, perhaps the son and his young brother.

"Timothy, O'Toole asked if you were married, your age. I felt compelled to tell him about Rachel, and that since then the school has been your life - in large measure. Hope you don't mind."

"No, of course not, and thank you. Rachel is never far away for me."

"Nor is Eunice from me. I know you have met others, but no one serious, I guess."

"No one serious. If it happens, it happens, but I'm not pressing."

"All right. Why don't you sleep on this school thing - but call then, either way. Even if you don't want it, we could give some counsel. Sleep on this, Timothy Jordan. Right now I can't imagine going on without you here. Also, know it is almost certain that in staying you would become Headmaster - unless, of course, the Trustees totally lose all judgment. I'm not to do this forever; you would be the logical choice. I must also honestly say you are ready. You have paid all the dues, and I know you have stayed when others beckoned. Your loyalty to Ashford, to me, has been incredibly faithful. What I mean is, you owe neither Ashford nor me a thing."

At the door we shook hands, and together looked at the clear night sky, the campus now quiet and otherwise dark.

"Sir, should I decide to give this new school a try, what would be your number-one piece of advice?"

"I assume there will be a Board of Trustees. My number one piece of advice is simple and to the point. Never trust a trustee!"

Then Henry Clare entered his house and closed his door.

Back at the car, I paused to look at it. It was the same one I had purchased from Father years before, a car I religiously cared for, so that it had served me well for a long time. As I stood looking at it, I began to feel the fetters loosen, my posture straighten, my heart beat more freely. Then I knew that somehow the contract was complete, my promise fulfilled, the guilt nearly expiated. When I looked again, the car seemed to have lost its nostalgic importance, and right there I decided I'd need a new one to travel all the way to Chicago.

Turning toward my place, I thought I could persuade Tony Donnelli to come help me at a new school. Donnelli taught and coached at Hartfield - very well, I had heard - and another Upstate New Yorker could have the right attitude, or at least not one that said anything worthwhile in the school business ended at the Hudson River!

When I reached my apartment, I sat in my big wingback, feeling a lassitude not likely from Henry Clare's bourbon, but more from a sense of peace, of quiet at the bottom of my being, bubbling quietly. I put my head back, closed my eyes, and after some moments against the inside of my lids, I saw the river. Then I stood, slowly, turned to the coat tree for my Ashford jacket and left, pulling it on as I strode quickly across the fields to the Housatonic. A three-quarter moon hung well down over Mt. Everett, but the light was enough to find my way easily to the river bank I had not visited since that dark time so long ago.

Now I found our log, still in place after so many years. I touched it with my hand, then sat astride the smooth wood and watched the strip of moonlight that reached across the water, pointing west.

About the Author

I grew up on an apple-dairy farm near Cazenovia, New York, one of five children, my education beginning in a one-room schoolhouse. Proceeding on to Colgate University, I majored in English and played varsity basketball, and then to Columbia for graduate school, with a thesis on Hawthorne's *The House of the Seven Gables.* I began teaching and coaching at Canterbury School in New Milford Conn., in 1950, married Billie Cooper, and after four children it's a communion that still lasts.

After thirteen years at Canterbury, I went on to LaLumiere School in LaPorte, Indiana, in 1963. In 1979 I became Headmaster of Berkshire School in Sheffield, Mass., but when LaLumiere faltered in admissions and finance I returned there in 1988. By 1994 I decided the school business and the students had seen or heard most of my ideas, and with one of our children in Vermont we moved to East Fairfield, VT, a widening in the road thirteen miles east of St. Albans.

I write daily, read, help with our local church, and with my wife Billie play as much golf and bridge as time permits. We are flatlanders, but very happy here in Vermont.

Lightning Source UK Ltd.
Milton Keynes UK
UKHW042051271022
411196UK00002B/592